Praise for The Killing Circle

National Bestseller
A *New York Times* Notable Crime Novel

"*The Killing Circle* is one great read: darkly lyrical and atmospheric, it's as haunting as it is gripping. Highly recommended." —Harlan Coben

"Very smart, very scary, very good: once I started I couldn't stop." —Peter Abrahams, author of *Oblivion* and *End of Story*

"Extraordinary. . . . This is easily Pyper's most ambitious—and absorbing—work to date." —*Publisher's Weekly* (Starred Review)

"Outstanding. . . . A riveting prologue, impossible to put down, quickens the beat and leaves you with a twist in the pit of your gut. . . . [A] compulsive read that clearly demonstrates Pyper is a unique storyteller on the Canadian scene." —*Hamilton Spectator*

"Pyper does an impressive job building suspense, offering enough narrative twists and turns to keep the reader nicely off balance. . . . A strong and compelling read with just enough thrills and chills to cool the dog days of summer." —*Vancouver Sun*

"Rising star [Pyper] doesn't disappoint in [this] fast-paced, funny thriller. A terrific ride of a mystery . . . the story hurtles along. Pyper is so good at dropping clues. The thing is, he's also good at introducing so many twists that you'd swear his plot was inspired by a bowl of rotini." —*Edmonton Journal*

"Ultra-creepy. . . . A thumping good read, a real creep-fest." —*The Ottawa Citizen*

"Pyper's early scenes with the writers' circle are sharp and witty, functioning as a pithy introduction to his cast of misfit protagonists, and as a send-up of the pretensions of various artistic personality types, especially of the Canadian genus." —*Quill & Quire*

"Transfixing in its handling of suspense, and thought provoking in its reflections of the seductive art of manufacturing fortune. Pyper delivers a dark, compelling read that occasionally—and refreshingly—steps outside itself and invites readers to think about the nature of fear and obsession." —*The Walrus*

"Deliciously vicious." —*Toronto Life*

"It's not for nothing that Pyper has been hailed as 'leading the way among the bright young things of new Canadian writing.'" —*The Gazette* (Montreal)

THE KILLING
CIRCLE

THE KILLING
CIRCLE

ANDREW PYPER

SEAL BOOKS

Seal Books and colophon are trademarks of
Random House of Canada Limited.

THE KILLING CIRCLE
Seal Books/published by arrangement with Doubleday Canada
Doubleday Canada edition published 2008
Seal Books edition published August 2009

ISBN: 978-1-4000-2608-1

This book is a work of fiction. Names, characters, places and
incidents are products of the author's imagination or are used
fictitiously. Any resemblance to actual events or locales or
persons, living or dead, is entirely coincidental.

Cover design by Terri Nimmo
Page design by Terra Page

Printed and bound in the USA

Seal Books are published by Random House of Canada Limited.
"Seal Books" and the portrayal of a seal are the property of
Random House of Canada Limited.

Visit Random House of Canada Limited's website:
www.randomhouse.ca

10 9 8 7 6 5 4 3 2 1

For Heidi

LABOUR DAY, 2007

I didn't know my son could tell directions from the stars.

Corona Austrina. Lyra. Delphinus.

Sam leaves noseprints on the passenger window as we highway out of the city, reciting the constellations and whispering "South" and "East" and "North" with each turn I make.

"Where'd you learn that?"

He gives me the same look as when I came into his room a couple nights ago and found him sling-shooting a platoon of plastic Marines, one by one, on to the neighbour's roof. "I'm a terrorist," he had answered when asked what he thought he was doing.

"Learn what?"

"The stars."

"Books."

"Which books?"

"Just *books*."

With Sam I know I'll get no further than this. It's because both of us are readers. Not by passion necessarily, but by character. Observers. Critics. Interpreters. Readers of books (most recently the later, furious Philip Roth for me, and *Robinson Crusoe*, told in bedtime snippets, for Sam). But also comics, travel brochures, bathroom-stall graffiti, owner's manuals, cereal-box recipes. The material doesn't matter. Reading is how we translate the world into a language we can at least partly understand.

"North," Sam says, his nose returned to the glass.

The two of us peer at the slab of shadow at the top of the rise. A square monolith jutting out of an Ontario corn field like the last remnant of an ancient wall.

"Mus-tang Drive-in. End of Sea-son. La-bour Day Dusk 'til Dawn," Sam reads as we pass the sign.

He leans forward to study the neon cowboy on a bucking bronco that is the Mustang's beacon, directing us in from the night roads.

"I've been here before," he says.

"You remember that?"

"The sign. The man on the horse."

"You were so little then."

"What am I now?"

"Now? Now you're a book-reading, star-gazing young man."

"No," he says, grimacing. "I'm eight years old. And I just remember things."

We have come out here, widower and son, to watch the last movie show of the summer at one of the last drive-ins in the country. The last of the lasts.

Tamara—Sam's mother, my wife—died eight months after Sam was born. Since then, I have found a parental usefulness in moviegoing. In a darkened cinema (or here, in a darkened corn field) Sam and I can find an intimacy without the dangers of talk. There's something distinctly male about it. The closeness fathers and sons find in passive, mostly silent hobbies, like fly fishing or watching baseball games.

The guy at the admission booth pauses when he spots Sam in the passenger seat. Tonight's main feature—a spooky Hollywood thriller currently raking in the last of the easy summer dollars—is R-rated. I hand the guy a bill that more than covers full price for two adults. He winks and waves us on, but offers no change.

The place is packed. The best spot left is in front of the concession stand, well off to the side. Sam wanted to try further back, but I know that's where the high school kids go. Pot and smuggled rye, teenaged boys and girls and all the things they get away with. It's not concern for Sam's moral education, but the nostalgic envy that being so close to these crimes would cause in me that makes me stay up here with the rest of the respectables.

"It's starting!" Sam announces as the floodlights cut out.

It leaves me to pull our chairs and mothballed sleeping bag out of the trunk with only the light of the commercials to see by. I slide along the side of the car keeping my eye on the screen. This, for me, is the best part of the whole drive-in experience: the vintage ad for junk food. A dancing hot dog, leering milkshake, a choir of french fries. And there's something about the tap-dancing onion ring that always breaks my heart.

I set up Sam's chair, then my own. Snuggle up next to each other under the sleeping bag.

"En-joy Our Fea-ture Pres-en-ta-tion!" Sam says, reading the screen.

The parked rows await the sky's final turn from purple to black. A single honk to our right, a minivan rollicking with sugar-freaked little leaguers, brings muffled laughter from the vehicles around us. But there's something nervous in these sounds—the bleat of alarm, the reply of hollow mirth. To make this impression go away I try at a laugh of my own. A dad laugh. And once it's out, I inhale the familiar mix of gas fumes, popcorn, burnt hamburger. Along with something else. Something like fear. Faint as the perfume a previous guest leaves on a motel pillow.

The movie starts. A scene of introductory horror: a dark figure pursuing its prey through a field at night. Flashes of desperate movement, swinging arms and boots and jangling keys on a belt. Jump edits between the killer's certain stride and the other's panicked run, fall, then sobbing, crab crawl forward. A brief shot of hands dripping with what may be oil, or wet earth, or blood. A close-up scream.

We don't know who this person is, this certain victim, but we recognize the context of hopeless struggle. It is the dream all of us have had, the one in which our legs refuse to carry us, the ground softened into black syrup, taking us down. And behind us is death. Faceless and sure, suffering no such handicaps.

We're so close to the screen that to look at anything

else forces me to turn all the way around in my chair. An audience of eyes. Looking back at me through bug-spattered windshields.

I sit forward again and tilt my head back. The autumn dome of night, endless and cold, lets me breathe. For a moment. Then even the stars crowd down.

"Dad?"

Sam has turned at all my fidgeting. I force myself to look straight ahead at the actors on the screen. Enormous, inescapable. Their words coming from every direction, as if spoken from within me. Soon the film becomes not just any dream, but a particular one I've had a thousand times.

I'm standing before I know I'm out of my chair. The sleeping bag spilling off my knees.

Sam looks up at me. Now, his face half in shadow, I can see his mother in him. It's what gives him his sweetness, his open vulnerability. Seeing her in his features brings the strange feeling of missing someone who is still here.

"You want anything?" I ask. "Tater tots?"

Sam nods. And when I reach my hand out to him, he takes it.

We shuffle toward the source of the projector's light. The blue beam and the glimpsed orange of matches lighting cigarettes in back seats—along with the dull glow of the quarter moon—the only illumination to see by. And the same dialogue broadcast from the speakers hooked to every car window.

It's him.

What are you talking about?

The thing that lives under your bed. The eyes in your closet at night, watching you. The dark. Whatever frightens you the most . . .

Somebody opens the door to the concession stand and a cone of light plays over our feet. Sam runs to stay within it. Pretending that if he touches the unlit gravel before he gets inside he'll be sucked into another dimension.

Which we are anyway. The Mustang's snack bar belongs to neither Sam's generation nor mine, but to whatever time it was when men wore ties to buy cheeseburgers. Just look at the posters on the walls: beaming sixties families stepping from their fin-tailed Fords to purchase treats for adorably ravenous Beaver Cleaver kids. It's almost enough to put you off the food.

But not quite.

In fact, we need a tray. On to which I pile cardboard boats of taters, foil-wrapped dogs, rings so greasy you can see through the paper plate they sit on, as well as a jumbo soda, two straws.

But before we can leave, we need to pay. The girl at the till is speaking into the air. "No way," she says, hang-jawed. "No *way*." And then I notice the cord coming out of her ear. The little mouthpiece thingy under her chin. "For *real*?"

"I'll meet you where we're sitting," Sam says, grabbing a hot dog off the tray.

"Just watch for cars."

"They're *parked*, Dad."

He gives me a pitying smile before running out the door.

Outside, after I've paid, the sudden dark leaves me blind. A tater tot leaps off the tray and squashes under my shoe. Where the hell did I park anyway? The movie tells me. The angle I'd been watching it from. Up a bit more, off to the side.

And there it is. My ancient Toyota. A car I should really think about replacing but can't yet. It's the lipstick and eyeliner Tamara left in the glove box. Every time I open it to grab my ownership certificate they spill out into my hand and she is with me. Sitting in the passenger seat, pulling down the visor mirror for a last-minute smearing. When we'd arrive at wherever we were headed to, she would turn to me and ask, "Do I look okay?" Every time I said yes, it was true.

I keep my eyes on the Toyota's outline and stumble toward it, right next to the van of little leaguers. Quiet now. Their attention held by the movie's suspense.

Why is he doing this? Why not just kill us when he had the chance?

The tray falls from my hands.

It's not the movie. It's what's in front of my car that does it.

There's our fold-out chairs. The sleeping bag.

Except the sleeping bag is lying on the ground. And both chairs are empty.

A couple of the minivan kids are sniggering at me, pointing at the unsheathed hot dog on the ground, the dixie cups of extra ketchup splashed gore over my pants. I look their way. And whatever shows on my face makes them slide the door shut.

I drift away from the Toyota, scuffing through the aisles between the cars. Slow, deliberate scans in every direction. Poking my head into the vehicles and noting the hundreds of North American lives in recreational progress—the dope-smoking kids, gluttonous adults, the couples slumped under comforters in the backs of pick-up trucks.

But no Sam.

For the first time the idea of calling the police comes to mind. Yet it remains only an idea. Sam's been gone three minutes at most. He has to be here. What *might* be happening is *not* happening. It can't be. It can't.

"Sam!"

My son's name comes to me from someone else. An alarmed third party.

"Sam!"

I start to run. As fast as I can at first. Then, realizing I won't make it the length of a single row, slow it to a jog. A pushing-forty man trotting his way through the parked cars in the middle of the main feature, rubber-necking this way and that. It's the sort of thing people notice. A teenager in his dad's convertible wolf whistles as I go by, and the girls bunched into the front with him offer an ironic wave. Without thinking, I wave back.

When I finish zigzagging all the rows, I start around the perimeter of the lot. Peering into the shadowed fields. Each line of corn another chance of seeing Sam standing there, hiding, waiting for me to find him. This anticipated image of him becomes so particular that I actually spot him a couple of times. But when I stop for a second look, he's gone.

I make it to the back of the lot where the light from the screen is dimmest, everything bathed in a deep-sea glow. The corn rows seem wider here, and darker. The roof of a distant farmhouse the only interruption on the horizon. No lights in its windows. I try to blink it into better focus, but my eyes are blurred by tears I hadn't felt coming.

I thought you were a ghost.

I was a ghost. But ghosts don't get to do things. It's much better being the monster. The kind you don't expect is a monster until it's too late.

I bend over and put my hands on my knees. Sucking air. A pause that lets the panic in. The horrific imaginings. Who he's with. What they will do. Are doing. How he will never come back.

I saw someone. Looking in the window.

Did you see who it was?

A man. A shadow.

I have already started to run back toward the concession stand when I see it.

A figure disappearing into the stands of corn. As tall as me, if not taller. There. And then not there.

I try to count the rows between where I was and where the figure entered the field. Seven? Eight? No more than ten. When I've passed nine I cut right and start in.

The fibrous leaves thrash against my face, the stalks cracking as I punch my way past. It looked like there was more room in the rows from outside, but now that I'm within them there's not near enough space for a man my size to move without being grabbed at, tripped, cut. Not so much running as swallowed by a constricting throat.

How is whoever I saw going any faster than me? The question makes me stop. I lie down flat and peer through the stalks. Down here, the only light is a grey, celestial dusting. With my open mouth pressed against the earth, it's as though the moonlight has assumed a taste. The mineral grit of steel shavings.

I teach my body to be still.

The thought occurs to me that I have gone mad between the time I left Sam and now. Sudden-onset insanity. It would explain crashing through a corn field at night. Chasing something that likely wasn't there in the first place.

And then it's there.

A pair of boots rushing toward the far end of the field. A hundred feet ahead and a couple rows to the left.

I scramble to my feet. Moaning at my locked knees, the muscles burning in my hips. I use my hands to pull me ahead. Ripping out ears of corn and tossing them to thud like another's steps behind me.

Every few strides offers a peek at the farmhouse in the distance, and I cut sideways to stay in line with it. As if I know this is where the figure is going. As if I have a plan.

I lift my head again, scanning for the gabled roof, and catch the figure instead. Rushing right-to-left across the gap. A glimpse of motion through the silk-topped ears. Darker than the night stretched tight over the corn.

I launch forward. Blinking my eyes clear to catch another sight of it down the rows. But what *was* it? Neither identifiably man nor woman, no notable clothing, no hat, no visible hair. No face. A scarecrow hopped off its post.

Now when I shout I'm no longer addressing Sam but whatever it is that's out here with me.

"Bring him back! Bring him *back*!"

There's no threat in it. No promise of vengeance. It's little more than a father's winded gasps shaped into words.

All at once I break through into the farmhouse's yard. The grass grown high around a rusted swing set. Paint chipping on the shutters. Smashed-out windows.

I go around the back of the place. No car parked anywhere. No sign that anyone has come or gone since whatever bad news ushered out the people who lived here last.

I stop for a second to think of what to do next. That's when my legs give out. I fall to my knees as though moved by a sudden need to pray. Over the pounding of my heart I listen for retreating footfall. Not even the movie voices can reach me. The only sound the electric buzz of crickets.

And the only thing to see is the Mustang's screen. An ocean of cornstalks away, but still clearly visible. A silent performance of terror so much more fluid and believable than my own.

It's as I watch that it comes to me. A truth I could never prove to anyone, but no less certain for that.

I know who has done this. Who has taken my son. I know its name.

I kneel in the high grass of the abandoned farmyard, staring at its face. Forty feet high and towering over the harvest fields, lips moving in silence, directly addressing the night like a god. A monstrous enlargement made of light on a white-washed screen.

The part all actors say is the best to play. The villain.

Part One
The Kensington Circle

VALENTINE'S DAY, 2003

"Love cards!"

This is Sam, my four-year-old son. Running into my room to jump on the bed and rain crayoned Valentines over my face.

"It's Love Day," I confirm. Lift his T-shirt to deliver fart kisses to his belly.

"Who's *your* Valentine, Daddy?"

"I suppose that would have to be Mommy."

"But she's not *here*."

"That doesn't matter. You can choose anyone you like."

"Really?"

"Absolutely."

Sam thinks on this. His fingers folding and unfolding a card. The sparkles stirred around in the still wet glue.

"So is Emmie your Valentine?" I ask him. Emmie being our regular nanny. "Maybe someone at daycare?"

And then he surprises me. He often does.

"No," he says, offering me his paper heart. "It's you."

Days like these, the unavoidable calendar celebrations—
Christmas, New Year's, Father's Day, Mother's Day—are
worse than others. They remind me how lonely I am. And
how, over time, this loneliness has burrowed deeper, down
into tissue and bone. A disease lurking in remission.

But lately, something has changed. An emerging emptiness. The full, vacant weight of loss. I thought that I'd been
grieving over the past three and a half years. But maybe
I'm only just now coming out of the shock. Maybe the real
grief has yet to arrive.

Sam is everything.

This one rule still helps. But in the months immediately following Tamara's death, it was more than just a
focus. It allowed me to survive. No one-way wants, no
me. Not permitting myself to dream had got me halfway
to not feeling—easier conditions to manage than feeling
and dreaming too much.

But maybe this has been a mistake. Maybe I was
wrong to believe you could get along without something
of your own. Eventually, if living requires being nothing,
then you're not even living any more.

Tamara's last days is something I'm not going to get into.
I will confess to all manner of poor behaviour and bad
judgment and broken laws. And I am prepared to
explore the nature of memory (as the cover bumpf on
those precious, gazing-out-to-sea sort of novels puts it)
even when it causes the brightest flashes of regret. But
I'm not going to tell you what it was like to watch my
wife's pain. To watch her die.

I will say this, however: losing her opened my eyes. To the thousands of hours spent gnawing on soured ambitions, petty office grievances, the seemingly outrageous everyday injustices. To all the wasted opportunities to not think, but do. Chances to change. To see that I could change.

I had just turned thirty-one when Tamara died. Not even half a life. But when she left, a cruel light was cast on how complete this life could have been. How complete it *was*, had I only seen it that way.

We bought the house on Euclid just off Queen as newlyweds, before the arrival of the yoga outfitters, the hundred-dollar-haircut salons, the erotic boutiques. Then, the only yoga being practiced was by the drunks folded up in store doorways, and the only erotica was a half-hour with one of the ladies pacing in heels at the corner. I could barely manage the down payment then, and can't afford to sell now. Not if I want to live anywhere near downtown.

Which I do. If for no other reason than I like to walk to work. Despite the comforts offered by all the new money washing in, Queen Street West still offers plenty of drama for the pedestrian. Punks cheering on a pair of snarling mastiffs outside the Big Bop. A chorus of self-talkers off their meds. The guy who follows me for a block every morning, asking me to buy him a prosciutto sandwich (he's very specific about this) and inexplicably calling me Steve-o. Not to mention the ambulances hauling off whoever missed the last bed in the shelter the night before.

It is a time in the city's history when everyone is pointing out the ways that Toronto is changing. More construction, more new arrivals, more ways to make it and spend it. And more to fear. The stories of random violence, home invasions, drive-bys, motiveless attacks. But it's not just that. It's not the threat that has always come from the *them* of our imaginations, but from potentially anyone, even ourselves.

There's a tension in the streets now, the aggression that comes with insatiable desires. Because there is more on offer than there was before, there is more to want. This kind of change, happening as it's happening here, fast and unmanageable, makes people see others in ways they hadn't before. As a market. A demographic. Points of access.

What all of us share is our wishing for more. But wishing has a dark side. It can turn those who were once merely strangers into the competition.

I follow Queen all the way to Spadina, then lakeward to the offices of the *National Star*—"*The New York Times* of Toronto" as one especially ill-conceived ad campaign called it. This is where I started out. An angry young man with no real grounds to be angry, quickly ascending from copy editor to the paper's youngest ever in-house book critic. My unforgiving standards buttressed by the conviction that one day all those tall poppies I had scythed to earth would see I had a right to my declarations. One day, I would produce a book of my own.

From as far back as I can remember I felt I had

something within me that would find its way out. This was likely the result of a solitary, only-child childhood, throughout which books were often my only friends. Weekends spent avoiding the out-of-doors, curled up like a cat on the rug's sunny squares, ripping into Greene, Leonard, Christie, mulling over the out-of-reach James, Faulkner, Dostoyevsky. Wondering how they did it. The making of *worlds*.

What was never in doubt was that I would be among them when I grew up. Not their equal necessarily, but participating in the same noble activity. I accepted that I might not be good at it. At first. But I could sense the hard work that had gone into my favourite works, and was prepared to devote myself to slow improvement.

Looking back on it, I must have seen writing as a sort of religious practice. A total commitment to craft and honest disclosure no less holy for its godlessness. There was the promise of salvation, after all. The possibility of creating a story that spoke for me, would be *better* than me. More compelling, more mysterious, more wise. I suppose, when they were still alive, I believed that writing a book would somehow keep my parents with me. And after they were gone, I simply changed my articles of faith: If I wrote a good enough book, it might bring them back.

But no book came.

Instead, after university, I started typing my way up the ladder of small-town weeklies and specialty magazine freelancing ("The New Dog, The New You" for *Puppy Love!* and "Carrots vs Beets?: The Root of the

Problem" for *Sustenance Gardening* being two prizewin-
ners in their fields). After I got married and was hired at
the *National Star*, I thought about my book less, and
about a flesh-and-blood future more. Children. Travel.
But the niggling idea that I was thwarting my destiny
with domestic comforts couldn't be wholly escaped. In
some private corner of my soul, I was still waiting. For
the opening line. For a *way in*.

But no line came.

Two things happened next, oddly related, and at the
same time: Tamara became pregnant, and I cancelled my
Sunday-only subscription to *The New York Times*. The
articulated reason for the latter decision was that I barely
found the time to peel apart its many sections and sup-
plements, never mind read any of them. And now, with
a baby on the way—it was a *waste*.

The truth had nothing to do with saving time or trees,
however. It had to do with my coming to the point where
I could no longer open the Book Review of the Sunday
Times without causing physical pain to myself. The *pub-
lishers*. The *authors' names*. The *titles*. All belonging to
books that weren't mine.

It hurt. Not emotionally, not a mere spanking of the
ego. It hurt in the same way kidney stones or a soccer
cleat to the balls hurts—instantly, indescribably, criti-
cally. The reviews themselves rarely mattered. In fact, I
usually couldn't finish reading the remotely positive
ones. As for the negative ones, they too often proved to
be insufficient salves to my suffering. Even the snarkiest
vandalism, the baldest runs at career enders, only acted

as reminders that their victims had produced something worth pissing on. Oh, to awaken on a rainy Sunday and refuse to get out of bed on account of being savaged in the *Times*! What a sweet agony *that* would be, compared to the slow haemorrhaging in No Man's Land it was to merely imagine creating words worthy of Newspaper of Record contempt.

Then Sam arrived, and the bad wanting went away.

I was in love—with Tamara, with my son, even with the world, which I hadn't really liked all that much before. I stopped trying to write. I was too busy being happy.

Eight months later Tamara was gone.

Sam was a baby. Too young to remember his mother, which left me to do all the remembering for the both of us.

It wasn't long after this that I started believing all over again. Waiting for a way to tell the one true story that might bring back the dead.

The demotions started some time after my return from bereavement leave. The dawning millennium, we were told, was ushering in a new breed of "user friendly" newspaper, one that could compete with the looming threats of the internet and cable news channels and widespread functional illiteracy. Readers had grown impatient. Words in too great a number only squandered their time. In response, the Arts section became the Entertainment section. Features were shrunk to make room for celebrity "news" and photos of movie stars walking, sunglassed, with a barbell-sized latte. Memos were circulated directing us to fashion our stories so as to no longer appeal to adults seeking information and analysis, but to adolescents with attention-deficit disorder.

Let's just say they weren't good days for the Books section.

Not that the ruin of my journalistic career happened overnight. I had slipped down the rungs of respectability one at a time, from literary columnist (gleeful, sarcastic trashings of almost everything) to entertainment writer-at-large (starlet profiles, tallying up the weekend box-office results), a couple months as "junior obituarist" (the "senior obituarist" being five years younger than me), before the inarguable end of the line, the universal newspaper grease-trap: TV critic. I had tried to talk my section editor into at least putting "Television Feature Writer" under my by-line, but instead, when I opened the *Tube News!* supplement the following weekend, I found that I didn't even have a name anymore, and that I was now, simply, "The Couch Potato."

Which is accurate enough. These past months of professional withering have found me spending more of my time on various recliners and mattresses: my bed, in which I linger later and later every morning, the chair in my therapist's office, which I leave shining with sweat, as well as the sofa in the basement, where I fast forward through the lobotomized sitcom pilots and crime dramas and reality shows that, put together, act on me as a kind of stupefying drug, the bye-bye pills they slip under the tongues of asylum inmates.

No shame in any of this, of course. Or no more shame than most of the things we do for money, the paid positions for Whale Saver or African Well Digger or Global Warming Activist being so lamentably few.

The problem is that, almost unnoticeably, the same notion from my childhood has returned to me like a lunatic whisper in my ear. A black magic spell. A devil's promise.

Maybe, if I could only put the right words in the right order, I would be saved. Maybe I could turn longing into art.

There is something unavoidably embittered in the long-exposure critic. It's because, at its heart, the practice is a daily reminder of one's secondary status. None start out wanting to review books, but to write them. To propose otherwise would be like trying to convince someone that as a child you dreamed of weighing jockeys instead of riding racehorses.

If you require proof, just look at the half-dozen souls keyboard clacking and middle-distance staring in the cubicles around mine. Together, we pick through the flotsam that the waves of pop culture wash in every morning. The CDs, DVDs, game software, movies, mags. Even the book desk. My former domain. Now responsible for assembling a single, ignored page on Saturday. But still a better place than where they've put me.

Here we are. Off in the corner, no window within stapler-throwing distance. A desk that my colleagues call the Porn Palace, on account of the teetering stacks of black video cassettes on every surface. And it *is* porn. It's

TV. An addictively shameful pleasure we all seem to want more of.

There's a box of new arrivals on my chair. I'm pulling out the first offering—a reality show where I'm promised contestants in bikinis eating live spiders—when Tim Earheart, one of the paper's investigative reporters, claps me on the back. You'd never know it, but Tim is my best friend here. It occurs to me now with a blunt surprise that he may be my best friend anywhere.

"You got any *Girls Gone Wild*?" he says, rummaging through the tapes.

"Thought you were more of a documentary guy."

"Wife's away this week. Actually, she might not be coming back."

"Janice left you?"

"She found out that my source on last week's Hell's Angels story was one of the bikers' old ladies," Tim says with a sad smile. "Let's just say I went more under-cover with her than Janice was comfortable with."

If it's true that his most recent wife has taken off, this will be marriage number three down the tubes for Tim. He turns thirty-six next week.

"Sorry to hear that," I say, but he's already waving off my sympathy.

"Drinks tonight?" he says, stepping away to re-join the hectic relevance of the news department. "Wait. It's Valentine's, isn't it? You got a date?"

"I don't date, Tim. I don't anything."

"It's been a while."

"Not so long."

"Some would say four years is enough to –"

"Three."

"*Three* years then. Eventually you're going to have to face the fact that you're still here, even if Tamara isn't."

"Trust me. I face that every day."

Tim nods. He's been to war zones. He knows a casualty when he sees one.

"Can I ask you something?" he says. "You think it's too late to ask out that new temp they've got down in Human Resources?"

It happened again on the walk home.

More and more these days, I'll be in the middle of something—dashing to the corner store, pounding out the day's word count at my desk, lining up for coffee—and the tears will come. So quiet and without warning I hardly notice.

And then today, walking along the sidewalk when I would have said "Nothing" if asked what was on my mind, it started again. Wet streaks freezing on my cheeks.

A rhyme pops into my head. An unconsoling singsong that carries me home.

> *I'm not well*
> *I'm not well*
> *But who in the hell*
> *Am I going to tell?*

By the time I get through the door, Sam's already finished his dinner and Emmie, the nanny, is drying him from his bath. Another irretrievable moment missed. I like bath-time with Sam more than any other part of the day. A little music. Epic sea battles waged with rubber ducks and old toothbrushes. All of it leading to bed. To stories.

"I'll take him," I tell Emmie, and she opens the towel she has wrapped around him. He rushes out of his cocoon and into my arms. A soapy angel.

I get him into pajamas. Open the book we're working through. But before I start reading, he studies me for a moment. Places a palm against my forehead.

"What do you think, doc? Am I going to make it?"

"You'll live," he says.

"But it's serious?"

"I'm not sure. Is it?"

"Nothing I can't handle."

"I don't want you to be sad."

"I miss your mom sometimes. That's all. It's normal."

"Normal."

"More or less."

Sam purses his lips. He's not sure whether to buy my pinched grin or not. The thing is, he needs me to be okay. And for him, I'll stay as okay as I can.

He yawns. Squirms in close, his head against my throat so that he can feel the vibrations of the words to come. Jabs his finger at the pages I hold open.

"Where were we?"

Once Sam is asleep it's down to the basement office. What Tamara used to call the Crypt. Which is a little too accurate to be wholly amusing. A low-ceilinged room that was a wine-making cellar for the previous owner. Even now, I can catch whiffs of fermented grapes. It makes me think of feet.

This is where I watch the tapes. A notebook on my knee, remote control in my hand.

I'm just three minutes into the spider-eating bikini babes when I hit Pause. Dig out of my pocket the ad I clipped from today's classifieds.

Tell the Story of Your Life

Open your soul. Bring your buried words to the page in this intensive workshop with Conrad White, published poet and novelist. Truly write. Write the truth.

I've never heard of Conrad White. Never attended a writers' workshop, circle, night class or retreat. It's been years since I've tried to write anything other than what I am contractually obliged to. But something about this day—about the taste of the air in this very room— has signalled that something is coming my way. Has already come.

I call the number at the bottom of the ad. When a voice at the other end asks me what he can do for me, I answer without hesitation.

"I want to write a book," I say.

People read less today than they used to. You've seen the studies, you've got teenagers, you've been to the mall—you know this already. But here's something you may not know:

The less people *read*, the more they want to *write*.

Creative writing workshops—within universities, libraries, night schools, mental hospitals, prisons—are the true growth industry in the ink-based sector. Not to mention the *ad hoc* circles of nervy aspirants, passing round their photocopied bundles. Each member claiming to seek feedback but secretly praying for a collective declaration of brilliance.

And now I'm one of them.

The address the voice on the phone gave me is in Kensington Market. Meetings to be held every Tuesday night for the next five Tuesdays. I was told I was the last to join the group. That is, I called it a group, and the voice corrected me.

"I prefer to think of it as a circle."

"Right. And how many will there be? In the circle?"

"Just seven. Any more, and I fear our focus may be lost."

After I hung up I realized that Conrad White—if that's who answered the phone—never asked for my name. I also realized I'd forgotten to find out if I should bring anything along to the first meeting—a pen, notebook, cash for the donation plate. But when I dialled the number again, it rang ten times without anyone answering. I suppose that now the circle was complete, Mr. White decided there was no point in picking up.

The next Tuesday, I walk up Spadina after work with my scarf turbaned around my ears. Despite the cold, most of the Chinatown grocers still have produce tables outside their doors. Frozen bok choy, starfruit, lemongrass. A dry powdering of snow over everything. At Dundas, nightfall arrives all at once. The giant screen atop the Dragon Mall casting a blue glow of advertising over the street.

I carry on another couple blocks north, past NO MSG noodle places and whole roast pigs hanging in butchers' windows, their mouths gaping in surprise. Then dash across the four lanes of traffic into the narrow lanes of the market.

Kensington means different things to different people, but for me, a walk through its streets always gives rise to the same question: How long can it last? Already some of the buildings are being turned into "live/work loft alternatives," promising a new "urban lifestyle" for people who are seeking "The Kind of Excitement that Comes with Walking on the Edge." I take out the tiny dictaphone recorder I always carry around (to capture any especially biting phrases for the next day's review) and read these words directly off the hoardings around the latest condo project. Some shoppers have also stopped to read the same come-hithers. But when they see me whispering into a tape recorder, they walk on. Another outpatient to be politely avoided.

On a bit, the old Portuguese fishmongers are lifting the slabs of cod and octopus off their beds of ice and waltzing them to the walk-ins for the night. The street still busy with safety-pinned punks and insane, year-round bicyclists, all dinnertime bargain hunting. Or simply congregating in one of the last places in the city where one can feel a resistance to the onslaught of generic upgrading, of globalized sameness, of money.

And then it strikes me, with an unsettling shiver, that some of the people bustling around me may be here for the same reason I am.

Some of them may be writers.

The address for the meeting brings me to a door next to The Fukhouse, a bar that, as far as I can see through the grimy window, has every wall, table surface, and both floor and ceiling painted in black gloss. Above the sign, on the second floor, stout candles flicker in the windows. If I wrote the number down right, it's up there that the Kensington Circle is to gather.

"Anarchists," a voice says behind me.

I turn to find a young woman in an oversized leather biker jacket. Her shoulders armoured with silver spikes. She doesn't seem to notice the cold, though below the jacket all she wears is a threadbare girls' school skirt and fishnets. And a raven tattooed over the back of her wrist.

"I'm sorry?"

"Just thought I'd warn you," she says, gesturing toward The Fukhouse's door. "That's kind of an anarchist clubhouse. And anarchists often don't take well to those not part of the revolution."

"I can imagine."

"Not that it matters. You're here for the circle. Am I right?"

"How'd you guess?"

"You look nervous."

"I *am* nervous."

She squints into my face through the looping snow. I have the same feeling I get when the customs officer at the border slides my passport through the computer and I have to wait to see if I'll be allowed through or placed under arrest.

"Evelyn," she says finally.

"Patrick Rush. A pleasure to meet you."

"Is it?"

And before I can tell if she's joking or not, she opens the door and starts up the stairs.

The room is so dark I can only stand at the entrance, hands feeling for walls, a light switch, the leather jacket girl. All I can see for sure are the candles oozing wax over the two distant window sills, the snow outside falling fast as TV static. Though I followed Evelyn up the stairs, she now seems to have disappeared into the void that yawns between the doorway and the windows.

"Glad you could come."

A male voice. I spin around, startled. This sudden movement, and my boots slipping on the puddle of snowmelt over the floorboards, makes me lose my footing. Someone releases a coquettish gasp. In the next instant I realize it was me.

"We're over here," the voice says.

The dark figure of a stooped man passes in front of me, drifting toward what I now can see is a circle of chairs in the centre of the room. Boots kicked off, I slide over to one of the two unoccupied places.

"We're just waiting for one more," the voice says, and I recognize it only now as the same as the one on the phone. Conrad White. Never-heard-of author and poet, now taking his seat across from mine. The sound of his lullaby voice also brings back the feeling I got when I first spoke my desire to write a book. There had been a pause, as though he was measuring the depth of my yearning. When he spoke again, I wrote down the details he gave me without really hearing them. His words seemed to come from somewhere else, a different time altogether.

All of us wait for the voice to begin again. If there really are six of us sitting here, we are still as dolls. Only the faint tide of our breaths to be heard, taking in the vapours of red wine and incense from the rug beneath our chair legs.

"Ah. Here he is."

Conrad White rises to welcome the last member of

the circle to arrive. I don't turn to see who it is at first. But as a second pair of feet step deliberately forward (and with boots left on), I sense some of the others shrink in their seats around me. Then I see why.

A sloped-shouldered giant steps forward from out of the darkness. At first he appears headless—there's a ridiculous second when I glance down to his hands to see if he carries his own skull—but it is only the full beard of black wires that obscures most of his face. Not his eyes though. The whites clear, unblinking.

"Thank you all for coming. My name is Conrad White," the old man says, sitting again. The bearded latecomer chooses the last chair—the one beside mine to the left. Though this saves me from having to look at him, it allows me a whiff of his clothes. A primitive mixture of wood smoke, sweat, boiled meat.

"I will be your facilitator over the next four weeks," Conrad continues. "Your guide. Perhaps even your friend. But I will not be your teacher. For writing of the truest kind—and *that*, I'm assuming, is what all of us aspire to—cannot be taught."

Conrad White looks around the circle, as though giving each of us the opportunity to correct him. None do.

He goes on to outline the ground rules for the meetings to come. The basic structure will involve weekly assignments ("Little exercises to help you *feel* what you *see*"), with the bulk of time spent on personal readings from each of our works-in-progress, followed by commentary from the other members. Trust is crucial. Special note is made that criticism, as such, will not be tolerated. Instead, there will be "conversations." Not between ourselves, but "between a reader and the words on the page." At this, I feel a couple of heads nodding in agreement off to my right, but I still don't look to see who it is. Somehow, so long as he's speaking, I can only look straight ahead at Conrad White. It makes me wonder if it's not only shyness that holds my stare. Perhaps there is something more deliberately occult in the arrangement of our chairs, the candles, the refusal of electric light. If not enchantment, there is definitely a lightheadedness that accompanies his words. A vertigo I can't shake.

When I'm able to focus again I pick up that we're now being told about honesty. It's the truth of the thing that is our quarry, not mastery of structure, not style. "Story is everything," the voice says. "It is our religions, our histories, our selves. Only through story can we hope to become acquainted with experiences other than our own."

In a different context—a room with enough light to show the details of faces, the hum of institutional central air, EXIT signs over the doors—this last promise might be overkill. Instead, we are moved. Or I am, anyway.

Now it's time for the obligatory "Tell us a little bit about yourself" roundabout. I'm terrified that Conrad will start with me. ("Hi. I'm Patrick. Widower, single dad. There was a time I dreamed of writing novels. Now I watch TV for a living.") Worse, he ends up choosing the woman sitting immediately to my right, someone I have so far sniffed (expensive perfume, tailored leather pants) but not fully seen. This means I will be last. The closer.

As each of the members speak, I play with the dictaphone in the outside pocket of my jacket. Push the Record button, Pause, then Record again, so that I create a randomly edited recording. It's only when they're halfway round the circle that I realize what I'm doing. Not that this stops me.

The good-smelling woman introduces herself as Petra Dunn. Divorced three years ago, and now that her one child has left for university, she has found herself "mostly alone" in the midtown family home. She names her neighbourhood—Rosedale—meaningfully, even guiltily, as she knows this address speaks of an attribute not lost on any of us: money. Now Mrs. Dunn spends her time on self-improvement. Long runs in the ravine. Charity volunteering. Night courses on arbitrary, cherry-picked subjects—Pre-Civil War American History, The Great Paintings of Europe Post-World War II, the 20 Classic Novels of the Twentieth Century. But she became tired of seeing "different versions of myself" in these classrooms, "second or third time around women" not seeking to be edified but asked out by the few men who prowled the Continuing Studies departments, men she calls "cougar hunters." More than this, she has felt the growing need to tell a story concerning the life she might have lived if she hadn't said yes when the older man who would become her husband offered to take her to dinner while she was working as a bartender at the Weston Country Club. An unlived existence that would have seen her return to her studies, a life of unpredictable freedoms, instead of marrying a man whose free use of his platinum card she'd mistaken for gentlemanly charm. A story concerning "A woman like me but not . . ."

And here Petra Dunn pauses. Long enough for me to steal a look at her face. I expect to see a woman in her fifties who's been silenced by her fight with tears. Instead, I'm met with a striking beauty not much older than forty. And it's not tears, but a choking rage that has stolen her words.

"I want to imagine who I really am," she says finally.

"Thank you, Petra," Conrad White says, sounding pleased at this start. "Who's next?"

That would be Ivan. The bald crown of his head shining faintly pink. Shoulders folded toward his chest, his frame too small for the plaid work shirt he has buttoned to his throat. A subway driver. A man who too rarely sees the light of day ("If I'm not sleeping, either it's night, or I'm underground"). And lonely. Though he doesn't confess to this outright, he's the sort who wears his chronic bachelorhood in the dark circles under his eyes, the tone of defeated apology in his voice. Not to mention the shyness that prevents him from making eye contact with any of the circle's women.

Conrad White asks him what he hopes to achieve over the course of the meetings to come, and Ivan considers his answer for a long moment. "When I bring my train into a station, I see the faces of all the people on the platform flash by," he says. "I just want to try and capture some of them. Turn them into something more than the passengers on the other side of the glass who get on, get off. Make whole people out of them. Something I can hold on to. Some*one*."

As soon as Ivan finishes speaking, he lowers his head, fearing he's said too much. I have to resist the impulse to go to him, offer a brotherly hand on his shoulder.

And then I notice his hands. Oversized gloves resting atop his knees. The skin stretched like aged leather over the bones. Something about those hands instantly dissolves the notion of going any closer to Ivan than is necessary.

The portly fellow beside Ivan introduces himself as Len. He looks around at each of us after this, grinning, as though his name alone suggests something naughty. "What I like about reading," he goes on, "is the way you can be different people. Do different things. Things you'd never do yourself. If you're good enough at it, it's like you're not even imagining any more."

This is why Len wants to write. To be transformed. A big kid who has the look of the stay-at-home gamer, the kind whose only friends are virtual, the other shut-ins he posts online messages to inquiring how to get to Level Nine on some shoot-the-zombies software. Who can blame him for wanting to become someone else?

The more Len talks about writing, the more physically agitated he becomes, wriggling his hefty hips forward to the edge of his chair, rubbing the armrests as though to dry his hands of sweat. But he only gets *really* excited once he confesses that his "big thing" is horror. Novels and short stories and movies, but especially comic books. Anything to do with "The undead. Presences. Werewolves, vampires, demons, poltergeists, witches. *Especially* witches. Don't ask me why."

Len shows all of us his loopy grin once more. It makes it hard not to like the guy. His passions worn so plainly, so shamelessly, I find myself almost envying him.

Sitting beside Len's nervous bulk, Angela looks small as a child. Part of this illusion is the result of her happening to occupy the largest chair in the room, a wing-backed lounger set so high the toes of her shoes scratch the floor. Other than this, what's notable about Angela's appearance is its lack of distinction. Even as I try to sketch her into my memory I recognize she has the kind of face that would be difficult to describe even a few hours from now. The angles of her features seem to change with the slightest shift, so that she gives the impression of being a living composite, the representative of a general strain of person rather than any person in particular.

Even what she says seems to evaporate as it drifts out into the room. Relatively new in the city, having arrived via "a bunch of different places out west." The only constant in her life is her journal. "Except it's not *really* a journal," she says, and makes an odd sound with her nose that might be a stifled laugh. "Most of it is made up, but some of it isn't. Which makes it more fiction than, like, a diary, I guess."

With this, she stops. Slides back into the chair and lets it swallow her. I keep watching her after she's finished. And though she doesn't meet eyes with anyone else in the circle, I have the notion that she's recording what everyone says just as deliberately as I am.

Next is Evelyn. The deadpan pixie in a biker jacket. I'm a little surprised to learn that she is a grad student at the University of Toronto. It isn't her youth. It's the outfit. She looks more like Courtney Love when she first fell for Kurt than the fellowship winner who can't decide between Yale, Cornell or Cambridge to do her Ph.D. Then the answer comes: her planned dissertation will be a study of "Dismemberment and Female Vengeance in the 1970s Slasher Film." I remember enough of university to know that such topics are best handled by those in costume.

We're now all the way around to the latecoming giant. When Evelyn's finished speaking, there's a subtle positioning of our bodies to take him in, more an adjustment of antennae to pick up a distant signal than the directness required in making eye contact. Still, all of the circle can steal a look at him except for me. Given his proximity, I would have to turn round and tuck my leg under to see him straight on. And this is something I don't want to do. It may only be the room's unfamiliarity, the awkwardness in meeting strangers who share little other than a craving for self-expression. But the man sitting to my left radiates a darkness of a different kind from the night outside. A strange vacancy of sympathy, of readable humanness. Despite his size, it's as though the space he occupies is only a denser form of nothing.

"And you?" Conrad White prompts him. "What brings you to our circle?"

The giant breathes. A whistling that comes up through his chest and, when exhaled, I can feel against the back of my hand.

"I was called," he says.

"'Called' in the sense of pursuing your destiny, I take it? Or perhaps a more literal calling?"

"In my dreams."

"You were summoned here in your dreams?"

"Sometimes –" the man says, and it seems like the beginning of a different thought altogether. "Sometimes I have bad dreams."

"That's fine. Perhaps you could just share your name with us?"

"William," he says, his voice rising slightly. "My name is William."

My turn.

I say my name aloud. The sound of those elementary syllables allows me to string together the point form brief on Patrick Rush. Father of a smart little boy lucky enough to take his mother's looks. A journalist who has always felt that something was missing from his writing. (I almost say "life" instead of "writing," a near-slip that is as telling as one might think). A man who isn't sure if he has something to say but who now feels he has to find out once and for all.

"Very good," Conrad White says, a note of relief in his voice. "I appreciate your being so frank. *All* of you. Under the circumstances, I think it only fair that I share with you who I am as well."

Conrad White tells us that he has recently "returned

from exile." A novelist and poet who was publishing in Toronto, back just before the cultural explosion of the late sixties that gave rise to a viable national literature. Or, as Conrad White puts it evenly (though no less bitterly), "The days when writing in this country was practiced by unaffiliated individuals, before it took a turn toward the closed door, the favoured few, the tribalistic." He carried on with his work, increasingly feeling like an outsider while some of his contemporaries did what was unimaginable among Canadian writers up to that point: they became famous. The same hippie poets and novelists that were in his classes at UofT and reading in the same coffee houses were now being published internationally, appearing as "celebrity guests" on CBC quiz shows, receiving government grants.

But not Conrad White. He was working on a different animal altogether. Something he knew would not dovetail neatly with the preferred subject matters and stylistic modes of his successful cohorts. A novel of "ugly revelations" that, once published, proved even more controversial than he'd anticipated. The writing community (as it had begun to regard itself) turned its back on him. Though he responded with critical counter-attacks in any journal or pamphlet that would have him, the rejection left him more broken-hearted than livid. It prompted his decision to live abroad. England, at first, before moving on to India, southeast Asia, Morocco. He had only returned to Toronto in the last year. Now he conducted writing workshops such as these to pay his rent.

"I say 'workshops,' but it would be more accurate to speak of them in the singular," Conrad White says. "For this is my first."

Outside, the snow has stopped falling. Beneath our feet the bass thud from The Fukhouse's speakers has begun to rattle the windows in their frames. From somewhere in the streets of the market, a madman screams.

Conrad White passes a bowl around to collect our weekly fee. Then he gives us our assignment for next week. A page of a work-in-progress. It needn't be polished, it needn't be the beginning. Just a page of *something*.

Class dismissed.

I fish around for my boots by the door. None of us speak on the way out. It's like whatever has passed between us in the preceding hour never happened at all.

When I get to the street I start homeward without a glance back at the others, and in my head, there's the conviction that I won't return. And yet, even as I have this thought, I know that I will. Whether the Kensington Circle can help me find my story, or whether the story is the Kensington Circle itself, I have to know how it turns out.

Emmie has Wednesday mornings off, so it's my day to work from home and look after Sam on my own. Just four years old and he sits up at the breakfast table, perusing the Business and Real Estate and International News sections right along with me. Though he can hardly understand a word of it, he puts on a stern face—just like his old man—as he licks his thumb to turn the grim pages.

As for me, I comb the classifieds to see if Conrad White's ad is still running, but can't find it anywhere. Perhaps he's decided that the one group who assembled in his apartment the night before will be all that he can handle.

Sam pushes the Mutual Funds Special Report away from him with a rueful sigh.

"Dad? Can I watch TV?"

"Ten minutes."

Sam retreats from the table and turns on a Japanimation robot laser war. I'm about to ask if he wouldn't mind turning it down when a short piece in the City section catches my attention.

A missing person story. The victim (is one a "victim" when only missing?) being one Carol Ulrich, who is presumed to have been forcibly taken from a neighbourhood playground. There were no witnesses to the abduction—including the woman's son, who was on the swings at the time. Residents have been advised to be alert to any strangers "acting in a stalking or otherwise suspicious manner." While authorities continue their search for the woman, they admit to having no leads in the case. The story ends ominously with the police spokesperson stating that "activity of this kind has been shown to indicate intent of repeated actions of a similar nature in the future."

It's the sort of creepy but sadly common item I would normally pass over. But what makes me read on to the end is that the neighbourhood in question is the one we live in. The playground where the woman was taken the same one where I take Sam.

"What are you *doing*, Daddy?"

Sam is standing at my side. That I'm also standing is something of a surprise. I look down to see my hands on the handle of the living room's sliding door.

"I'm locking the door."

"But we *never* lock *that* door."

"We don't?"

I peer through the glass at our snow-covered garden. Checking for footprints.

"Show's over," Sam says, pulling on my pant leg and pointing at the TV.

"Ten more minutes."

As Sam runs off, I pull the dictaphone out of my pocket.

"Note to self," I whisper. "Buy padlock for back gate."

It's the weekend already, and Tuesday's deadline requiring a page from my nonexistent work-in-progress is fast approaching. I've made a couple stabs at something during the week, but the surroundings of either the Crypt at home or the cubicle at work have spooked any inspiration that might be waiting to show itself. I need to find the right space. A laptop of one's own.

Once Tamara's out-of-town sister, Stacey, has come by to take Sam and his cousins to see the dinosaurs at the museum, I hit the Starbucks around the corner. It's a sunny Saturday, which means that, after noon, Queen Street will be clogged with shoppers and gawkers. But it's only just turned ten, and the line-up isn't yet out the door. I secure a table, pop the lid on my computer, and stare at a freshly created word-processing file. Except for the blinking cursor, a virgin screen of grey. Its purity stops me from touching the keys. The idea of typing a word on to it seems as crude as stepping outside and pissing into a snowbank. And the dentist office grind of the cappuccino machine is starting to get on my nerves. Not to mention the orders shouted back and forth between the barista kids behind the counter. Who wouldn't raise their head to see what sort of person orders a venti decaf cap with half skim, half soy and *extra whipped cream*?

I pack up and walk crosstown to the Reference Library on Yonge. The main floor entrance is crowded, as it always is, with the homeless, the new-in-town, the dwindling souls without a cellphone who need to make a call. Through the turnstiles, the building opens into an atrium that cuts through the five floors above. I choose the least occupied level and find a long work table all to myself. Lean back, and think of a single word that might stride forth to lead others into battle.

Nothing.

All around me are tens of thousands of volumes, each containing tens of thousands of printed words, and not *one* of them is prepared to come forward when I need it most.

Why?

The thing is, I *know* why.

I don't have a story to tell.

But Conrad White did, once upon a time. Seeing as I'm in the Reference Library, I decide to take a break and do a bit of research. On Mr. White, ringleader of the Kensington Circle.

It takes a little digging, but some of the memoirs and cultural histories from the time of sixties Toronto make footnoted mention of him. From old money, privately schooled, and author of a debatably promising novel before going into hiding overseas. As one commentator tartly put it, "Mr. White, for those who know his name at all, is more likely remembered for his leaving his home-land than any work he published while living here."

What's intriguing about the incomplete biography of Conrad White are the hints at darker corners. The con-ventional take has it that he left because of the critical reception given his book, *Jarvis and Wellesley*, the fractured, interior monologue of a man walking the streets of the city on a quest to find a prostitute who most closely resembles his daughter, recently killed in a car accident. An idealized figure he calls the "perfect girl." To anyone's knowledge, Conrad White hasn't written anything since.

But it's the echoes of the author's actual life to be found in the storyline of *Jarvis and Wellesley* that gives bite to his bio. He *had* lost a daughter, his only child, in the year prior to his embarking on the novel. And there is mention of White's exile being precipitated by his relationship with a very real teenage girl, and the resulting threats of legal action, both civil and criminal. A literary recluse on the one hand, girl-chasing perv on the other. Thomas Pynchon meets Humbert Humbert.

I go back to my table to find my laptop screen has fallen asleep. It knows as well as I do that there will be no writing today. But that needn't mean there can't be reading.

The edition of *Jarvis and Wellesley* I pull off the shelf hasn't been signed out in over four years. Its spine creaks when I open it. The pages crisp as potato chips.

Two hours later, I return it to where I found it.

The prose ahead of its time, no doubt. Some explicit sex scenes involving the older protagonist and young streetwalkers lend a certain smutty energy to the proceedings, if only passingly. And throughout, the unspoken grief is palpable, an account of loss made all the more powerful by narrating its effects, not its cause.

But it's the description of the protagonist's "perfect girl" that leaves the biggest impression. The way she is conjured so vividly, but using little or no specific details. You know exactly what she looks like, how she behaves, how she feels, though she is nowhere to be found on the page.

What's stranger still is the certainty that I will one day meet her myself.

4

Tuesday brings a cold snap with it. A low of minus eighteen, with a wind chill making it feel nearly double that. The talk-radio chatter warns everyone against going outside unless absolutely necessary. It makes me think—not for the first time—that I can be counted among the thirty million who voluntarily live in a country with annual plagues. A black death called winter that descends upon us all.

Down in the Crypt I dash off a column covering two new personal makeover shows, a cosmetic surgeon drama, and five (yes, *five*) new series in which an interior designer invades people's homes and turns their living rooms into what look like airport lounges. Once this is behind me, I get to work on my assignment for the evening's circle. By the end of the day I've managed to squeeze out a couple hundred words of shambling introduction—*Tuesday brings a cold snap with it*, etc. It'll have to do.

Upstairs, as I heat up leftovers in the microwave, Sam comes to show me something from today's paper.

"Doesn't she look like Mommy?"

He points to a photo of Carol Ulrich. The woman who was abducted from our neighbourhood playground. The one snatched away as her child played on the swings.

"You think so?" I say, taking the paper from him and pretending to study the woman's features. It gives me a chance to hide my face from Sam for a second. He only knows what his mother looks like from pictures, but he's right. Carol Ulrich and Tamara could be sisters.

"I remember her," Sam says.

"You do?"

"At the corner store. She was in the line-up at the bank machine once too."

"That so."

Sam pulls the newspaper down from my eyes. Reads me.

"They look the same. Don't they?"

"Your mother was more beautiful."

The microwave beeps. Both of us ignore it.

"Was that lady . . . did somebody hurt her?"

"Where'd you hear that?"

"I can *read*, Dad."

"She's only missing."

"Why would somebody *make* her missing?"

I pull the newspaper from Sam's hands. Fold it into a square and tuck it under my arm. A clumsy magician trying to make the bad news disappear.

Conrad White's apartment is no brighter, though a good deal colder than the week before. Evelyn has kept her jacket on, and the rest of us glance at the coats we left on the hooks by the door. William is the only one who appears not to notice the chill. Over the sides of his chair his T-shirted arms hang white and straight as cement pipes.

What's also noticeably different about the circle this time round is that each of us have come armed: a plastic shopping bag, a binder, a sealed envelope, two file folders, a leatherbound journal, and a single paper clip used to contain our first written offerings. Our work trembles on our laps like nervous cats.

Conrad White welcomes us, reminds us of the way the circle will work. As his accentless voice goes on, I try to match the elderly man speaking to us with the literary bad boy of forty years ago. If it was anger that motivated his exile, I can't detect any of it in his face today. Instead, there's only a shopworn sadness, which may be what anger becomes eventually, if it shows itself early enough.

Tonight's game plan calls for each of us to read what we've brought with us aloud for no more than fifteen minutes, then the other members will have a chance to comment for another fifteen. Interruption of responses is permitted, but not of the readers themselves. Our minds should be open as wide as possible when listening to others, so that their words are free from comparison to anything that has come before.

"You are the children in the Garden," Conrad White tells us. "Innocent of experience or history or shame. There is only the story you bring. And we shall hear it as though it is the first ever told."

With that, we're off.

The first readers are mostly reassuring. With each new voice trying their words out for size, the insecurities I have about my own tortured scribbles are relieved, albeit only slightly. By the halfway point (when Conrad White calls a smoke break) I am emboldened by the confirmation that there are no undiscovered Nabokovs, Fitzgeralds or Munros—nor a Le Carré or Rowling or King—among us. And there are few surprises, in terms of subject matter. Petra has a bit of *As the World Turns* meets *Who's Afraid of Virginia Woolf?* husband-and-wife dialogue that captures certain verbal cruelties in such detail I assume they are taken straight from a loop of memory. Ivan, the subway driver, tells a tale of a man who awakens to find he's been transformed into a rat, and must find a way into the sewers beneath the city that he intuitively knows is his new home of pestilence and filth. (When, after his reading, I compliment him on his re-working of Kafka, Ivan looks at me quizzically and says, "I'm sorry. *Kafka?*"). Though Len feels that only the opening paragraph of a proposed "epic horror trilogy" is ready for presentation, it nevertheless goes on forever, a description of night that is a long walk through the thesaurus entry for "dark." And Evelyn promisingly starts her story with a female grad student being screwed by her thesis advisor on the floor of his office while she daydreams about her father teaching her how to skip stones on the lake at the family cottage.

Over the smoke break, those not slipping on their coats get up to stretch. We shuffle around the room without looking at each other or being the first to start up a conversation. All of us steal glances, however. And note where William stands at all times, so we know what corner to avoid.

It's over these awkward minutes of feeling others' eyes on me that I ask myself: How does the rest of the circle see me? Most favourably, how I see myself on the best of days, I suppose: an endearingly rumpled Preppie that Time Forgot. Most unfavourably, how I see myself on the worst of days: a dandruffy channel flipper fast approaching the point of no return. Beyond debate are the wide shoulders that lend the illusion of one-time athleticism. And good teeth. A set of ivory chompers that always impress when encountered in *Say Cheese!* snaps.

Once the smokers return, we get started on the readers who remain.

And this is where things get a little foggy.

I must have read the page I brought with me, as I remember bits of what the other members said afterwards. (Evelyn found the first-person mode "captures your character's sense of being trapped in himself," and Petra could detect a "hidden suffering.") William requested a pass on reading his own work, or I think he did, as I only recall the sound of his voice and not its words. A low grinding, like air forced through wet sand.

But all I really preserve from the second half of the meeting is Angela.

My first thought, as she opens the cracked leather journal on her knees and lifts it slowly, even reluctantly to her eyes, is that she appears younger than I'd guessed the week before. What I took to be the indistinct features of an adult may instead be the unblemished, baby-fat smoothness of a girl coming out of her teens.

And yet, even as she reads, this impression of girlish youth turns into something else. Her face is difficult to describe, to remember, to *see*, because it's not a face at all. It is a mask. One that never sharpens into full focus, like an unfinished sculpture in which you can recognize the subject is human, but beyond this, taken at different points of view, it could be a representation of virtually anyone.

These considerations of Angela's appearance come and go within seconds. Soon, all of my attention is on what she reads. We listen without shifting in our seats, without crossing or uncrossing our legs. Even our breathing is calmed to the smallest sips.

It's not the virtuosity of her writing that dazzles us, as her style is simple as a child's. Indeed, the overall effect is that of a strange sort of fairy tale. One that lulls for a time, then breaks its spell with the suggestion of an awaiting threat. It is the voice of youth taking its final turn into the world of adult corruption, of foul, grown-up desire.

I have been playing with the dictaphone in my pocket this meeting as I had at the last, clicking the Record button on and off. Unthinkingly, a nervous tic. Now I press it down and leave it running.

Once she begins her reading I have no other thoughts except for one: I will not attempt to write again. There will be what I do for the newspaper, of course. And I can always force out a page here and there, whatever it takes to bluff my way through the next four sessions. But Angela's story blots out whatever creative light that might have shown itself from within.

It's not envy that makes me so sure of this. It's not the poor sport's refusal to play if he can't win. I know I won't try to write for the circle again because until Angela's journal comes to its end, I am only a reader.

After the meeting, I have a drink with Len at The Fukhouse. That is, I'm the first to nip into the bar below Conrad White's apartment, and Len follows me a moment later. He takes the stool two over from mine, as if we are going to entertain the pretence of not knowing who the other is. A couple minutes after our facially tattooed bartender delivers our drinks—beer for me, orange juice for Len—the space between us becomes too ridiculous to maintain.

"You enjoying the class so far?" I ask.

"Oh yeah. I think this might turn out to be the best."

"You've done a writing workshop before?"

"Plenty. Like, a *lot*."

"You're an old pro then."

"Never had anything published, though. Not like you."

This takes me by surprise. It does every time someone recognizes me, before I remember that my Prime Time Picks of the Week column on Fridays has a tiny picture of me next to the by-line. A pixillated smirk.

"There's published, and then there's published," I say.

I'm thinking that's about it. Politeness has been maintained, my beer almost guzzled. I'm about to throw my coat on and steel myself for the cold walk home when Len ventures a question of his own.

"That guy's pretty weird, don't you think?"

He could be speaking of Conrad White, or Ivan, or the bartender with a lizard inked into his cheek, or the leader of the free world warning of nerve gas delivered in briefcases on the TV over the bar, but he isn't.

"William's quite a character, alright."

"I bet he's done time. Prison, I mean."

"Looks like the sort."

"He scares me a bit." Len shifts his gaze from his orange juice to me. "What about you?"

"Me?"

"Doesn't he give you the creeps?"

I could admit the truth. And with another man, one I knew better or longer, I would. But Len is a little too openly eager for company to be dealt any favours just yet.

"You should use him as material." I flatten a bill on to the bar sufficient to cover both our drinks. "I thought you *liked* horror stories."

"Definitely. But there's a difference between imagining bad things and doing bad things."

"I hope you're right. Or some of us would be in real trouble," I say, and give Len a comradely pat on the shoulder as I go. The big kid smiles. And damn if I don't feel a smile of my own doing its thing too.

5

Angela's Story
Transcribed from Tape Recording No. 1

There once was a girl who was haunted by a ghost.
A terrible man who does terrible things who would
visit her in her dreams. The girl had never had a
friend, but she knew enough to know this wasn't
what he was. No matter how much she prayed or
how good she was or how she tried to believe it was
true when others would tell her there was no such
thing as ghosts, the terrible man would come and
prove that all the wishing and prayers in the world
could never wish or pray him away. This was why the
girl had to keep her ghost to herself.

The only connection, the only intimacy she would
allow herself with him was to give him a name.
The Sandman.

Everyone has parents. Knowing this is like knowing
that, one day, all of us will die. Two things common to
every person in the world.

But there were times when the girl thought she was the singular exception to this supposedly inescapable rule. Times she felt certain she was the only person who'd ever lived who had neither a mother nor a father. She simply appeared in the middle of her own story, just as the terrible man who does terrible things walked into the middle of her dreams. The girl is real, but only in the way that a character in a story is real. If she *were* a character in a story, it would explain how she had no parents, as characters aren't born but just *are*, brought into being on the whim of their authors.

What troubled the girl almost as much as being haunted by the terrible man who does terrible things was that she had no idea who her author might be. If she knew that, she'd at least know who to blame.

Even characters have a past, though they may not have lived it as the living do. The girl, for instance, was an orphan. People never spoke of where she came from, and the girl never asked, and in this way it was never known. She was a mystery to others as much as to herself. She was a problem that needed solving.

There were books the girl had read where orphans such as herself lived in homes with other orphans. And although these homes were often places of longing and cruelty, the girl wished she could live in one, so that she was not the only one like herself. Instead, she was sent to live in foster homes, which are not like the orphanages in books, but just regular homes with people who are paid to look after someone like the girl. When she was ten, she moved four times. When she was eleven, twice more. When she was twelve, she moved once a month for a year. And all along the Sandman followed her. Showing her the things he would do if he were real, and continued to do in her dreams.

And then, when she was thirteen, she was sent to live in an old farmhouse in the dark forests to the north, further north than most farms were ever meant to be. Her foster parents there were the oldest she'd had yet. Edra was the wife's name, and Jacob the husband's. They had no children of their own, only their hardscrabble farm, which yielded just enough to feed them through the long winters. Perhaps it was their childlessness that made them so happy when the girl came to them. She was still a mystery, still a problem. But Edra and Jacob loved her before they had any reason to, loved her more than if they'd had a child of their own. It was the suffering the girl had seen that prompted their love, for they were farmers of land that fought them over everything they took from it. Edra and Jacob knew suffering, and had some idea of what it could do to a girl, alone.

For a time, the girl was as happy—or as close to happy—as she'd ever been. There was comfort in the kindness her elderly foster parents showed her. She had a home in which she might live for years instead of weeks. There was a school in the town down the road she took the bus to every day, and where there were books for her to read, and fellow students she dreamed of one day making friends of. It was, for a time, what she'd imagined normal might be like.

Her contentment had been so great and without precedent that she'd almost forgotten about the terrible man who does terrible things. It had been a while since her night thoughts had been interrupted by his appearance. So it is with the most awful kind of surprise when she comes home from school one afternoon in late autumn to overhear Edra and Jacob talking about a little girl who'd disappeared from town.

Thirteen years old. The same age as her. Playing outside in the yard one minute, gone the next. The police and volunteer search parties had looked everywhere for her, but for three days the missing girl remained missing. The authorities were forced to presume foul play. They had no suspect in mind. Their only lead was that some in town had lately noticed a stranger walking the cracked sidewalks at night. A tall, sloped-shouldered man, a figure who kept to the shadows. "A man with no face," was how one witness put it. Another said it seemed the man was searching for something, though this was an impression and nothing more. Aside from this, no details were known of him.

But they were known to the girl. For she knew who the dark figure was even though she wasn't there to see him. She knew who had taken a girl in town the same age as her. The Sandman. Except now he'd escaped the constraints of her dream world and entered the real, where he could do all the terrible things he desired to do.

The girl was certain of all this, along with something else. She knew what the Sandman searched for as he walked in the night shadows.

He searched for her.

6

Write What You Know.

This is one of the primary Writers' Rules, though an unnecessary one, as the initial inclination of most is toward autobiography anyway. The imagination comes later, if it comes at all, after all the pages of the family photo album have been turned, love affairs autopsied, coming-of-age revelations and domestic tragedies rehashed on the page. Usually, people find their own lives sufficiently fascinating to never have to confront the problem of making things up. The Kensington Circle is no exception. Evelyn's campus sexcapade, Petra's marital breakdown, Ivan's sewer-rat metamorphosis. I'm jealous of them. It would make writing so much easier if I never tired of seeing the same face in the mirror.

But what if you don't particularly find the life you know all that interesting? *Real*, yes. And marked by its share of loss, redeemed by the love of a son with eyes the colour of his mother's. It's just that I don't see my life as satisfactory material to present as fiction. I find it challenge enough just muddling along as who I am, never mind casting myself as hero.

This is the reasoning I call on when, as now, I try to squeeze out a paragraph to be read at the next circle meeting, and nothing comes. I'm taking lunch at my desk, gnawing on a cafeteria ham-and-cheese, randomly pecking at the keys of my computer. Tim Earheart, who finds my literary aspirations perplexing ("Why do you think anybody would pay to read the shit you're pulling out of your ass?" is how he put it to me, unanswerably, when I told him of my attendance at a fiction-writing circle), comes by to read over my shoulder.

"I'm no judge," he says, "but I'm not sure you're going anywhere with this."

He's right. Over the next hour and a half, only a few sentences remain on the screen.

Here's what good Write What You Know has done for me today:

> After my wife died I started hearing voices. Just hers at first. And then others I've never heard before. Strangers. I can't know this for sure but I have the feeling that all of them are dead.
>
> They come to me before I go to sleep. This is what frightens me. Not that they're dead, or that I can hear them. But that I'm awake when I do.

Once this passage of luminous prose has been accomplished, I turn my mind to my Couch Potato column for the weekend edition. This week it's a gloves-off attack on the Canadian franchise of *American MegaStar!*, a talent show that is the top-rated program in this country, as well as the fourteen others it has colonized. An entire, worldwide generation being led to believe they are entitled to be famous. It's toxic. A lie. It's *wrong*. And it's also how my frustration with Writing What I Know opens the gates to Writing How the World Has Gone to Crap, which has never been much of a problem for me.

Even though I know that *Canadian MegaStar!* is owned by the same multinational media behemoth that owns the paper I work for, and even though there have been ominous hints from the section editor to "go easy" on "content" which is produced by said behemoth, I let slip the dogs of war on *MegaStar!* as if it is single-handedly responsible for carrying out a cultural atrocity. In fact, this last phrase makes it into the lede. From this measured opening, the column goes on to be brutal, hyperbolic and libellous, all leading to the kind of hysterical finish where you're actually a little concerned about the mental health of the column's author. It's *personal*.

I stay at work late (Thursdays keep me at the office at least until midnight copyediting the Best on the Box listings) and walk home wondering if today will prove to be my last in my current position. Or, come to think of it, my last in *any* position. It's almost amusing to wonder what else I might be qualified to do. I've always rather liked the idea of running my own business. Something very hands off. Automated, preferably. A laundromat. A spray-it-yourself car wash.

I round the corner on to my street speculating over what kind of pay cut, if any, would be involved in delivering newspapers instead of writing for them, when I notice the yellow police tape around the house across from mine. It is the neighbouring family at 147, and not my own family at 146 that the four police cruisers are parked in front of. But I still run the half-block up Euclid, ring the bell at my front door after twice dropping the keys, and confirm my son is safe with Emmie before going back out to ask the cop turning traffic back toward Queen what's going on.

"Break and enter," he says, chewing the inside of his cheek.

"What'd they take?"

"Didn't touch a thing. The kid was the only one who saw him."

"Joseph. My boy plays with him sometimes."

"Yeah? Well, when Joseph woke up tonight some son of a bitch was standing over his bed."

"Was he able to give a description?"

"All he can say is the guy's a shadow."

"A shadow?"

"Went downstairs to the living room with the kid following behind him. Just stood at the front window, staring out at the street. Then, after a while, he walked out the front door as if he owned the place. Turn it *around*, buddy! Yeah, *you!*"

The cop steps away to have a word with whoever's behind the wheel of the SUV that refuses to head back to Queen. It gives me a chance to walk up on to the neighbour's patch of lawn and stand with my back to their front window. The same view the shadow would have had, standing behind the glass.

Staring at my place.

Where Sam is now. Standing next to Emmie on the porch, squinting over at me.

I read the nanny's lips—*Wave to Daddy!*—and Sam raises his chubby arm in salute. And as I wave back I wonder if he can see how bad Daddy's shaking.

The next circle meeting is at Petra's house. She had kindly offered to host all of us the week before, though as I step out of my cab at her Rosedale address, I see she was being modest to the point of insult when she described her digs as "Nothing too fancy." The place is a mansion. Copper roof, terraced landscaping that looks expensive even under a couple inches of snow, matching Mercedes coupés (one red, one black) docked in the carport. It makes me wonder how much the husband had before the divorce if this is Petra's cut.

Inside the door, my coat is taken by a silver-haired man wearing a better suit than any I have ever owned. A man who serves not only a different class, but a different century. My first honest-to-God butler.

"The group is assembling in the Rose Room," he says, and leads me over marble floors to a sunken lounge of leather chairs, each with their own side table, and a snapping fire in the hearth. At the door, the butler discreetly inquires as to whether I would like a drink. He says it in a way that makes it clear real drinks are included in the offer.

"Scotch?" I say, and he nods, as though my choice had confirmed a suspicion he'd had on first sight.

Most of the other members are already here. Conrad White has chosen a chair near the fire, its orange flickers lending him a devilish air which is only enhanced by the smirk he barely manages to conceal as he notes the room's incoherent collection of Inuit sculptures, garish abstracts and bookshelves lined with leather-bound "classics." In this context of stage-set wealth, the rest of us look like hired help sneaking a break, holding our crystal goblets with both hands so nothing might spill on the rug.

Len in particular seems out of place. Or perhaps this is because he's the only one talking.

"You should come. You *all* should. How about you, Patrick?"

"How about me what?"

"The open mic. There's a launch party for a new litmag, and then afterwards they open the floor to anyone who wants to read."

"I don't know, Len."

"C'mon. You can check out what's *going on* out there."

"They have a bar?"

"Half-price beer if you buy the zine."

"Now you're talking."

All of us are here now except for William and Petra, the latter clipping back and forth to the kitchen on high heels, touchingly anxious about burning the shrimp skewers. When our hostess finally sits, Conrad White decides to go ahead without William. There's a subtle easing in all of our postures at this. I would be surprised if any of us didn't hope that William has moved on to other creative endeavours, if not a different area code altogether.

I'm first, which is something of a relief, as the sooner I can get through the miserable couple of paragraphs I've brought along, the sooner I can get to work on the quadruple single malt Jeeves has poured for me.

Besides, I'm only here for one reason anyway.

Angela.

She doesn't disappoint. I say this even though I'm not really listening. After I click my dictaphone on, I pay less attention to her words than how she speaks them. I have assumed all along that Angela was using a voice distinct from her own in her readings. Now I realize that I have virtually no idea what her "real" voice is like, or whether it would be different from the one I listen to now. She has said so little in the circle (her responses to the other readers little more than a murmured "I liked it a lot") that it may be the at once innocent and debauched little girl tone she uses is the same as her everyday speech.

When she's finished, no one says anything for what may be a minute. The fire hissing like a punctured tire. An ice cube cracks in Len's tumbler of apple juice. And from the moment Angela closes the cover of her journal to the moment Conrad White invites the circle to comment on what we've just heard, she looks at me.

More active than staring. A *taking in*. Every blink marking some new observation. And I do the same. Or try to. To see inside, sort her truth from the make believe. Figure out whether she can spot anything worthwhile in me. Anything she might like.

"Wonderful, Angela. Truly *wonderful*," Conrad White says.

Everyone raises their heads. No one had noticed our silent exchange except for Conrad himself. And Ivan. Both men shifting in their chairs to find relief from an affliction I immediately recognize. A thought that, for the lonely like us, passes more than any other.

Why not me?

After the meeting, we step out into the cold night, none of us knowing which way will lead us out of the enclave's curving streets and cul-de-sacs that discourage entry or exit. I look around for Angela, but she must have grabbed her coat before us. In any case, there's no sign of her now.

"So, Patrick, we're on for Tuesday?" Len asks. I look at him like I don't have a clue what he's talking about. Which I don't. "The open mic?"

"Right. Yes. Absolutely."

"'Night then," he says, and scuffs off in the opposite direction I would guess to be the way out of here. Leaving just me and Ivan standing there.

"I know the way," Ivan says.

"You're familiar with this neighbourhood?"

"No," he says, exhaling a long, yogic breath. "I can hear the trains."

Ivan tilts his head back, eyes squeezed shut, as though savouring the melody of a violin concerto, when all there is to hear is the clacking of the subway train emerging out of the tunnel somewhere in the ravine below.

"Follow me," Ivan says, and starts out toward the nearest doors to the underworld.

———

On our walk out of Rosedale's labyrinth of old-money chateaux and new-money castles, enveloped in a cold-hardened March darkness, Ivan tells me he's never hit a jumper. For a subway driver with his years of seniority, this is a rare claim. Not once has one of the bodies standing behind the yellow warning line on the platform made that incongruous leap forward. Yet every time his train bursts out of the tunnel and into the next station lit bright as a surgery theatre, he wonders who it will be to break his good record.

"Every day I see someone who thinks about it," Ivan says as we cross the bridge over the tracks. "The little moves they make. A half step closer to the edge, or putting their briefcase down at their side, or swinging their arms like they're at the end of a diving board. Getting ready. Sometimes you can only read it in their faces. They look at the front of the train—at me behind the glass—and there's this calm that comes over them. How *simple* it would be. But in the next second, they're thinking, 'Why *this* train? If there's another just as good coming along, why not wait? Make sure everything's right.' I can hear them like they're whispering in my ear."

"And then they change their minds."

"Sometimes," Ivan says, spitting over the side of the bridge on to the rails below. "And sometimes the next train *is* the right train."

We walk on toward Yonge Street where it breaks free of the downtown stretch of head shops and souvenir fly-by-nights, and heads endlessly north. Ivan talks without provocation, laying out his thoughts in organized capsules. Even when we come to stand outside the doors to the station he continues on, never looking at me directly, as though he has memorized this speech by heart and cannot allow himself to be distracted. It leaves me to study his head. Hatless and bald. A vulnerable cap of skin turned the blue-veined white of Roquefort.

And what does Ivan tell me? Things I would have already guessed, more or less. Son of Ukrainian immigrants. His father a steel cutter with a temper, his mother an under-the-table seamstress, mending the clothes of the neighbourhood labourers in their flat over what was then a butcher's, now an organic tea shop on Roncesvalles. Never married. Lives alone in a basement apartment, where he writes in the off-hours. Meandering stories that follow the imagined lives of those he shuttles here and there under the city.

"This is the first time I've been with people in a long time," he says. It takes a moment to realize he's talking about the circle. About me.

"It's hard to meet strangers in this town," I say.

"It's not that. It's that I haven't allowed myself to be around others."

"Why not?"

"I was accused of something once," he says. Looks at me straight. "Have you ever been accused of something?"

A rip of freezing wind comes out of nowhere. A furious howl that leaves me with instant headache.

What I took to be Ivan's shyness has dropped away. He reads my face, numbed by the cold so that I have no idea what shape my features have taken. What I do know for sure is that, all at once, the fact that nobody has come in or out of the subway in the time we've been standing here makes me more than a little uncomfortable.

"I suppose I have," I say.

"You suppose you have."

"I mean, I'm not sure what context –"

"The context of being accused of *harming* someone."

Ivan steps away from me. He had meant to have a normal conversation with someone who struck him as normal too, but he'd lost his balance on the home stretch. Yet it's not embarrassment or apology that plays over his face now. It's anger. At me, at himself. At the whole accusing world.

"Better start home," he mumbles, leaning his back into the subway's door. The warmer air from underground moans out through the gap. "I can get you on free if you want."

"No, thanks. I like to walk."

"On a night like this?"

"I'm not too far."

"Yeah? Where?"

"Close enough."

I could tell Ivan where I live, and I almost do. But I just wave vaguely westward instead.

Ivan nods. I can feel him wanting to ask me to keep the last part of our conversation to ourselves. But in the end, he just slips through the door and stands on the descending escalator. His head an empty cartoon thought bubble following him down.

I walk to Bloor and start west, past the funny-money block of Gucci and Chanel and Cartier, then left at the museum. Entering the university campus at Harbord, the traffic is hushed. I'm alone on the street, which invites the return of a habit I've indulged since childhood. Talking to myself. Back then, it was whole conversations carried on with characters from the books I was reading. Now I restrict myself to certain phrases that catch in my mind. Tonight, it's some things from Angela's reading.

Dirty hands.

These two words alone frighten me.

Fear made them see the town, the world, in a way they'd never seen it before.

I try to leave these incantations behind in the dissolving fog of my breath. Work to turn my mind to real concerns. No progress on my writing to speak of. The thinning thread that connects me to my job. Dark feelings that have me wondering: *Is this it?* Is it days like this that start the slide into a hole you can't climb out of?

A smell that soldiers and surgeons would recognize.

Last night Sam awoke from a nightmare. I went to him. Stroked the damp hair back from his forehead. Once I'd settled him down, I asked what his dream was about.

"A man," he said.

"What kind of man?"

"A bad man."

"There's no bad man in here. I wouldn't let anyone bad in this house."

"He's not in *this* house. He's in *that* house."

With his *that*, Sam sat straight and pointed out the window. His finger lined up with the neighbour's house across the street. The window where the shadow had stood a few nights back. Looking out.

"Did you see the bad man who was there?" I asked him, but he heard in my very question the concession that what I'd just assured him didn't exist may in fact be real, and he turned his back to me. What good were a father's empty promises against the bogeyman? He would face any further nightmares on his own.

Blood tattooed on the curtains.

It's on my shortcut through Chinatown that I start to feel less alone. Not because of the few others shuffling homeward on the sidewalks, heads down. It's because I'm being followed.

Past the karaoke bars along Dundas, then the foolish turn south straight through the housing projects between here and Queen. That's when I hear the footsteps echoing my own. There are reports in the City pages of frequent shootings on this very block, yet I'm certain that whatever shadows me isn't interested in my wallet. It wants to see what I will do when I know it is there.

And what do I do?

I run.

A headlong sprint. I'm wearing the wrong shoes for it, so that within the first block my shins send bolts of pain up to the back of my head. Eyes stinging with wind-burned tears. Lungs crackling like a pair of plastic bags in my chest.

Courage is not a matter of will, but of the body.

I take the alley that runs behind the businesses along Queen. The shortest way to my house. But a *dark alley?* What was I thinking? I *wasn't* thinking. I was running. Past walls and fences built against the rats and crackheads. No light to see by. Just the darker outline of the buildings and the square of black that is the alley opening on to the street at the far end.

I don't stop. I don't look back.

Not until I stop and look back.

Standing under the block's lone working streetlight. My house within snowball-throwing distance. The light on in my son's room. Sam up late. Sneak reading. And all I want is to sit on the edge of his bed, close his book, turn off the light. Listen to him breathe.

He is my son.

I love my son.

I would die to protect him.

These conclusions come fast and terse as lightning. Along with one other.

The alley is empty.

7

Angela's Story
Transcribed from Tape Recording No. 2

The girl doesn't tell anyone what she knows of the
Sandman and the terrible thing he's done. In part,
this is because she doesn't actually *know* anything
about the missing girl, not in a way she could ever
prove. Not to mention that a declaration of this kind
might just label her as crazy once and for all. She'd
be taken away from Edra and Jacob and put in a
place far worse than any foster home or orphanage.
Someplace she would never come out of again.

But more frightening than even the consideration
of being taken away is the idea of hurting Edra and
Jacob. Her well-being was all they cared about. To
show them that she believed in dark figures born in
her dreams, a monster who had come from the
darkest place to hunt her down, would break both
their hearts. The girl resolved to protect them from
this no matter what.

For the next few days, ignoring the fact that

something was wrong seemed to work. No more
children disappeared. No dark figures were spotted
in town. The girl's dreams were the same irrational
puzzles that others have, free of any terrible men
who do terrible things. It felt like the news of a
stranger with no face escaping from the confines of
a nightmare was *itself* a nightmare, and no more
real than that.

Then the girl sees him.

Not in a dream, but through the window of her
classroom at school. She has been sitting at her desk,
working through a math quiz. Multiplying fractions.
At one equation more difficult than the others, she
raises her head to clear her mind of the numbers atop
numbers collapsing into a confused pile. She sees
him right away. Standing in the shade of the schoolyard's solitary elm. As tall as the lowest limb that,
the girl knows from trying, is too high to reach, even when
one of the boys offered her a boost. The Sandman's
face is obscured by the leaves' latticework of shadow,
though the girl has the impression he is staring
directly at her. And that he's smiling.

She bends over her quiz again. The fractions
have doubled in the time she'd taken her eyes
from the page, so that the numbers are now a
mocking jumble.

He would still be there if she looked. She doesn't
look.

Outside, a lawn mower roars to life. The sound
makes the girl gasp. A flare of pain. She feels the

lawn mower's blades cutting into her side, halving her. Turning her into a fraction.

Later, sitting in the back row of the school bus on the ride home, the girl tries to remember what the Sandman looked like. How could she see him smile without seeing his face? Was this a detail she'd added after the moment had passed? Was she making him up, just as she sometimes thought *she'd* been made up? Was she the author of the terrible man who does terrible things?

As if in answer to all of these questions, the girl looks out the school bus window and he is there. Sitting on a swing in the playground. His legs held out straight before him, his boots touching the grass border around the sand. A sloped-shouldered man out of scale on the children's swing set, so that he looks even more enormous.

The girl turns to the other students on the bus, but none of them are looking out their windows. All of them laughing and blowing goobered paper out of straws. For a moment, the girl is knocked breathless by the recognition of how little these other children know. Of what awaits them, watches them. If not the Sandman then some other reshaped darkness.

The bus grinds into gear and lurches forward. Still sitting on the swing, the Sandman turns to watch them go. Even from this distance the girl notices his hands. The fingers swollen and thick as sausages, gripped round the chain. Dirty hands.

Before the bus turns a corner on to the road out

of town, the girl squints hard and sees that she
was wrong.

It's not dirt that fills the creases and sticks to the
hair on the backs of the Sandman's hands. It's blood.

They find the missing girl the next day. Her remains.
Down in the trees by the river beyond the graveyard.
A place the older kids call the Old Grove, famous for
bush parties. Now and forever to be known as the
place where a girl, too young for bush parties, was
found in pieces, buried in a layer of scattered leaves,
as though her murderer had grown bored at the end
and cast a handful of deadfall over her just to be
done with it.

Because of where they found her, the police
turned their suspicions toward the older boys at
school who'd gotten in trouble in the past. Perhaps
one of them had been in contact with the girl? Had a
crush on her, been following her around? But even
the most trouble-prone boys at the school had done
nothing worse than pocket candy bars or egg
windows on Halloween. It was near impossible to
imagine any of them had graduated from such crimes
to the one in question.

After they found the missing girl, the talk in town
shifted from suspicion to fear. It mattered less who
had done this terrible thing, and more that a terrible
thing not be visited on anyone else. An unofficial
curfew was put in place. Lights burned in the houses
through the night. Groups of townsmen—doctors and

shop owners and tradesmen and drunks, a strange mix that would otherwise be unlikely to associate with each other—patrolled the streets with flashlights and, it was said, shotguns hidden beneath some of their long coats. They had no idea what they might be looking for. Fear made them see the town, the world, in a way they'd never seen it before.

The second girl went missing the same night the first was found. As the men cast their flashlights over lawns and cellar doors and shrub rows, as the lights burned in all the homes, as most stayed up late, unable to sleep, another girl, the same age as the other, was snatched directly out of her bed before dawn. Her ground-floor window left open. Boot prints in the soil by the trampled rose bush. Sheets on the floor. Blood tattooed on the curtains.

They closed the school for the day. Not that the students would be any safer at home. The decision came by way of the instinct to stop whatever had been considered normal, if for no other reason than to match the abnormality of what was happening around them. Edra and Jacob were glad, nevertheless. It was late enough in the season that the crops (however meagre) were already in. There were no church services on Tuesday. And now they'd closed the school. Which meant that the two of them could afford to stay indoors with their adopted daughter, whom they now wanted to protect as much as love.

It was an odd sort of holiday. They baked candied

apples. Played cards. Built a fire they didn't really need just to smell the cherry smoke through the house. The girl's thoughts turned to the terrible man who does terrible things only a few times over the course of the entire day. She would sneak long looks at Jacob and Edra, and ventured to think the word *family* as an invisible cord connecting the three of them.

That night she is awakened by the tap of stones against her bedroom window. She hears the first, but only opens her eyes on the second. There is a rule the girl has arrived at through her experience of being haunted. Once could be anything. Two times makes it real.

She's aware that she's making a mistake even as she rises from her bed and goes to the window. What compels her isn't curiosity but duty. She must keep whatever darkness she has brought to this place from touching Edra or Jacob. It isn't their fault that the girl they've shown such kindness to has let her worst dreams free from her head. They mustn't see what she is about to see.

The girl slides her feet over the bare floorboards and the whole house seems to groan a warning at her movement. Her room is small. But the effort it takes to reach the window exhausts her. Courage, she realizes, is not a matter of will but of the body.

When she reaches the window she has to grip the frame with both hands for balance. There is the sickening stillness that precedes a fainting spell. She makes herself take a breath. As she looks outside, she wonders if her heart has stopped.

The Sandman stands in the yard below. When he sees her, he tosses another stone up at the glass. It is a gesture the girl has seen in old movies. A suitor signalling his arrival for a midnight tryst.

Once he's sure that she's watching, he turns and walks toward the barn. There is a scuffing slowness to his gait that one might mistake for regret. But the girl sees it instead as an expression of his self-certainty, the ease with which he sets about his actions. It's what makes his kind of badness so unpredictable.

He reaches the barn doors and pauses. There's an opening wide enough for him to enter, but he doesn't. He only wants her to see that he's been in there.

The man turns, keeping his back to her. Steps around the side of the barn and is gone.

The girl knows what she must do. That is, what he wants her to do.

She carries her boots down the stairs to quiet her descent. In her haste, she forgets to put her coat on, so that when she steps out the back door and starts into the yard, the cold bites straight through her cotton pajamas. A wind dances dried leaves in figure eights over the dirt. The paper shuffle sound covers her footfall, so that she's able to half-run to the barn.

A step inside the doors and the thicker darkness stops her. She comes into the barn almost every day (it's where she's assigned most of her after-school chores) so she could navigate her way around its stalls and tools hanging on hooks without light. But there is something different about the space she cannot identify at first. It's because it isn't something she can see, but something she can smell.

A trace of the Sandman's scent left hanging in the air. Stronger than the hay and mouldy wood and cow manure, even without him here. It makes her cough. The cough turns into a gag. A smell that soldiers and surgeons would recognize, but that a girl like her would have no reason to have encountered before.

She fights her revulsion and starts toward the stall at the far end. This is where he wants her to go. She knows this as well as if he'd taken her by the hand to lead her there.

As her eyes become used to the dark, faint threads of moonlight find their way in through the slats. When she opens the gate to the stall, she discovers that it's enough light to see by.

The girl in the stall looks like her. He'd likely chosen her because of this. She'd known the second missing girl from her class at school, but had never realized the similar colour of her hair, the round face. For a second, she thinks it may be her own body lying in pieces amongst the spattered clumps of straw. Which would make her a ghost now too.

She sets to digging before there is anything like a plan in her mind. Just beyond the edge of the forest that borders Jacob's unyielding acreage, she goes as deep as the hard earth and time allows her. There's not even the opportunity to be scared. Though more than once she's certain the canvas sack she'd dragged here from the barn jostles with movement from within.

Even as she pushes the seeping bag into the hole and begins to throw spadefuls of soil back in the place it came from, it only vaguely occurs to her that she's doing this to make sure Jacob won't be blamed. Which of course would be the result if they ever found the second girl in his barn. The terrible man who does terrible things forced her into making this decision, which wasn't much of a decision at all. She would rather be an accomplice to the Sandman than allow the man who is as close to a father as she's ever known wrongly go to prison for the rest of his days.

By the time the first pencil line of dawn appears on the horizon, she is patting the mound of the second girl's grave down firm with the back of the spade.

Later, the horror of this night will revisit her in different forms. The girl has enough experience with dreams to know this much.

What she isn't certain of yet is what the Sandman wants from her. He has discovered where she lives. He could take her as easily as he's taken these others any time he felt inclined. But there is a different wish he wishes from her. And though she tries to tell herself that she couldn't possibly imagine what this might be, the truth is she has an idea.

8

Two days after the circle's meeting at Petra's house, the morning paper brings news of another missing person. A man this time. Ronald Pevencey, twenty-four. A hairdresser at one of the avant-garde salons on Queen who hadn't shown up for work all week. When the police were finally alerted, they discovered that the door to his second-floor apartment was left ajar, though no evidence of forced entry or struggle within could be found. This led investigators to a relatively safe assumption. Whoever had come knocking, Ronald had let in.

The reason authorities are announcing suspicions of foul play at all is not only based on Ronald Pevencey's unusual absence from work, but disturbing remarks he'd recently shared with co-workers. His belief he was being followed. Here and there over the past weeks a figure seemed to be watching him. While he didn't say whether he knew who this stalker was, one of his colleagues suspected that Ronald had a theory, and it scared the bejesus out of him. "He wanted to talk about it, but *didn't* want to talk about it," is how his confidante put it.

The rest of the piece, which appears under the by-line of my drinking buddy Tim Earheart, has the police spokesperson bending over backwards to dismiss any speculation that there may be a serial killer at large. First off, there was nothing to indicate that either Carol Ulrich or Ronald Pevencey have been murdered. And while neither had any motive for being a runaway or suicide, there is always the possibility that they just took off for a spontaneous vacation. Postpartum depression. A crystal meth bender. It happened.

It's further pointed out that there is no connection between the two missing persons. A hairdresser. A stay-at-home mom. Different ages, different social circle. Carol had never set foot in the salon where Ronald worked. The only commonality is their residence within six blocks of each other. Within six blocks of us.

If Ronald Pevencey and Carol Ulrich are both dead, odds are they met their ends by different means. Serial killers work in patterns, as the police were at pains to point out. A psychotic glitch in their software makes them seek out versions of the same victim, over and over. In this case, all the two missing persons shared was the city in which they lived.

Yet for all this, I'm certain that whatever hunted these two was the same in both cases. I'm also certain that neither is still alive. Despite what all the forensic psychiatrists and criminologists say, it seems to me that, at least some of the time, unpredictability must be as likely a motivation for murder as any other. A twist. Maybe this is what whoever is doing this likes. Not any one perversity, but the far more unsettling variance afforded by anonymity. If you don't know why a killer does what he does, it makes him more of a threat. It also makes him harder to catch.

But it's not the killer's hypothetical motivation that has me convinced. It's that I believe whatever followed me home the other night is the same shadow that followed Ronald Pevencey and Carol Ulrich. The bad man from my son's nightmares who is now making appearances in my own.

I give Emmie the morning off and walk Sam to daycare myself. Every half-block I turn and scan the street to catch the eyes I feel upon us. Sam doesn't ask why I stop. He just takes my gloved hand in his mitten and holds it, even as he comes within view of his friends in the fenced-in play area, a point at which he would normally run off to join them.

"See you later," he says. And though I intend to say the same thing, an "I love you" slips out instead. But even this is permitted today.

"Ditto," Sam says, with a punch to the elbow before stepping through the daycare's doors.

There's a new box of video cassettes sitting on my chair at the office. More cable freakshows and wife swaps and snuff amateur video compilations with titles like *Falling from Buildings!* and *Animals that Kill!* But it's what I find under the box that is truly disturbing. A Post-it Note from the Managing Editor. *Come see me. M.* It's the longest piece of correspondence I've ever received from her.

The Managing Editor's office is a glassed-in box in the opposite corner of the newsroom from where I sit. But this is not why I so rarely have any contact with her. She is more a memo drafter, an executive conference attender, an advertiser luncher than a manager of human beings. She has been so successful in this position, it is rumoured that she is currently being headhunted by American TV networks. She is twenty-eight years old.

For now, however, she's still the one who does the hiring and firing at the *National Star*. And I'm fully aware, as I approach her glass cube (bulletproof, it is said), that she is more inclined toward the firing than the hiring.

"Patrick. Sit," she says when I come in, a canine command that is obeyed. She raises an index finger without looking my way, a gesture that indicates she's in the middle of a thought that could make or break the sentence she's halfway through. I watch her type out the words she finally harnesses—*symbiotic revenue stream*—and tap a button to replace her memo-in-progress with a Tahitian beach screensaver.

"I'm sure you know why you're here," she says, turning to face me. Her eyes do a quick scan of my person. I seem to disappoint her, as expected.

"No, I don't, actually."

"There's been a complaint."

"From a reader?"

The Managing Editor smiles at this. "No, not a reader. A real complaint. Quite real."

"How real are we talking?"

She rolls her eyes ceilingward. A signal that she means an office high up the ladder. So high up, she dare not speak its name.

"We have to look out for our properties. Our brands. And when one of those brands is undermined from within one of our own properties . . ." She lets this thought go unfinished, as though where it leads is too unsavoury to even consider.

"You're talking about the *MegaStar!* review."

"It was upsetting. People were upset."

"You don't look upset."

"But I am."

"So this is serious."

"There are certain calls from certain offices I don't like to get."

"Should I be calling my lawyer?"

"You have a lawyer?"

"No."

The Managing Editor pushes a stray hair off her forehead. A brief, but distinctly female motion that, I regret to say, makes me like her a little.

"Are we clear on all this then?"

This question would be funny, given the preceding conversation, if my answer weren't yes. She's made herself perfectly clear.

I stop by Tim Earheart's desk on the way back to my own. I'm not really expecting to find him there. He usually prefers to work in the reeking, greasy bunker that goes by the name of the Smoking Room. Tim doesn't think of himself as a smoker, though he'd eat cigarettes if he couldn't smoke them when he's up against a deadline. Which he must be today, given the talk of a potential killer on the loose. Yet here he is. Throwing the reporter's tools of pen, notepad, dictaphone and digital camera into the knapsack he proudly brought back with him from Afghanistan, complete with bullet hole. A prop he says has got him more "intern action" than he knows what to do with.

"She fire you?" he asks. This is the question first asked of anyone caught walking out of the Managing Editor's office.

"Not yet. Where you off to?"

"Ward's Island. They found one of the missing persons."

"Which one?"

"The Ulrich woman. A dozen or so parts of her, anyway. Spread out over a hundred-foot stretch of beach."

"Oh my God."

"Yessir. It's ugly."

"They know who did it?"

"Right now all they're saying is they're following up on every lead. Which means they don't have a clue."

"He *cut her up*?"

"He. She. They."

"Who would *do* that?"

"Somebody bad."

"It's insane."

"Or not. Just got off the phone with the police profiler guy. He's thinking there's a point to the way the body was on display like that. Some sort of announcement."

"Saying what?"

"How the fuck do I know? 'I'm here,' I guess. 'Come and get me, assholes.'"

Tim slings the knapsack over his shoulders. Even through his aviator sunglasses you can see the excited gleam in his eyes.

"She lived near you, didn't she?" he says.

"Sam recognized her. She had a kid about his age. They went to the same playground."

"Creepy."

"It is."

"I'm going over there now on the ferry. Wanna come?"

"I wouldn't want to spoil it for you."

"Could be great material for your novel."

"It's not that kind of novel," I say, which makes me wonder what kind of novel I *would* write, if I ever could.

By the time I leave work, shortly after five, the day has already taken its wintry turn toward night. The backed-up traffic along King a red line of brake lights as far as the horizon, the only colour against the dusk. The new restaurants that have moved into the former textile warehouses are already full of besuited diners, each of them plunking down the equivalent of my biweekly mortgage payment to taste the dainty constructions of overnight superstar chefs. And what will the Rush boys be eating this evening? One sag paneer, one butter chicken roti, medium spicy, from Gandhi take-out. Sam's favourite.

It's the choice of tonight's menu, however, that leads to my seeing him.

There is the usual clog of people in Gandhi, either eating from styrofoam containers at one of its two tables, or standing close together, waiting to hear our number called and make the last dash home. The air is steamy from the bubbling pans of curry on the stove, the open pot of boiling potatoes, the breath of everyone in here. It makes the windows that look on to Queen cloud and drip with condensation. Through the glass, the bodies of passers-by merge into a single, mutating form.

My number's up. Now that I've sidestepped my way to the front, claustrophobia tickles a mild panic in my chest. One of those momentary near freak-outs I have a couple times a day negotiating my way through the city. A struggle I almost always win by telling myself to hold on. Just do the next thing—*pay for food*—and then the next—*grab the bag, turn, squeeze toward the door*—and everything will be okay.

At the door, I pause to pull my gloves out of my jacket pocket. It allows me to take a last look through the clouded glass.

It is only a darkened outline among other darkened outlines. But I know it's him.

Standing on the far side of the street. Unmoving as the other sidewalkers pass in both directions around him. Taller than any of them.

As I push the door open and the street is brought into

sudden focus, William turns his back to me and joins the others heading east.

I don't get a good look at his face. That's not how I know. It's his *presence*. A menacing energy that radiates from him so strongly it knocks me back a few inches, so that I have to lean against the door for balance. Even as he turns the corner at the end of the block and disappears, the density of the space he leaves in his wake holds me where I stand. It's as though the air is turned to black water, taking on a sludgy, unbreathable weight.

Someone pushes against the door and I step aside, murmuring an apology. All around me the inching traffic and striding pedestrians carry on their homeward journeys, oblivious. William had no effect on them. Perhaps this is because *he wasn't there*. A hallucination formed out of the day's gloom, the news of violence, an empty stomach.

But these are only the rationalizations I need to get my feet moving again. Whatever I just saw, just felt, was not a product of the imagination. I'm not sure I even *have* an imagination.

It was William, watching me. Which means it was William, following me.

There is one further possibility, of course.

One day I will look back and recall that tonight, outside Gandhi with a bag of take-out in my hand, was the first step on the road to losing my mind.

Sam and I eat our dinners by candlelight, the good silver and wedding-present wine glasses brought out for the hell of it. Curry on the plate, beer and ginger ale in the crystal.

We talk about things. The proto-bullies who terrorize his daycare. A kid who had an allergic reaction at the playground and whose face "got fat and red like a giant zit" before an ambulance took him away.

As for me, I do my best to cushion each of these fears. But even as I do, I wrestle with my own nightmare material. The Managing Editor's warning shot. The picture of Carol Ulrich on the TV, the lady who looks like Tamara. The parts of her found on the beach. Which leads my private thoughts to the larger, geopolitical worries of the day. The fallen towers. Sleeper cells, alternate targets, promises of more trouble to come issued from Afghan caves. How our corner of the world is less and less safe the richer it becomes.

After a while, what Sam is speaking about and what it makes me think of seem like parts of the same observation. *Even here*, we say. *Even here evil can find you.*

Of course I don't tell Sam about seeing William across the street on my way home. What occurs to me now is that it's not just William I'm keeping from him. Since I started going to the meetings at Conrad White's, I have held the Kensington Circle out of his reach. Sam wouldn't be interested. These Tuesday evenings when Emmie stayed late and Daddy went out for some grown-up time were so harmless, so dull, they weren't worth the breath required to explain them.

Yet now I feel the restraint, the mental work required in keeping a certain topic covered over. What goes on in the writing circle has become a secret. And as with most secrets, it is meant to protect as much as conceal.

9

I arrive early the following Tuesday. I'm hoping for a moment to speak with Conrad White on his own. I begin with the irresistible bait of flattery. At least, *I've* always found it irresistible, on the rare occasions it's come my way.

"I'm glad you enjoyed it," the old man says in reply to my praise of *Jarvis and Wellesley*. "It cost me a great deal."

"The controversy."

"That, yes," he says, looking up at me to gauge how much of that I might know. "It would be a lie to say I wasn't inconvenienced by my banishment. But I was thinking more of the cost of writing the thing in the first place."

"It's taxing. The process. I mean, it *must* be taxing."

"It needn't be. That book spilled forth with the ease of a sin in the confessional box. Which turned out to be my mistake. I should have held something back. Saved it for later. The total revelation of our selves in one go does not make for long careers."

Conrad White pushes the room's chairs into their circle formation for the meeting. Even this minor task leaves him winded. I try to help him, but he waves me off the moment I step forward.

"I suppose, in a way, you must be grateful to be out of it," I say, expecting easy agreement. Instead, the old man's knees stiffen, as though preparing to absorb or deliver a blow.

"Out of what?"

"You know. The whole game, the schoolyard politics. Attention/neglect, praise/attack. The so-called rewards of fame."

"You're quite wrong. I would do anything to have it back. Just as you, I suspect, would do anything to have it."

I'm about to object—how could he know what I want?—when he releases a gusting sigh and falls back into his chair.

"Tell me," he says, showing a pair of nicotined incisors to signal a change of subject. "Have you found our meetings edifying?"

"It's been interesting."

"I understand from what you've brought to read that you are a critic by profession."

"I'm paid to watch television."

"So. What do your slumming critical faculties make of your classmates?"

Conrad White's lips part fully into a smile. His question is an amusing parry. But it's also a test.

"A mixed bag. As one would expect," I say. "There are a couple of pieces I think show special merit."

"A couple?"

"No. Not a couple."

Conrad White sits forward. The smile drops so quickly I can't be sure it was ever there.

"You never know who might have it," he says.

"Have what?"

"That thing that keeps bringing you to this place week after week, even though you have no faith whatsoever that what I or anyone else might say will assist you. The reason you're sitting here right now."

"What reason is that?"

"You want to know if someone else has been involved in the way you have been involved."

"Sorry. Not following you."

"The only vital currency is story. And yet we spend most of our time blowing flatus about theme or symbol or political context or structural messing about. Why?" The old man's smile returns. "I believe it's because it distracts us from the inadequacies of our own narrative. We avoid speaking of stories *as* stories for the same reason we avoid contemplating the inevitability of death. It can be unpleasant. It can *hurt*."

"I think the story Angela's telling is *about* death."

"Ghost stories usually are."

"How much of it do you think is real?"

"Perhaps the better question is how much of it you have *made* real."

"That's not up to me."

"It's not?"

"It's her story, not mine."

"So you say."

"We're talking about Angela."

"Really? I thought we were talking about you."

I would be lying if I said that Conrad White correctly guessing my involvement (as he called it) in Angela's story didn't catch me a little off guard. I'm not surprised by how intelligent a man he is, but by how much of this intelligence he has applied to me, to us, his raggedy group of bookish refugees. He knows I've been bluffing my way along right from the start, just as he knows that Angela is in possession of a "vital currency". Vital to the people like me and him, anyway. Popcorn crunchers, channel changers, paperback devourers. The hungry audience.

There's a knock at the door. Conrad White gets to his feet. I can hear Len's voice excitedly telling him about a breakthrough in his zombie apocalypse ("I've set it in a prison, because, after the dead rise, prisoners will be the only ones still alive *inside* the walls, and the society that has judged them left *outside*!") followed by Ivan, who slips by them both and takes a seat across from me. I nod at him in welcome, but since our conversation outside the subway station he's pretending he can't see me. It leaves me to measure the hands capped over his knees. Too big for the wrists they're attached to, so that they appear taken from another body altogether, grave-robbed. An impression that reminds me of Ivan telling me what it's like to be accused of harming someone. Those hands could do harm without much effort. They could do it all on their own.

The rest of the circle arrives in a pack. Petra taking the chair next to Len's and politely listening to his how-to remarks on decapitating the undead. Angela slips by Evelyn and Conrad White to sit next to me. We smile hello at each other. It allows me the closest look at her yet. In the room's dimness, a distance of more than a couple feet makes our faces susceptible to distortion, the misreadings of candlelight. Now, however, I can see her more or less as she is. But what strikes me isn't any aspect of her appearance. It's the disarming certainty that *she* is seeing *me* with far greater accuracy than what I can only guess about her. She isn't dreamy or wounded or bashful. She's *working*.

William arrives last. I force myself to take him in at more than a glance, to confirm or dispel my suspicion that it had been him watching me across the street from the Indian take-out. He's the right size, that's for sure. A threat in the very space he occupies, consuming more than his fair share of light, of air. Still, I can't be sure it was him. His beard even thicker now, so that the true shape of his face is impossible to outline. And unlike Angela, a direct look into his eyes reveals nothing. Where she is busy, William is lifeless. There is no more outward compassion in him than the zombies of Len's stories.

William takes his seat. Each of us slide an inch away from him, and each of us notices it. An instinct of the herd that communicates there is a wolf among us.

It is our second to last meeting, and Conrad White wants to get through as many of our pieces today as possible. We begin with Ivan, who takes his rat character into the tunnels beneath the city, where he watches the humans on the train platforms with the same revulsion that he, as a man, once viewed the vermin skittering around the rails. Evelyn returns her prof-bonking grad student to the family cottage, where she goes for a swim alone at night and symbolically ends up on an island, naked, "baptized by moonlight." Petra's domestic drama leads to her female character making a courageous call to a divorce lawyer. As for me, I nudge along my account of a frustrated TV critic just far enough to satisfy the rules.

Angela is next. Once I've turned on the dictaphone, I *feel* her reading more than anything else. It's as though I am within her, at once distinct and fused as Siamese twins. And this time there's something entirely new, a crackling energy in the inches between us that, for the first time, I interpret in purely physical terms. A literal attraction. I want to be closer to her mouth, look down upon the same scribbled pages she reads from, cheek to cheek. It takes a concerted effort to not let myself drift into her.

When she's finished, it's William's turn. This time, he's actually brought something with him. We soon wish he hadn't.

In his flat voice, he begins his account of "the summer when something broke" in the life of a boy, growing up in "the poorest part of a poor town." Avoiding the house where his father drank and his mother "did what she called her 'day job' in her bedroom," the friendless boy wanders through the dusty streets, bored and furious, like "he was buried under something heavy he couldn't crawl out from under."

One day, the boy picked up the neighbour's cat, took

it out to a shed at the far end of an empty lot, and skinned it alive. The animal's cries are "the sound he would make if he could. But he has never cried in his life. It's something that's missing from him. Everything is missing from him." After burying the cat, the boy listens to the woman next door, calling her pet's name in the night, and he sees that "this is something he could do. Something he was good at. He could take things away."

The rest of the story goes on to describe, in the same bland language, the boy's successive graduation from cats to dogs to the horse in the stable at the edge of town, wanting to see if it "was filled with glue, because that's what he'd heard they turned dead horses into."

Eventually, Conrad White breaks his own rule. He interrupts William in the middle of his reading.

"Thank you. I'm sorry, but we have run out of time," the old man lies. A trembling hand smoothing back his remaining wisps of hair. "Perhaps we can return to William's piece at our final meeting."

William folds his papers into a square and returns it to the pocket of his jeans. Looks around at the rest of us, who are now getting up, turning our backs to him. I may be the only one who doesn't move. And while I cannot say I notice anything change in his expression, I sense something that makes me certain it was William who stared at me across the street the other night. The same cruel aura he had then as now. A calmness that speaks not of contentment, but how, as with the boy in his story, everything is missing.

After the meeting, Len reminds me of our plans to check out the litmag launch and open mic at a bar up on College Street. On the way, as he shuffles a few steps ahead of me, anxious to get good seats, Len asks if I've noticed something between Evelyn and Conrad White.

"Something?"

"I don't know. They're always whispering to each other. Making eyes."

"I hadn't noticed."

"Who do you think she's with right now?"

"You mean *with* with?"

"Answer the question."

"Conrad?"

"It's kind of *sick*."

"There's got to be forty years between them."

"I told you."

"How do you know?"

"I don't. But what's a writing circle without a little scandal?"

The open mic is on the second floor of a Mexican restaurant, a long, dark-panelled room that smells of sawdust and refried beans. At the door, Len and I buy a copy of the stapled zine on offer, *Brain Pudding*, which entitles us to the beer discount.

"Not much of a turn-out."

"There's a serial killer out there somewhere," Len says. "It can make people stay in and order pizza."

"What are you talking about?"

Len gives me a hopeless, get-with-the-program look.

"The missing hairdresser," he says.

"Ronald Pevencey."

"The police found his body in a dumpster in Chinatown this afternoon. In pieces. Just like that woman on Ward's Island. So now they're thinking the same guy did them both. Two is a series. Thus, serial killer. Which is bad for business."

"We'll just have to do our best to help," I say, ordering a round.

The emcee thanks us for coming. But before he opens the floor to all comers, he has a special announcement. Congratulations for one of *Brain Pudding*'s contributors, Rosalind Canon, a mousy girl sitting with mousy boys in the front. Apparently she learned just this morning that the manuscript for her first novel had been accepted for publication in New York. A bidding war. World rights sold. Film option.

"And as if that wasn't enough," he says, "it's her birthday! Happy twenty-fourth, Rosalind!"

The emcee steps back from the mic, beams down at Rosalind, and starts to clap.

And in the next second, something interesting happens.

A drop in the room's barometric pressure, the sudden hollowness that precedes a thunderstorm. Aside from the emcee's two hands clapping, there is no sound other than our collectively held breath. It leaves each of us exposed. Caught on the coruscated edges of the same desire. Despite our differences of age, of costume, of genre, we are here because we all share the longing to be writers. But in this moment, what we more immediately wish is to be Rosalind. A surge of not-yet-rationalized jealousy powerful enough to alter the composition of the very environment we occupy.

And then, when our limbs finally accept the command given them, we join in the applause. A round of whistles and hearty good wishes you'd never suspect of the effort they required.

"That's great! Wow!" Len says.

"Oh yeah. It's so wow great I could kill her."

I wave my arm barward. From here on, my beers are coupled with bourbon shots. It eases things somewhat. The flatulent sound poetry and same-sex erotica and hate-my-parents short stories that follow pass in a benumbed succession. I even *like* some of it. Or at least, I admire that their authors are here, putting their name in the emcee's hat and, when called upon, ascending the plywood riser and letting it fly. Good or bad, they *made* this stuff. Which is more than I can say for myself.

Some time later, Rosalind Canon's name is called over the PA. She's come to these things before. She even knows the right way to approach the stage: with a slouch, as though her real thoughts are elsewhere, puzzling out some far deeper question than *How do I look?*

As she murmurs on, I resolve that, once she's finished, I will start home. The flush of goodwill that came with the first wave of alcohol is already passing, and I know from experience it will soon leave only regret and self-pity behind. Just one more drink in case the killer out there decides I'm to be next. I'd rather not see it coming. What kind of blade would he have to use to do what he does? Something motorized, perhaps. Or perhaps he is just incredibly strong. What had the monster in Angela's story liked to do? Turn people into fractions.

I'm about to tell Len I'm going to leave when I'm stopped by the realization that half the people in the room have turned in their chairs to look my way.

"Sorry to wake you," Len is saying, his hand on my arm. "But you were snoring."

In my cubicle at the *National Star* the next morning, Tim Earheart stops by to deliver coffee. It will be my fourth of the day, and it's only just turned ten. But I need all the help I can get. The many beers and only slightly fewer Wild Turkeys of the night before have left me fuzzy-headed and furry-mouthed. I take a couple scalding gulps before I'm able to read Tim's lips.

"Let's go down for a smoke," he's saying for the second time, glancing over his shoulder to see if anyone's listening.

"I don't smoke."

"I'll give you one."

"Quit. More or less. Thought you knew –"

Tim raises the back of his hand and for a second I'm sure he's going to slap me. Instead, he bends close to my ear.

"What I've got isn't for general consumption," he whispers, and walks away toward the doors to the main stairwell.

The basement of the *National Star* is the exclusive domain of two species of dinosaur: smokers and historians. It's down here where the pre-electronic database issues of the paper are stored, as well as some archival bric-à-brac including, I have heard, the shrunken head of the newspaper's founder. Aside from a few postgrad researchers the only people who come down here are the last of the nicotine wretches. A dwindling number, even among reporters. The kids coming out of journalism school these days are more likely to carry a yoga mat and an Evian bottle than a flask and a pack of smokes.

It leaves the Smoking Room one of the last places in the building where you can hope to have a private conversation. Sure enough, when I close the door behind me and feel my stomach clench at the carcinogenic stink, it's only Tim Earheart in here with me.

"They're not running it. They're not fucking *running* it," he says, literally fuming, grey exhaust spilling out his nose.

"What aren't they running?"

"The note."

I know that Tim is enough of an obsessive that if he's this excited, he's talking about a story. And his story right now is Carol Ulrich and Ronald Pevencey.

"Left it by her body," he goes on. "A *part* of her body. Her head, as a matter of grotesque fact. Typed out nice and neat for whoever found her."

"You have possession of this note?"

"Sadly, no. One of the cops on the scene told me what it said. He shouldn't have, but he did."

"And you brought it to the suits."

"Expecting it to go A1. Because if this isn't front page, what is? But the police caught wind of it, and they begged us to muzzle it. Ongoing investigation, lives at risk, an eventual arrest could be jeopardized, blah blah blah. Just throw a blanket on it for a few days. So now they're not running it."

"Does it say who wrote it?"

"It's not *signed*. But I think it's pretty damn clear."

Tim finishes his cigarette, grinds the butt under his heel and has another in his mouth in less time than it takes me to speak.

"What did it say?"

"That's the reason I'm telling you. I was hoping you might have some literary insight."

"You're talking about a serial killer's note, not *Finnegans Wake*."

Tim takes a step closer. Smoke rising from his hair.

"It's a *poem*," he says.

The Smoking Room door opens and a lifer from Sports comes in, gives us a distasteful glance and lights up. Tim makes a zipper motion across his lips. I'm about to step outside when he grabs my wrist. Presses something into my palm.

"Call me later about those Leafs tickets," he says. Winks a secret wink.

A business card. Tim Earheart's writing squeezed on to the back. I read it over a few times in my cubicle, then tear it into confetti and let it fall into my recycling box.

I am the ground beneath your feet
The man in dark alleys you don't want to meet
I live in the Kingdom of Not What It Seems
Close your eyes, you will see me—here in your dreams.

Not much, as poems go. Just a pair of rhyming couplets, a Mother Goose simplicity that gives it the sing-song of nursery doggerel. Perhaps this is the point. Given the grisly context in which the poem was found, the childish tone makes it all the more threatening. The kind of thing you need only read once and it, or some part of it, remains hooked in your mind. A poem meant not to be admired but remembered.

So what does it say about its author? First, whoever did this to Carol Ulrich also wrote these lines. One an act of assembly, the other of dismemberment. Creator and Destroyer in one. *Somebody bad*, as Tim Earheart had guessed.

Second, he wanted the poem to be read. It could have been kept to himself, but instead it was left by the victim's corpse. A killer who—like all writers—wants an *audience* for their work. To make us feel something. To invite the kind of scrutiny I am giving his poem right now. To be understood.

Third, while it is only a four-line ditty, there are indications of some intelligence. That a poem would occur to him at all puts him at a creative level above the everyday backstreet butcher. And the composition itself offers some indication of talent. It rhymes, for one thing. A rhythm that's not accidental. Good enough that it would likely achieve its macabre effect even if it wasn't deposited next to a corpse.

And then there are the words themselves.

The first line sets out the poem's purpose: the poet seeks to introduce himself. He is the ground beneath our feet. That is, he's everywhere. The next line establishes the character of this presence as menacing, hostile, the "man in dark alleys." Naturally, the mention of alleys rings especially loud for me, as it was only a few days ago that I ran home through one, fearing something that likely wasn't there. But "dark alleys" are universally regarded as places to fear. He wants us to know that he is the one who waits for us there.

The third line introduces a note of dark whimsy. The "Kingdom of Not What It Seems" is where he *lives*, but he is also able to materialize in the ground beneath our feet. At once real and an illusion. A shape shifter.

All of which is reinforced in the poem's concluding line. If we wish to see him, we must turn not to whatever clues have been left behind, but to our dreams. And these dreams aren't only imagined, but "here," in the real world. We are all part of the same dream whether we like it or not. And it's *his*.

It's not until my walk home that another interpretation occurs to me. "Occurs to me" might not be strong enough. In fact, it almost knocks me over. I have to sit on the curb with my head between my legs to prevent myself from blacking out.

When I'm partly recovered I speak into the dictaphone, still slouched on the curb as cars pass within inches of my feet.

TRANSCRIPT FROM TAPE

March 12, 2003

[Sounds of passing traffic]
I am the ground beneath your feet.
Literally. Whoever first read the poem would have
been on Ward's Island. Standing on a beach. On
sand.
[Aside]
Oh, shit.
[Kid in background]
Look at this pisstank! He's gonna lose . . .
[Car horn]
. . . if he doesn't watch it!
[Background laughter]
Close your eyes, you will see me.
Okay. To know who he is, we have to dream. But
who delivers our thoughts while we sleep?
[Singing]
Mr. Sandman, bring me a dream . . .

10

Angela's Story
Transcribed from Tape Recording No. 3

The next week, after the school was re-opened
despite the second missing girl remaining missing
and no leads being discovered as to the perpetrator
of what the town's Chief of Police called "these
heinous crimes" (a word the girl had never heard
before and spelled in her mind as "hayness," which
only reminded her of what she discovered in the
barn), Edra had to go into the hospital a hundred
and sixty miles down the road for surgery. Her gallbladder. Nothing to worry about, Jacob assured the
girl. Edra would be just fine without it. Which, if this
was true, made the girl wonder why God gave us
gallbladders in the first place.

Edra is taken to the hospital on a Friday, which
leaves Jacob and the girl alone in the farmhouse until
Edra is brought home, all being well, on Sunday. The
old man and the girl have the weekend to themselves.

As much as the girl is delighted by the idea of exclusive attention from Jacob, part of her dreads their number being reduced from three to two. She wonders if the invisible cord that connected them as a family also acted as a spell, a force field that kept out the terrible man who does terrible things. With Edra gone, a door might be opened. For the sake of her foster parents, the girl would keep a vile secret. She would bury someone in the night and suffer the nightmares that followed. But she isn't sure she could ever close a door to the Sandman once it was opened.

Soon her worry over all of this could be read in every look and gesture the girl makes. No matter how she tries to keep her burden hidden, she wears her trouble like a cloak. Jacob knows her too well not to notice. And when he asks the girl what's wrong, this simple provocation triggers an explosion of tears.

She tells him almost everything. That there's a terrible man who does terrible things who used to live only in her dreams, but has now taken form in the real world. That she believes this man took the two girls from town because they were the same age and general appearance as she.

What she doesn't tell him is what she found in the barn, and what she did with it.

Jacob doesn't speak for a long time after the girl is finished. When he finally finds the words he's looking for, the girl expects him to explain how what she's said could not be possible. But instead he surprises her.

"I have seen him too," the old man says.

The girl can hardly believe it. What was he like? Where did Jacob see him?

"I could not describe him to you any more than I could say what shape the wind takes," the old man answers. "It is something I have *felt*. Moving around the house as though what he seeks is within, but he cannot enter. Not yet."

Perhaps the girl should go to him. If it's only her that the Sandman wants, why risk him doing harm to another girl? Or worse, to Jacob or Edra.

"You mustn't speak like that," Jacob implores her. "Never *ever*. Understand? He will not have you so long as I live. And after I'm gone, you must still resist him. Promise me this."

The girl promises. But what is left for them to do? The girl can't imagine how they might attempt to fight him. How can you kill what may already be dead?

"I cannot say if he is alive or dead. But I believe I can say who he is."

Jacob holds the girl firm by the shoulders as though to prevent her from falling.

"It's your father," he says.

After Jacob failed to pick her up, Edra returned from the hospital in a taxi on Sunday to find the farmhouse empty. The back door left wide open. If someone had come in or gone out by this point of entry there was no way of knowing. Over the last twenty-four hours, the whole county had been buried under three feet of snow. The arrival of winter announced in a

November blizzard. Any tracks that might have been left now filled in and sculpted into fin-tailed drifts.

When the police arrive Edra is frantic for them to find the girl. They don't have far to look. Huddled in the corner of the last stall in the barn. Glass-eyed, blue-skinned. Shaking from the hypothermia caused by staying outside all night when the temperature dipped as low as ten below.

They ask her where Jacob is. The girl's only answer is to slip into unconsciousness. For a time, it's judged to be even odds if she will survive or not. Three of her toes are removed, turned black from frostbite. Her brain monitored to determine what parts have died from lack of oxygen while she sleeps.

But the girl doesn't die.

When she comes to the next day, she will not speak to anyone but Edra, and even then, it's not about what happened over the preceding days. Edra buffers the girl from their queries, putting her anxieties regarding her husband second to the girl's need for protection. The police are left to look for Jacob on their own.

After it is determined that Jacob's truck was parked in the farmyard the entire weekend, and there is no sign of a struggle or suicide note inside the house, the forest that borders the end of his fields and carries on for five hundred miles north into the Canadian Shield becomes the prime area of concentration for the police search.

The snowfall from the blizzard, however, makes it

difficult. Helicopter fly-overs can spot little more than trees sprouting up from a blanket of white. The dogs they use to track Jacob's scent run a hundred yards into the woods only to sink up to their muzzles, and then must be carried out, whimpering, by their trainers. By the fourth day, the search's urgency is downgraded from a rescue operation to evidence collection. If Jacob is to be found somewhere out in the endless woods, there is no expectation that he will be alive.

It takes another two weeks of mild weather for the snow to melt enough to expose Jacob's body. Four miles from the farm. Lying face down, arms sprawled out at his sides. No injuries aside from cuts to his face and arms that came from branches slashing his skin as he ran. Just socks on his feet, and not wearing any outerwear (his boots and coat were in their usual places in the house). The cause of death determined to be exposure following a collapse from exhaustion. The coroner is amazed that a man of Jacob's age was capable of getting as far as he did. A four-mile run through a blizzard in the night woods. Only someone in a state of mortal panic would be capable of it.

But the questions that followed from this were beyond both the coroner's and forensic investigators' capacity to answer. Was Jacob running *from* or *toward* something? If he had been the one in pursuit, what quarry would have driven him into the forest dressed as he was during the first big snowfall of the year? And if he was the pursued, what would have terrified him enough to run so far he let himself fall and die without anything laying a hand on him?

The police all agreed that if Jacob had been murdered, it was a perfect crime. No suspect. No witness. No tracks left after the snow had filled them in. No weapon to be found aside from the cold.

Only the girl knew—or might know—what happened over the time she and Jacob were alone in the farmhouse. But no matter how many times she was asked, she would not speak of it.

Shock, the doctors said. Extreme emotional trauma. It can cut the tongue out of a child as sure as any blade. She's of no use now, they concluded. You'd have as good a chance asking the trees in Jacob's forest what they saw as this poor girl.

The girl heard everything they said about her, though she acted as though she was deaf. She resolved that there are some things you cannot speak of. But she would record what she knew in a different way from speech. She would write it down. Later, when she was older and on her own, she would tell the truth, if only to herself.

Here, in the pages of this very book.

She even knows how it will begin.

There once was a girl who was haunted by a ghost . . .

11

"City in Fear" reads the banner headline of the next day's *National Star*, and for me, at least, it's not over-statement. The accompanying piece is one of those "man on the street," mood-gauging surveys that only retreads what is already known of the two recent victims—unrelated, no known involvements in crime, no indication of sexual assault, nothing of value taken from their persons. Indeed, there is no reason to believe their killer to be the same person. This report is followed by interviews with people in the neighbourhood who admit they're not planning to go out at night until "they catch whatever sick bastard that would do this." I read the article to the end to see if there's any mention of the poem found next to Carol Ulrich's body, but it looks like Tim was right. The editors killed it.

And then, perhaps most troubling of all, there is an account of the various eyewitness statements and anonymous call-in tips received by police. A well-dressed, bald white man says one. Two black men are cited—one with gold teeth and a Raiders toque, the other grey-haired, nice-looking, a "Denzel Washington look-alike." A pair of curly-haired men who "may be twins." An elderly Portuguese lady in mourning black.

"People are seeing killers in whoever sits next to them on the subway," one policeman points out.

And why not? It *could* be them.

The morning's walk through the City of Fear confirms that the three million hearts pounding their way to work all around me have turned a darker shade of worry. Each cluster of newspaper boxes shows that the *National Star*'s competition have run similarly alarmist pieces, the always hysterical tabloid putting smiling photos of Carol Ulrich and Ronald Pevencey side by side under the headline "Are You Next?" A question that's impossible not to give some thought to. Everyone getting off the streetcars or emerging from the mouths of subway entrances sees these front-page faces and, through them, sees themselves. Not stony-faced mobsters or gangland hoods (the kinds who had it coming), but the faces of those whose primary goal was the avoidance of trouble. That's the security most of us count on: we belong to the majority who never go looking for it. Yet all of us know at the same time that this is an increasingly hollow assurance. Fear is always there, looking for a way to the surface.

No matter how we might keep to ourselves, sometimes the Sandman finds us anyway.

The Quotidian Award, affectionately known as the Dickie, is the nation's second-richest literary prize. The honour was established by Richard "Dickie" Barnham, a Presbyterian minister who, in his retirement, became an enthusiastic memoirist, recounting the mild eccentricities of his quaint Ontario parsonage. He was also, in the year before his death, the purchaser of a $12-million-winning lottery ticket. The Dickie is today awarded to the work of fiction that "best reflects the domestic heritage of Canadian family life," which has led to a series of hushed, defiantly uneventful winners. A rainy-day parade of stolid farmers and fishermen's widows.

It also happens to be one of the gala events of the season. A ticket to the Dickie marks one's membership in the nation's elite, a Who's Who of country club philanthropists, TV talking heads, corporate barons. The *National Star*'s publisher has never missed it. It's in part why, each year, a photo of the winner and a hyperventilating description of the menu and ladies' gowns appear on the front page.

It's the sort of assignment I'm no longer considered for. Even when I was the literary columnist, the paper preferred to send one of the party girls from the Style section who could recognize not only the celebrities in attendance, but the designers who did their outfits. This year, however, the reporter they had in mind called in sick four hours before the event. The Managing Editor was out of town at one of her executive retreats, so the task of choosing a last-minute alternative came down to the News Editor who asked if I could do it for him. I accepted.

The press pass allows me to take a guest. The wise course would be to go alone, write the story they're looking for, and be in bed by midnight. Instead, I call Len.

"You could slip someone your manuscript," I tell him.

"You think?"

"Every editor in town is going to be there."

"Maybe just a couple short stories," he decides after a moment. "Something that could fit under my jacket."

By the time I rent a tux and spin by in a cab to pick up Len (who has also been fitted in black tie, though for someone a foot shorter and thirty pounds lighter than he) we arrive at the Royal York just in time to catch the last half of the cocktail hour.

"Look!" Len whispers on our way into the Imperial Room. "There's Grant Duguay!"

I follow Len's pointing finger and find the emcee of tonight's proceedings. The same waxy catalogue model with a used car salesman grin who acts as host of *Canadian MegaStar!*

"That's him alright."

"And there! That's Rosalind Canon!"

"Who?"

Len looks at me to make sure I'm being serious. "At the *Brain Pudding* launch. The one who got half a million for her first novel."

I get Len to point Rosalind out to me. And there she is, the mousy girl who is now shaking hands with every culturecrat and society wife who make their way to her. Even from across the room I can lip-read the same earnest *Thank you* in reply to the congratulations, over and over. It makes me want to say the same thing to someone. A passing waiter will have to do.

"Thank you," I say, plucking a pair of martinis, one for each hand, from his tray.

We settle at the press table before the other hacks arrive. It allows me to stick one of the two bottles of wine on the table between my feet, just in case the steward is unavailable at a crisis point later on. Then the *MegaStar!* guy is up at the lectern saying something about how reading made him what he is today, which seems reasonably true, given that managing a teleprompter would be tricky for an illiterate. Following this, as the dinner begins to be served, each of the nominated authors take the stage to talk about the genesis of their work. The bottle between my feet is empty before the caribou tartare is cleared.

It's absurd and I know it. It's shallow and unfounded and generally reflects poorly on my character. Because I haven't published a book. Haven't written a book. I don't have anything in mind to one day turn *into* a book. But in the spirit of full and honest disclosure, I'll tell you what I'm thinking as I sit in the Imperial Room in my itchy tux watching the night's honourees bow into the waves of applause.

Why not me?

Luck. Pulled strings. Marketability. Maybe they have this on their side. Though there is always something else, too. A compelling order to things, a story's *beginning, middle and end.* Me? All I have is all most of us have. The messy garble of a life-in-progress.

To turn my mind from such thoughts, I lean over and share with Len the killer's secret poem. It leaves him goggle-eyed. Encouraged, I go on to outline my interpretation of the poem's meanings, including the unlikely hint at the author's identity.

"You think there's a connection?" he asks, wiping the sweat from his lip.

"I think it's a coincidence."

"Hold on, hold *on*." Len fusses with the cutlery set out in front of him as though it represents the thoughts in his head. "If you're right, then it means whoever's been doing those things is either in our writing circle, or has read Angela's story."

"No, it doesn't. Anyone can call themselves the Sandman. And he doesn't call himself *anything* in the poem. It's just a theory."

"And my theory is it's William."

"Slow down. It's not –"

"Hello! A kid who disembowels cats and horses for fun? He's basically *telling* us what he's capable of."

"It's a *story*, Len."

"Some stories are true."

"If writing fiction about serial killers makes you a murder suspect, there'd be a hundred freaks within ten blocks of here the police would want to talk to."

"Still. *Still*," Len says, chewing his lip. "I wonder what Angela would think if she –"

"You can't tell anyone."

Len is crestfallen. A real horror story dropped in his lap, and he's not allowed to run with it.

"I mean it, Len. I only told you because –"

Why *did* I tell Len? The martinis helped. And I suppose I wanted him to be impressed. I'm a journalist at a real newspaper. I *know* things. But more than this, I think I wanted to *entertain* the big geek.

"Because I believe you can be trusted," I say finally, finishing the sentence Len has been waiting for. And he looks away, visibly touched by the compliment.

After dessert, Mr. *MegaStar!* announces the winner. And once I've jotted the name down, I'm out of there.

"I'm off, Len. Got to write this thing up lickety-split."

Len eyes my untouched maple syrup cheesecake. "You going to eat that?"

"All yours."

I squeeze his shoulder as I get up from the table. And although Len smiles in acknowledgment of the gesture, the fact is if I hadn't grabbed him I would have fallen face first into a passing tray of beaver-shaped shortbreads.

After a couple hours punching keys on my laptop, keeping focused with the help of the Library Bar's Manhattans, I hit Send and start the long stagger home. It's not easy. My legs, lazy rascals, won't do what I tell them. Pretzelling around each other, taking sudden turns toward walls or parking meters. It takes me a half-hour to get two blocks behind me. At least my arms seem to be working. One hugging a lamp-post and the other hailing a cab.

Despite the cold, I roll the window down as the driver rockets us past the Richmond Street nightclubs that, at this late hour, are only now disgorging the sweaty telemarketers, admin assistants and retail slaves who've come downtown to blow half their week's pay on cover, parking and a half-dozen vodka coolers. I hang my elbow out and let the air numb my face. Sleep coils up from the bottoms of my feet.

But it's interrupted by a news reader's voice coming from the speaker behind my head. I roll up the window to hear him tell of a third victim in a murder spree police continue to publicly deny believing is the work of a single killer. Like Carol Ulrich and Ronald Pevencey, the body was found dismembered. A woman again, her name not yet released by investigators. The additionally puzzling twist is that she had only arrived in Toronto the day before from Vancouver. No known relation to the first two victims. Indeed, police have yet to determine if she knew anyone in town at all.

And then, right at the end of the report, come the details that chill me more than if I was being driven home tied to the roof rack.

The victim's body was found in the playground around the corner from us. The one where I take Sam.

And not just anywhere in the playground. The sand box.

"Eight fiddy," the driver says.

"Home. Right. I need to pay you now."

"That's how it works."

I'm stretching out over the back bench, grunting to pull out my wallet when the driver informs me the whole city's gone crazy.

"Kids got guns in the schools. Cops takin' money on the side. And the *drugs?* They sellin' shit that turn people into *robots*. Robots that stick a knife in your gut for pocket change."

"I know it."

"And now this insane motherfucker—'scuse me—

goes round and chops up three people in three weeks. Three *weeks!* What, he don't take no holidays?"

I hand the driver a piece of paper that, in the dark and with my Manhattan-blurred vision, could be either a twenty-dollar bill or a dry-cleaning receipt. It seems to satisfy him, whatever it is.

"I been out here drivin' nights for eight years," he says as I shoulder the door open and spill out into the street. "But I never been scared before."

"Well, you take care then."

The driver looks me up and down. "How 'bout this? How 'bout *you* take care."

I watch the taxi drive up Euclid until its brake lights shrink to nothing. Snow suspended under the street-lights, neither falling nor rising.

In the next moment, there is the certainty that I must not turn around. Not if I want to preserve the illusion that I am alone. So I step off the street, lurch toward my door. Only to see that this is a journey someone has already made.

Boot prints. At least two sizes larger than mine. Leading across the postage-stamp lawn and into the narrow walkway between our house and the house next door.

At least, this is the trail I think I'm following. When I look back, the prints, both mine and the boots', are already obscured by powdery snow.

I am the ground beneath your feet . . .

I could pull out my keys, unlock the front door, and put this skittishness behind me. Instead, something starts me down the unlit walk between the houses. If there is a danger here, it is my job to face it. No matter how unsteady I am. No matter how frightened.

But it's darker than night in here. A strip of sky running twenty feet over my head and no other way for the light of the city to get in. My heart accelerated to the point it hurts. Hands running over the brick on either side, making sure the walls don't close in on me. It's only thirty feet away, but the space at the far end that is our backyard feels like it's triple that. Uphill.

Along with another impression. This one telling me that someone else was here only moments ago.

The man in dark alleys you don't want to meet.

Once out, I slide my back along the rear wall. The branches of perennials reaching up from the snow like skeletal fingers. The old garden shed I keep meaning to tear down leans against the back fence to remain standing, much as I do using the wall behind me.

I sidestep up on to the deck. The sliding glass door is closed. Inside, the living room is illuminated by the TV. An infomercial demonstrating the amazing utility of a slicer-and-dicer gadget. It may be the booze, or the comforting images of advertising, but something holds me here for a moment, peering into my own darkened home. Taking in the mismatched furniture, the frayed rug, the overstuffed bookshelves, as though they are someone else's. As they could well be.

Except the room is not empty.

Sam. Asleep with a *Fantastic Four* comic open on his lap, his hands still gripping the cover. Emmie has let him stay up, having retired to the spare room awaiting my return. I look at my son and see the worry in his pose, the evidence of his struggle against sleep. Nightmares. It makes my heart hurt all over again.

I pull my hands from where they were resting against the glass. Step away and search my pockets for the keys to the house. Find them at the same instant I find something else that stops me cold.

A different pair of hand prints above mine on the sliding door. Visible only now I've moved away from the glass and the condensation of my breath has frozen them into silver. Ten fingertips and two smudges of palm that, when I place my own hands on top of them, extend an inch further from every edge.

He was here.

Looking into my home just as I am now, gauging the ease of entering. His eyes studying my sleeping son.

This time, when I push away from the sliding door, my hands smear the glass so that the other's prints are wiped away. Another filled-in boot print, a misguided intuition. A dubious creation of my non-creative mind.

Yet no matter how rational they sound, none of these explanations come close to being believed.

"I'm curious," the Managing Editor says, her face approximating an expression of real curiosity. "What were you thinking when you wrote this?"

It's the next morning. The Managing Editor has the front page of today's *National Star* laid out over her desk. My by-line under the lead story. "Prodigious Pay-Off for Pedantic Prizewinner."

"You mean the headline?" I say. "I've always been a sucker for alliteration."

"I'm speaking of the piece itself."

"I thought it needed some colour, I suppose."

The Managing Editor looks down at the paper. Reads aloud some of the lines she has highlighted.

"'Proceedings interrupted by coughing fits from an audience choking on air thick with hypocrisy.' 'The real prize should have gone to the jury for managing to read the shortlist.' 'There was more irony in listening to the host of an execrable TV show preach the virtues of reading than in the past dozen Dickie winners.' And so on."

The Managing Editor lifts her eyes from the page.

"*Colour*, Patrick?"

I search for a way to apologize. Because I *am* sorry. And I have a handful of excuses to back up my regret. The grief that seems to be turning into something else, something worse. Inoperable writer's block. A ghoul circling my house.

"I haven't been myself lately," I say.

"Oh?"

"It feels like I'm *losing hold* of things. But I can't let myself. I have a son, he's still little, and I'm the only one who –"

"So this," the Managing Editor interrupts, touching a finger to my article, "could be interpreted as a cry for help?"

"Yes. In a way, I think it could."

The Managing Editor reaches for the phone.

"Who are you calling?"

"Security."

"That won't be necessary."

"I know. I just rather *like* the idea of having you escorted out."

"This is it, then?"

"Very much so."

"Would it make any difference if I said I was sorry?"

"None whatsoever." She raises a finger to silence me. "Could you please have Patrick Rush removed from the building? That's right, this is a permanent access denial situation. Thank you."

The Managing Editor hangs up. Gives me a smile that's actually something else. The bared teeth dogs use to show their willingness to rip another's lungs out.

"So, Patrick. How's the family?"

12

Even with all my new free time, my final offering to the circle is no better than my previous scraps. Four whole days of wide-open unemployment and I've managed to produce little more than a To Do list stretched into full sentences. Patrick takes a nap. Patrick picks up long-forgotten dry cleaning. Patrick heats a can of soup for his lunch. If I'd set it during a war or the Depression and kept it up for a hundred thousand words, I'd have a shot at the Dickie.

Still, I make my way into Kensington with a fluttery anticipation, the winter showing signs of retreat, an almost clear March afternoon doing its best to lift the temperature past zero. A double espresso along the way has offered a jolt of hope. A caffeinated reminder there are blessings to be counted.

For one, Sam took my dismissal as well as could be expected for a four-year-old. He doesn't understand money. Or mortgages. Or the prospects for unemployed writers. But he seems to think old Dad can pull a few rabbits out of his hat if he puts his mind to it.

The other good news is that I've been doing a half

decent job of talking myself out of my Sandman theories. Getting away from the newsroom and Tim Earheart's grisly scoops has downgraded my paranoia to milder levels. My evidence of a connection between Angela's story and the killings of Carol Ulrich, Ronald Pevencey and the unnamed woman from Vancouver amounts to little when considered in the light of day. An over-interpreted four-line poem. Bodies found on a beach and a sand box. Hand prints on glass. That's it. Curious bits and pieces that can be strung together only through the most elastic logic, and even then, outstanding questions remain. Why would someone in the Kensington Circle be inspired to brutally murder complete strangers? Even if there is a Sandman that has walked out of the pages of Angela's journal, what would it want from me?

Tonight is our last meeting. Once we leave Conrad White's drafty apartment we will go our separate ways, to dissolve back into the city and take our places among the other undeclared novelists, secret poets, closeted chroniclers. Whatever peculiarities have animated my dreams since I first heard Angela tell her tale of a haunted little girl will come to an end. And I will be glad when it does. I like a good ghost story as much as anyone. But there comes a time when one must wake up and return to the everyday, to the world in which shadows are only shadows, and dark is nothing more than the absence of light.

We go around the circle one last time, and to my surprise, there has been some improvement from where we started. Ivan's rat, for instance, has become a fully developed character. There's a melancholy that comes out of the writing that I don't remember the first go round. Even Len's horror tales have been revised to be a little less repetitive, their author having learned that not every victim of a zombie attack need have their brains scooped out of their skulls for us to understand the undead's motivations.

As we proceed, I pay extra attention to Conrad White, looking for any sign that might confirm his relationship with Evelyn. Yet the old man maintains the same benign gaze on her while she reads as he does for everyone else. Perhaps the attraction only runs the other way. Evelyn doesn't strike me as the sort for him anyway. I'd imagined the "perfect girl" in *Jarvis and Wellesley* as softer, waifish, an innocent (even if this innocence was feigned). Someone who thought less and felt more. Someone like Angela.

If Conrad White shows any special attention to a circle member over the course of the meeting, it's her. I even think I catch him at it at one point, his eyes resting on her in the middle of Len's reading, when her head is turned in profile and she can be observed without detection. His expression isn't lustful. There is something in Angela he has seen before, or at least imagined. It's surprised him. And perhaps it has even frightened him a little too.

In the next second he catches me watching him.

That's when I think I see it. Something I can't be sure of, not in this light. But as his eyes pass over me, I have the idea that his world has been visited by the Sandman as well as mine.

Angela's turn. She apologizes that she brought nothing new with her this week. There is a moan of disappointment from the rest of us, followed by jokey complaints of how now we'll never know how Jacob died, what really happened over the time Edra was in the hospital, who the Sandman was. Conrad White asks if she'd made any changes to her previous draft, and she admits she hadn't found the time. Or this is what she tells us. If I were to guess, I'd say she'd never intended to make any revisions. She hasn't come here for editorial guidance, but to share her story with others. Without an audience, the little girl, Edra and Jacob, and the terrible man who does terrible things are only dead words on the page. Now they live in us.

Following this, we do everything we can—repeat comments we've already made, request a second smoke break—but there is still enough time for William to read. He has been sitting in the chair closest to the door, a few feet back from the others. It has made it almost possible to forget he is here. But now that Conrad White has called on him, he leans forward so that his eyes catch the candlelight, as though emerging from behind a velvet curtain.

His reading is once again brutal, but mercifully short. Another page in the lost summer of a cat-skinning boy. This time, the boy has taken to watching his mother at her "day job" through her bedroom window. He observes "what the men do to her, lying on top with their pants around their ankles, and he sees how they are only animals." The boy doesn't feel shame or disgust, only a clarity, "the discovery of a truth. One that has been hidden by a lie told over and over." If we are all of us animals, the boy concludes, then what difference is there between slicing the throat of a dog and doing the same to one of the men who visit his mother's bedroom? For that matter, what difference would there be in doing such a thing to his mother?

Soon, however, this idle contemplation demands to be tested. The boy feels like "a scientist, an astronaut, a discoverer of something no one had ever seen or thought of before." Proceeding from the assumption that we are all creatures of equal inclinations, it would follow that this makes us worth nothing more than the ants "we step out of our way just to crunch under our shoe." He could prove it. All he had to do was "something he had been taught was very, very wrong." If he was still himself afterward, if nothing changed in the world, then he would be right. The prospect "fills him with an excitement he guesses is the same as the other boys in school have felt kissing girls. But this was not what he had in mind at all."

William leans back in his chair and the light in his eyes is extinguished again. This is as far as his story goes. It's my turn to respond first, and though I'm usually good at coming up with empty comments, in this case I'm stumped.

"This feels very close to the surface to me," I manage finally.

"What does that mean?"

"I suppose it means that it feels real."

"What does real feel like?"

"Like right now."

"What does he do?" a female voice says, and all of us turn to face Angela. She is peering into the dark where William sits. "The boy. Does he carry out his . . . experiment?"

That's when William makes a sound all of us immediately regret ever hearing. He laughs.

"I'll show you mine if you show me yours," he says.

After we finish up, Conrad White suggests all of us go out to "whatever ale house may be nearby" to celebrate our accomplishments. We decide on Grossman's Tavern, a blues bar on Spadina I haven't been to since I was an undergrad. Little has changed. The house band working away in the corner, the red streak of streetcars passing the picture window at the front. This is where we push a couple of tables together and order pitchers, all of us a little nervous about speaking of ourselves and not our stories, which despite the similarities in most cases, is still a different matter.

The beer helps. As well as the absence of William, who walked away in the opposite direction outside Conrad White's apartment. It's nearly impossible to imagine how he would act in a social setting, whether he would eat the stale popcorn the waitress brings, how he would bring the little draft glasses to find his lips in his beard. Even more difficult to guess is what he might contribute to the first topic we naturally fall upon. The murders.

I'm giving this some consideration when my thoughts are interrupted by Len shouting at me over a note-for-note T-Bone Walker solo.

"Tell them your theory, Patrick."

"Sorry?"

"The *poem*. Tell them what you told me. About the Sandman."

The circle has turned to look at me. And there is Len, bobbing about in his chair like an ape at feeding time.

"That's a secret, Len."

"It *was*. Didn't you read the paper this morning? I thought you *worked* there."

"Not any more."

"Oh. Wow. That's too bad. I really liked that Couch Potato thing."

"I'm touched."

"That poem? The one they found by the Ulrich woman's body? They published it today."

I haven't looked at the *National Star* since being given the heave-ho, so I hadn't noticed Tim Earheart's triumph. It means two things are quite certain. First, my friend is out there somewhere, getting drunk as a donkey in celebration of his exclusive. Second, the police are no closer to finding the killer than they were when they asked the paper to hold off on running the poem.

"So? What's your Sandman theory?" Petra asks, looking first to me, then Angela, who has been watching me with an unsettling steadiness.

"It's nothing."

"C'mon! It's *good!*" Len says.

I continue to refuse. And then Angela leans forward, places an upturned hand on the table as though inviting me to place mine in hers.

"Please, Patrick," she says. "We'd be very interested."
So I tell her. Tell them.

My Sandman interpretation sounds even more ridiculous when shouted aloud in a bar, the circle leaning forward to hear, an almost comically incongruous bunch who, if you were to walk in right now, you'd wonder what they could possibly have in common. The absurdity makes it easier to make my case, on account of it's an argument that knows it has little chance of being right.

Trouble is, the others take it seriously. I can see I'm convincing them even as I try to laugh it off. What is clear in each of their faces is that they have had similar thoughts these past weeks. They came here believing in the Sandman as much as I do.

Once I'm finished, I excuse myself to call Sam and catch him as Emmie is putting him to bed. (I wish him sweet dreams, and he requests pancakes in the morning.) When I return to our table, the conversation has moved on to domestic complaint (Petra unable to believe how much she had to pay a plumber to replace the faucet on her jacuzzi) and sports (Ivan pleading the case for the Leafs to trade that big Russian kid who can't skate). More pitchers, cigarettes on the sidewalk. Me eventually ordering a round of shots for everyone, and having to down Angela's and Len's when she'd pushed hers aside and he'd reminded me he doesn't drink (I'd remembered, of course, and figured it was an easy way to double up).

Yet even through the increasingly fuzzy proceedings, there are some moments that demand mention.

At one point, there is only myself and Len at one end of the table and Conrad White and Evelyn at the other. The two of them almost cheek to cheek, whispering. Perhaps Len was right after all. Lovers would behave this way after a few drinks, wouldn't they? And yet there is something grave in the secrets they share, a seriousness that doesn't match any form of flirtation I'm familiar with. Not that I'm an expert.

I'm pouring myself another, studying the two of them, when Len leans over with a secret whisper of his own.

"I was followed last night. I think it was You Know Who."

"You *saw* him?"

"More like I felt him. His . . . *hunger*. You know what I mean?"

"As a matter of fact, I don't."

"I don't believe you."

"No? Well, let me tell you what I believe. You're taking my read on that poem too seriously. It's bullshit. I was just kidding around."

"No you weren't. And I know what I felt. It was him."

"Him?"

"The bogeyman."

"Look at me, Len. I'm not laughing."

"Whatever it was, it wasn't like you or me."

"I take it that you're talking about William."

"I might have *thought* it was William, but only because it can take different shapes. It's why there haven't been any witnesses. Think about it. Who knows what the bogeyman looks like? Nobody. Because it's whatever scares you the most."

I have to admit this last bit unsettles me enough that I'm not sure I manage to keep it hidden. But it's what Len says next that makes my calm act fall away completely.

"I'm not the only one."

"You told the others what you're telling me?"

"They've told *me*."

"And?"

"Petra saw someone out in her backyard two nights ago," he goes on, sliding even closer, so that now Evelyn and Conrad White are watching. "And last week, Ivan was taking his subway train into the yards at the end of the night, all the stations closed. He's just whizzing through, nobody's supposed to be there. And at one of the stops he sees someone right at the edge of the platform, all alone, like he's going to jump. Except he *can't* be there, right? All the stations are locked up for the night. And this guy, he's not security, he isn't wearing one of those fluorescent maintenance vests. So when Ivan goes by he tries to see his face. And you know what Ivan said? *He didn't have one.*"

"You've got to take a little time away from those *Tales from the Crypt* comics," I say, forcing out a laugh as the others join us from outside. Len wants to say more, but I steal a cigarette from the pack Evelyn left on the table and head outside before he has the chance.

It's only when I'm on the street, trying to light a match with shaking hands, that I allow myself to consider what Len's disclosures might mean. The first possibility is that he's nuts. The other option is he's telling the truth. At best, the Sandman story has got us all jumping at shadows. At worst, he's real.

These worries are interrupted by the sense that I'm not alone. It's Petra. Behind me, just around the corner, speaking with some urgency into a cellphone. She went out earlier with the other smokers apparently. A bit odd in itself, as she doesn't smoke, and now she's standing outside in the cold she often complains about. Thinking she's alone.

And then the Lincoln pulls up. One among the city's fleet of black Continentals that prowl the streets, chauffeuring bank tower barons and executive princes between their corner offices, restaurants, mistresses, the opera, and home again. This one, however, has come for Petra.

She snaps her cellphone shut and the back door is pushed open from within. A glimpse of black leather and capped driver behind the wheel. Petra seems to speak to whoever sits in the back seat for a moment. A reluctance that shows itself in her glance back at the doors to Grossman's—then she's spoken to from inside the car again. This time she gets in. The limo speeds away down a Chinatown side street with the assurance of a shark that has swallowed a smaller fish whole.

What stays with me about Petra's departure is how she left without saying goodbye. This, and how she entered the Lincoln as though she had no choice.

The rest of the Kensington Circle's final evening together goes on as one would expect. More drinks, more inevitable celebrity gossip, even some recommendations of good books we'd recently read. One by one the circle dwindles as someone else announces they have to get up in the morning. I, of course, being recently liberated from professional obligation, stay on. Pitchers keep turning up that I manage single-handedly. I must admit that my farewells become so protracted that, by the end, I'm surprised to find Angela and I the last ones here.

"Looks like we're closing the place," I say, offering her what's left in my pitcher. She passes her hand over her glass in refusal.

"I should be getting home."

"Wait. I wanted to ask you something."

This is out before I know what's coming next. The sudden intimacy of sitting next to Angela has left me thrilled, tongue-tied.

"Your story. It's most . . . impressive," I go on. "I mean, I think it's great. Really great."

"That's not a question."

"I'm just stalling for time. My therapist told me that among the first warning signs for alcoholism is drinking alone. That was my last visit to *him*, naturally."

"Can I ask you something, Patrick?"

"Fire away."

"Why do you think you were the only one in the circle not to have a story?"

"Lack of imagination, I guess."

"There's always your own life."

"I know I may *seem* rather fascinating. But, trust me, beneath this mysterious exterior, I'm Mr. Boring."

"Nobody's boring. Not if they go deep enough."

"Easy for you to say."

"How's that?"

"That journal of yours. Even if only a tenth of it's true, you're still miles ahead of me."

"You make it sound like a competition."

"Well it *is*, isn't it?" I hear the squeak of self-pity in my voice that a cleared throat doesn't make go away. But there's no stopping me now. "Most great writers have had something *happen* to them. Something out of the ordinary. Not me. *Loss*, yes. Bad luck. But nothing *uncommon*. Which would be fine if you're just trying to stay out of trouble. But if you want to be an artist? Not so good."

"Everyone has a secret."

"There are exceptions."

"Not a surprise in you, not a single twist. Is that it?"

"That's it. A hundred per cent What-you-see-is-what-you-get."

It's a staring contest. Angela not just meeting my eyes but measuring the depth of what lies behind them.

"I believe you," she says finally, and drains the last inch of beer in her glass. "So here's hoping something happens to you sometime."

It's late. The band is packing up, the bartender casting impatient glances our way. But there's something in Angela's veiled intensity that holds me here, the suggestion of unseen angles she almost dares me to guess at. It reminds me that there is so much I need to know. Questions I hadn't realized have been rolling around since the Kensington Circle's first meeting. In the end, I manage to voice only one.

"The little girl. In your piece. Is she really you?"

The waitress takes our empty glasses away. Sprays vinegar on the table and wipes it clean. Angela rises to her feet.

"Have you ever had a dream where you're falling?" she says. "Tumbling through space, the ground rushing up at you, but you can't wake up?"

"Yes."

"Is that falling person really you?"

Angela nearly smiles.

She slips her coat on and leaves. Walks by the window without turning to look in. From where I sit, she is visible only from the shoulders up, so that she passes against the backdrop of night like an apparition. A girl with her head down against the wind, someone at once plainly visible and hidden, so that after she's gone, you wouldn't be entirely certain if she was there at all.

Part Two
The Sandman

13

MAY, 2007

Victoria Day Weekend

It's the fourth interview of the last five hours and I'm not sure I'm making sense any more. A *New Yorker* staffer doing a 2,000-word profile. A documentary crew from Sweden. *USA Today* wanting a "sneak peek" on what my next book is about.

"I'm retired," I insist, and the reporter smiles, as though to say *Hey, I get it. Us writers like to hold our cards close.*

And now a kid from the *National Star* who I can tell is planning a snark attack from the second he sits across from me and refuses to meet my eyes. A boneless handshake, dewy sweat twinkling over lips and cheeks. I vaguely remember him—a copy editor who was very touchy about having grown up in Swift Current.

"So," he says, clicking the Record button on the dictaphone he has placed on the table. "You've been on the London *Times'* bestseller list since the pub date. Film deal with stars attached. And you've hit six weeks on the

New York Times list. Was all this your plan from the beginning?"

"Plan?"

"To what extent were you aware of the market factors in advance?"

"I didn't really think about –"

"It's okay. There's no need to be defensive. I believe there should always be a place for pulp fiction."

"That's generous of you."

"I mean, your book—it's not *serious* or anything."

"Of course not. I wouldn't know serious if it kissed me on the lips."

The kid snorts. Flips his notebook closed.

"Do you really think you *deserve* all this? Do you think what you've done –"

He pauses here to toss my book on to the table like a turd he's only now realized he's been holding. "Do you actually think this *thing* is *literature*?"

His lips keep smacking, but no more words come. I watch as the visible effort of searching for the meanest thing he could say squeezes his forehead into red folds. As for me, I squint, making a show of searching through my memory. Click my fingers when it comes to me.

"Swift Current."

"What?"

"I couldn't get the accent at first. But I'm definitely certain now. Swift Current! Must have been such an exciting place to grow up. Exposed to all that *culture*."

I'll give the kid credit. After he storms toward the exit, but is forced to turn back to retrieve the still recording dictaphone that I hold out to him, he has the manners to say thank you.

The thing is, the kid was right to ask if I thought I deserved all this. Because the answer is no. And even as the publicist who's been shuttling me around in a limo from interview to bookstore to TV chat show fills my glass and Sam's with more sparkling water, I feel only the hollowness of the vampire, a man who has achieved immortality but at a monstrous cost.

"Are you nervous, Dad?" Sam asks.

More disgraced than anything. Disgraced and sorry.

"A little," I say.

"But this is your last reading, right?"

"That's right."

"*I'd* be nervous if *I* was you."

The two of us look out at Toronto passing by, at once familiar and new. A North American Everycity. Or Anycity. But this one happens to be home. The limo gliding past the cluster of glass condos and over the rail-yards toward Harbourfront, where in just a few minutes I, Patrick Rush, am to give a reading from my embarrassingly successful first novel.

It was four years ago that the Kensington Circle gathered for the last time. Then, I was the only aspiring fictioneer among us who was without a story to tell. I never attended another workshop or writing class again. My dream of birthing a novel had been snuffed out once and for all. And I was grateful. Liberated. To be unburdened of an impossible goal is a blessing, believe me, though it admittedly leaves a few scars behind.

Yet here I am. Travel to the foreign nations whose languages my words have been translated into. Dinners and drinks with famous novelists—no, *colleagues*—I have long read and admired from afar. Invitations to write opinion pieces in publications I had previously received only junk mail from. The kind of breakthrough one is obliged to describe as "surreal" in one's *Vanity Fair* write-up, as I did.

And even today, on the occasion of my triumphant homecoming, when nothing I would have dreamed of has been denied me, I know that none of it is real.

"We're almost there, Mr. Rush," the publicist says.

She looks concerned. More and more I'm lost in what she likely thinks are pensive moments of creativity, an artist's mulling. Maybe I should tell her. Maybe I should come clean, here in the plush confessional of a limo. And maybe I would, if Sam weren't here. If I did, I'd tell her that my silences aren't caused by the churnings of the imagination. The truth is I'm just trying to hold the shame at bay long enough to get through the next smile, the next thank you, the next signature on the title page of a book that bears my name but isn't really mine.

Backstage I'm given bottled water, a bowl of fruit, a pee break. I'm told it's a full house, asked if I would answer questions from the audience following my reading. People would love to know what it's like to have a first book do what mine has done. I agree, I perfectly understand. I'd love to know the same thing.

Then I'm being guided down the hall into the darkened wings. Whispered voices tell me to watch my step. An opening appears in a velvet curtain and I step through, alone. There's my place in the front row. The publicist is in the seat next to Sam's, waving at me, as though there is some threat I might turn and walk out.

The director of the reading series appears at the lectern. He begins by thanking the corporate sponsors and moneyed donors who make such things possible. Then he starts on his introduction. A funny anecdote involving an exchange between himself and the featured author backstage just moments ago. I laugh along with everyone else, thinking how nice it would be if the charming guest he's just described actually existed. If he could be me.

And then I'm into dangerous territory again. Wishing Tamara were here. A wallop of grief that chokes the breath out of my throat.

"Ladies and gentlemen, without further ado, it gives me great pleasure to present Toronto's own Patrick Rush, reading from his sensational first novel, *The Sandman*!"

Applause. My hands raised against the spotlight in protest at too much love. Along with a private struggle to not be sick all over the front row.

Silence. Clear my throat. Adjust glasses.

Begin.

"There once was a girl who was haunted by a ghost . . ."

14

A plain envelope bearing a Toronto postmark. Inside, a newspaper clipping. No note attached. A piece from the *Whitley Register*, the local weekly of a northern Ontario town. A pin prick along the rugged, unpeopled spine of Lake Superior.

The story dated Friday, August 24, 2003.

CRASH KILLS TWO ON TRANS-CANADA

Author and Companion in 'Puzzling' Auto Accident

By Carl Luben, Staff Reporter

Whitley, Ont.—An automobile's crash into a stone cliffside on the Trans-Canada twenty minutes outside Whitley has resulted in the death of both its passengers early Tuesday morning.

Conrad White, 69, and Angela Whitmore (age unknown) are believed to have died on impact between the hours of 1 a.m. and 3 a.m. when their car left the highway. At press time, Ms. Whitmore's place of residence has yet to be determined, but it is believed that Mr. White's current address was in Toronto. It is unknown what purpose had brought them to the Whitley area.

Mr. White is the author of the novel *Jarvis and Wellesley*, a controversial work at the time of its publication in 1972. He had been living overseas for the last few decades, and only recently returned to reside in Canada.

So far, the police have yet to contact Angela Whitmore's immediate family, as available identification did not contain next-of-kin information. Readers who are able to provide more information on Ms. Whitmore's relations are asked to contact the Ontario Provincial Police, Whitley Detachment.

Police are still at work determining the precise cause of the accident. "It's a little puzzling," commented Constable Dennis Peet at the scene. "There were no other cars involved, and no skid marks, so the chances they went off the road to avoid colliding with an oncoming vehicle or animal crossing seems unlikely."

Investigators have estimated the car's speed on impact in excess of 140 km/hr. This velocity, taken together with the accident occurring along a relatively straight stretch of highway, reduces the possibility of the driver, Ms. Whitmore, falling asleep at the wheel.

"Sometimes, with incidents like these, all you know is that you'll never know," Constable Peet concluded.

My first thoughts after learning of the accident weren't for the loss of the two lives involved, but who might have sent me the clipping. I was pretty sure it had to be someone in the circle, as my connection to Angela and Conrad White would have been known to few outside of its members. But, if one of them, why the anonymity? Perhaps whoever sent the envelope wanted to be the bearer of bad tidings and nothing more. Petra, maybe, who would feel obliged to share what she had learned, but didn't want visitors showing up at her door. Or Evelyn, who would be too cool to write a dorky note. And then there was the odds-on favourite: Len. He'd have the time to scour whatever obscure database allowed him to learn of such things, and would appreciate how leaving his name off the envelope would lend the message a mysterious edginess.

Yet these practical explanations inevitably gave way—as all speculations about the circle eventually did—to more fanciful theories. Namely, to William. Once he entered my mind, the secondary questions posed by the article came rushing to the forefront. What were Conrad White and Angela doing travelling together through the bush outside Whitley in the first place? And why did Angela drive off the highway sixty kilometres over the speed limit? By factoring William into these queries, the notion that he was not only the sender of the clipping, but somehow the author of the crash itself, became a leading, if unlikely, hypothesis.

It was only sometime later, sitting on my own in the Crypt, that the fact Conrad and Angela were dead struck me with unexpected force. I lowered the three-month-old *Time* I'd been pretending to read to find my heart drum-rolling against my ribs, an instant sweat collaring the back of my neck. Panic. Out-of-nowhere, suffocating. The sort of attack I'd succumbed to on more than a few occasions since Tamara died. But this time it was different. This time, my shock was at the loss of two people I hardly knew.

Hold on. That last bit's not quite true.

It was the thought of Angela alone that stole all the air from the room. The girl with a story I would now never get to the end of.

After the night at Grossman's Tavern, the murderer I'd come to think of as the Sandman stopped killing. The police never arrested anyone for the deaths of Carol Ulrich, Ronald Pevencey and the Vancouver woman eventually identified as Jane Whirter. Though a $50,000 reward was offered for information leading to a conviction and occasional police press releases were issued insisting they were working on the case with unprecedented diligence, the authorities were forced to admit they had no real leads, never mind suspects. It was proposed that the killer had moved on. A drifter with no links to family or friends who would probably continue his work somewhere else down the line.

For a time, though, I couldn't stop feeling that the Pevencey, Ulrich and Whirter deaths were somehow connected to the circle. This is only a side effect of coincidence, of course. It's the egocentric seduction of coincidence that personalizes larger tragedies, so that we feel what we were doing when the twin towers came down or when JFK was shot or when a serial killer butchered someone in the playground around the corner is, ultimately, *our* story.

I know all this, and yet even after the Sandman was declared to be retired I never believed he was finished. The dark shape I would sometimes catch in my peripheral vision could never simply be nothing, but was always the *something* of coincidence. The lingering trace of fate.

I spotted Ivan on Yonge Street once. Standing on the sidewalk and looking northward, then southward, as though uncertain which way to go. I crossed the street to say hello, and he had turned to look at me, blank-faced. Behind him, the lurid marquee of the Zanzibar strip club blinked and strobed.

"Ivan," I said, touching my hand to his elbow. He looked at me like I was an undercover cop. One he'd been expecting to take him down for some time. "It's Patrick."

"Patrick."

"From the circle. The *writing* circle?"

Ivan glanced over my shoulder. At the doors to the Zanzibar.

"Up for a drink?" he said.

We put the daylight behind us and took a table in the corner. The afternoon girls rehearsing their pole work on the stage. Adjusting their implants in the smoked mirrors. Smearing on the baby oil.

I did the talking. Asked after his writing (he'd been "sitting on" some ideas) and work ("Same tracks, same tunnels"). There was a long silence after that, during which I was waiting for Ivan to ask similar questions of me. But he didn't. At first I assumed this was a symptom of strip-bar shyness. Yet now, looking back on it, I was wrong to think that. It was only the same awkwardness I'd felt the first time I spoke with Ivan, when he'd confessed to having been accused of hurting someone. His loneliness was stealing his voice from him. Driving the underground trains, staring at the walls in his basement flat, paying for a table dance. None of it required speech.

I excused myself to the men's room, and to my discomfort, Ivan followed me. It was only standing side by side at the urinals that he spoke.

Usually, exchanges that take place with another fellow in such a context, dicks in hand, requires strict limits of the subject matter. The barmaid's assets or the game on the big screen are safe bets. But not Ivan's admission that he's been afraid to get close to anyone since he was accused of killing his niece fourteen years ago.

"Her name was Pam. My sister's first born," he started. "Five years old. The father'd left the year before. Scumbag. So my sister, Julie, she's working days, and because I'm driving trains at night, she asks me to stay at her place sometimes to look after Pam. Happy to do it. The kind of kid I'd like to have if I ever had kids. Which I *won't*. Anyways, I was over at Julie's this one time and Pam asks if she can go down to the basement to get some toy of hers. I watched her run off down the hall and start down the stairs and I thought *That's the last time you're ever going to see her alive*. I mean, when you look after kids, you have these thoughts all the time. Yet this time I think *Well, that's it, little Pam is gone*, and it stuck with me a couple seconds longer than usual. Long enough to hear her miss a step. I go to the top of the stairs and turn on the light. And there she is on the floor. Blood. Because she came down on something. A rake somebody'd left on the floor. One of the old kind, y'know? Like a comb except with metal teeth. *Pointing up*. But that's not where it ends. Because Julie thinks I did it. The only family I got. So the police look into it, can't make any conclusions, they're suspicious but they've got to let it slide. But Julie hasn't spoken to me since. I don't even know where she lives any more. That's how a life ends. *Two* lives. It just happens. Except I'm still here."

He shakes. Zips. Leaves without washing his hands.

By the time I made it back to our table, Ivan is ordering another round. I told the waitress one was enough for me.

"I'll see you around then," I said to him. But Ivan's eyes remained fixed on the slippery doings onstage.

A few strides on I turned to wave (a gesture I hoped would communicate my need to rush on to some other appointment) but he was still sitting there, looking not, I noticed, at the dancer, but at the ceiling, at nothing at all. His hands hanging cold and white at his sides.

Len, the only one I'd given my home number to, called once. Asked if I wanted to get together to "talk shop," and for some reason I accepted. Perhaps I was lonelier than I thought.

I arranged to meet him at the Starbucks around the corner. As soon as the lumbering kid pushed his way through the doors I knew it was a mistake. Not that things went badly. We spoke of his efforts to give up on horror and "go legit" with his writing. He'd been sending his stories to university journals and magazines, and was heartened by "some pretty good rejection letters."

It was over the same coffee that Len shared the gossip about Petra. Her ex-husband, Leonard Dunn, had been arrested for a whack of fraud schemes, blackmail, and extortion. More than this, reports had suggested that Mr. Dunn had close connections to organized crime. Len and I joked about Petra's Rosedale mansion standing on the foundations of laundered money, but I kept to myself my last glimpse of Petra outside Grossman's, stepping into a black Lincoln she seemed reluctant to enter.

That was about it. Neither of us mentioned William or Angela or any of the others (I had not yet learned of the car accident outside Whitley). Even the apparent end to the Sandman's career was mentioned only in passing. It struck me that Len was as unsure of the police's presumption that we would never hear of him again as I was.

Afterwards, standing outside, Len and I agreed to get together again sometime soon. I think both of us recognized this as a promise best unkept. And as it turned out, it was only some years later, and under circumstances that had nothing to do with fostering a tentative friendship, that we saw each other again.

In interviews, I have repeatedly stated that I only started writing *The Sandman* after my severance pay from the *National Star* had run out, but this is not exactly true. If writing is at least partly a task undertaken in the mind alone, well away from pens or keyboards, then I had started filling in the spaces in Angela's story from the last night I saw her.

Even after the circle and the long, worried days that followed, even as the bank started sending its notices of arrears followed by their lawyers' announcements of fore-closure, some part of my mind was occupied in teasing out possible pasts and futures for the orphan girl, Jacob, Edra, and the terrible man who does terrible things.

It wasn't that these considerations were a comfort. It would be more accurate to say that I returned to Angela's story because I needed it to survive. To be present for my son, I required a fictional tale of horror to visit as an alternative to the real horrors that kept coming at us. I had Sam—but I was *alone*. We'd already lost Tamara. Now here goes the house. Here go Daddy's marbles. And I couldn't tell Sam about any of it.

This is how I thought *The Sandman* could save me. It gave me somewhere to go, something that was mine.

But I was wrong. It was never mine. And it could never save me.

The Sandman had plans of its own. All it needed me for was to set it free.

15

I admit to stealing Angela's story. Even so, it still wasn't a novel. While I used her characters, premise, setting, mimicked her tone, even copied whole pages from her recorded readings, viewed strictly on the basis of a word count, the bulk of *The Sandman* could technically be described as mine.

There was much I needed to add to give it the necessary weight of a book. Whatever it took to roll out what I already had with a minimum of actual *creating*, so that the result had been thinned to cover a couple hundred pages. But what the book still needed was the very thing Angela's story didn't provide. An ending.

After long months of scratching ideas on to index cards and dropping most of them into the recycling box, I managed to wring out a few concluding turns of the screw of my own, though there's little point in going into that here.

Let's just say I decided to make it a ghost story.

I knew it was plagiarism. There wasn't a moment I thought enough of *The Sandman* was invented that it could be truly considered my own. What relieved me of the crime was that I was only playing around. It was a distraction and nothing else. A kind of therapy during those hours when Sam was asleep, the TV spewed its usual rot, the sentences of my favourite books swam unreadably before my eyes.

Even when it was done, I still had no plans to present it as though I was its sole author. This was partly because I *wasn't*. But there was another reason.

I always saw the writing of the book as a kind of communication, an exchange between Angela and myself. I have read dozens of interviews with real writers who say that, throughout the process, they have in mind an audience of one for their work, an ideal reader who fully understands their intentions. For me, that's who Angela was. The extra set of eyes looking over my shoulder as the words crept down the screen. As I wrote our ghost story, Angela was the one phantom who was with me the whole time.

And then I started wondering if it might not be good. Our book. Angela's and mine. Except Angela was dead now.

What would *someone else* think of what we'd made together?

But even this self-deceiving line of thought wasn't my undoing. My real mistake was printing it out, buying envelopes to slip it into, and telling myself *I'm just curious* as I dropped them in the mail addressed to the biggest literary agents in New York.

That was a mistake.

16

I say now what all those in my position say in response to
the most commonly asked question of the after-reading
Q&A: *I had always wanted to be a writer*. But in my case,
this answer is not precisely true. I had wanted to write,
yes, but more primary than this, I had always wanted to
be an *author*. Nothing counted unless you were published.
I longed to be an embossed name on a spine, to belong to
the knighthood of those selected to stand alongside their
alphabetical neighbours on bookshop and library shelves.
The great and nearly so, the famous and wrongly over-
looked. The living and the dead.

But now, all I wanted was to be out of it.

What had seemed so important then now struck me
as a contrivance, an invention whose purpose was to
complicate that which was, if left alone, cruelly simple.
Life's a bitch and then you die, as the T-shirts used to say.

I would make do with keeping both hands on
the wheel of fatherhood, with weekend barbecues
and package beach holidays and rented Westerns and
Hitchcock. I would no longer feel the need to *say
something*, to stand isolated and furious outside the

anesthetized mainstream. Instead I would be among them, my consumer brothers and sisters. The search called off.

There are times I'm walking with Sam, or reading to him, or scrambling an egg for him, and I will be seized mid-step, mid-page-turn, mid-scramble, with paralytic love. For his sake, I try to keep such moments under control. Even at his age he has a keen sensitivity to embarrassment, and me blubbering about what a perfect little fellow he is, how like his mother— well, it's right off the chart. Not that it stops me. Not every time.

It is these pleasures that *The Sandman*'s publication has denied me. All the attention afforded the break-out first novelist—the church basement talks, forty-second syndicated morning radio interviews ("So, Pat, *loved* the book—but, let me ask you, who do you like in the Super Bowl?"), even a few bedroom invitations (politely declined) from book club hostesses and college campus Sylvia Plaths—was poisoned by the fact that I was alone, miles from my son.

"Where *are* you, Dad?" I remember Sam asking over the phone at one of the campaign's low points.

"Kansas City."

"Where's that?"

"I'm not sure. Kansas, maybe?"

"*The Wizard of Oz*."

"That's right. Dorothy. Toto. Over the rainbow."

There was a silence for a time after that.

"Dad?"

"Yes?"

"Remember when Dorothy clicked her heels together three times? *Remember?* Remember what she said?"

That *The Sandman* wasn't my own book didn't help things. Just when a glowing review or snaking bookstore line-up or letter from a high school kid relating how much he thought I was the shit came close to making me forget, Angela's recorded voice reading from her journal in Conrad White's apartment would return to me, and any comfort the moment might have brought was instantly stolen away.

There was also the worry I would be found out. Although I hadn't heard from any of them since *The Sandman* was published, it was entirely conceivable that one of the Kensington Circle would come across it, recognize its source material, and go to the press. Perhaps worse, Evelyn or Len would come knocking on my door with my book in their hands, demanding hush money. Worse yet, it would be William. And I would pay no matter who it was. I'd done a wrongful thing. I'm not denying it. But if there was ever a victimless crime, this was it. Now, in order to walk quietly away from my fraudulent, non-starter of a writing career as planned, four people had to keep a secret.

When I finally returned to Toronto, I went through the mail piled on my desk in the Crypt expecting at least one of the envelopes to contain a blackmail letter. But there was only the usual bills.

Life returned to normal, or whatever shape normal was going to take for Sam and me. We watched a lot of movies. Ate out at neighbourhood places, sitting side by side at the bar. For a while, it was like a holiday neither of us had asked for.

And the whole time I waited to walk into someone from the circle. Toronto is a big city, but not so big that you could forever avoid the very people you'd most like to never see again. Eventually, I'd be caught.

I started wearing ball caps and sunglasses everywhere I went. Took side streets. Avoided eye contact. It was like being followed by the Sandman all over again. Every shadow on the city's pavement a hole in the earth waiting to swallow me down. And what, I couldn't help wondering, would be waiting for me at the bottom?

17

I raise my eyes from the page. Squint into the lights. Dust orbiting like atoms in the white beams. If there are people out there, I can't see them. Perhaps they have learned that I'm not what I've claimed to be, and have left the hall in disgust. Perhaps they are still here, waiting for the police to click the cuffs around my wrists.

But they are only waiting for me. For the words every audience to Angela's story requires to lift the spell that's been cast on them.

"Thank you," I say.

Yellow, flickering movement like the beating of hummingbird wings. Hundreds of hands clapping together.

Sam is there at the side of the stage, smiling at his dad with relief.

I pick him up and kiss him. "It's over," I whisper. And even though there's people watching, he kisses me back.

"We should make our way to the signing table," the publicist says, taking me by the elbow.

I put Sam down to be driven home in the waiting limo and let the publicist guide me through a side door. A brightly lit room with a table at the far end with nothing but a fountain pen, bottle of water and a single rose in a glass vase on its surface. A pair of young men behind a cash register. Copies of *The Sandman* piled around them in teetering stacks. A cover design I've looked at a thousand times and a name I've spelled my whole life, but it still looks unfamiliar, as though I'm confronting both for the first time.

The auditorium doors are already opening as I make my way around the velvet ropes that will organize the autograph seekers into the tidy rows that always make me think of cattle being led to slaughter. In this case, all that will await them at the end is me. My face frozen in a rictus of alarm, or whatever is left of the expression that started out a smile.

And here they come. Not a mob (they are *readers*, after all, the last floral-skirted and corduroyed, canvas bag-clutching defenders of civilization) but a little anxious nevertheless, elbowing to buy their hardcover, have me do my thing, and get out before the parking lot gets too snarled.

What would this labour feel like if the book were wholly mine? Pretty damn pleasant would be my guess. A meeting of increasingly rare birds, writer and reader, acknowledging a mutual engagement in a kind of secret Resistance. There's even little side servings of flirtation, encouragement. Instead, all I'm doing now is defacing private property. More vandal than artist.

I'm really going now. Head down, cutting off any conversation before it has a chance to get started. All I want is to go home. Catch Sam before Emmie puts him to bed. There might even be time for a story.

Another book slides over the table at me. I've got the cover open, pen poised.

"Whatever you do, just don't give me the 'Best Wishes' brush-off."

A female voice. Cheeky and mocking and something else. Or perhaps missing something. The roundness words have when they are intended to cause no harm.

I look up. The book folds shut with a sigh.

Angela. Standing over me with a carnivorous smile on her face. Angela, but a different Angela. A professional suit, hair expensively clipped. Confident, brisk, sexy. Angela's older sister. The one who didn't die in a car crash with a dirty old novelist, and who could never see the big deal about wanting to write novels in the first place.

You're dead, I almost say.

"What, no 'How's the writing coming?'" the living Angela says.

"How's the writing coming?"

"Not as well as yours, by the looks of things."

The publicist makes an almost imperceptible sidestep closer to the table. The woman next in line behind Angela shuffles forward. Coughs more loudly than necessary. Taps the toe of a Birkenstock on the floor.

Angela remains smiling, but something changes in her pose. A stiffening at the corners of her mouth.

"Have you –?" she starts, and seems to lose her thought. She bends closer. "Have you *seen* any of them?"

"A couple. Here and there."

Angela ponders this response as though I'd answered in the form of a riddle. The woman behind her takes a full step forward. Her reddening face now just inches from sitting atop Angela's shoulder.

"Perhaps you'd like to speak to Mr. Rush *after* the signing?" the publicist says, as pleasantly as an obvious warning could be stated.

"I think –" Angela starts again. I wonder if she is steeling herself to launch some kind of attack. Slap me across the face. Serve a court summons. But it's not that. With her next words she reveals that she isn't angry. She's frightened.

"I think something's . . . *happening*."

The publicist tries to squeeze between Angela and the table. "May I *help* you?" she asks, reaching toward Angela's arm. But Angela rears back, as though to be touched by another would burn her skin.

"Sorry. Oh. I'm *sorry*," she murmurs, nudging the book another inch closer to me. "I suppose I should have this signed."

Now the entire line is getting antsy. The woman behind Angela has come around to stand next to her, an act of rebellion that threatens to create a second line. Fearing the chaos that would result, the publicist pulls back the cover for me, holds the book open to the title page.

"Here we are," she says.

I sign. Just my signature at first. Then, seeing this as too hopelessly impersonal, I scribble a dedication above my name.

To the Living,
Patrick Rush

"Hope you enjoy it," I say, handing the book back to Angela. She takes it, but remains staring at me.

"I'm sure I will," she says. "I'm particularly intrigued by the title."

The Birkenstock woman has heard enough. Drops her copy on to the table from three feet in the air. A single crack on impact that draws gasps from the line.

At the same time, Angela grips the front of the table with her free hand. Whispers something so low I rise out of my chair to hear her.

"I need to *talk* to you," she says. Opens the palm of her hand so that I have to reach into it and take the card she's offered me.

Then all at once she pushes aside the publicist who attempts to usher her toward the exit, makes her way unsteadily around the corner and is gone.

"I liked it," the Birkenstock woman says when my hands steady enough to open her copy. "Didn't totally buy the ending, though."

Part Three
Story Thieves

18

SUMMER, 2007

You wouldn't say climate is Toronto's strong point. Not if you appreciate seasons as they are normally understood as quarters of transition. Instead, the city endures long months of swampy, equatorial heat, and longer months of ear-aching cold, each separated by three pleasant days in a row, one called spring, the other fall.

This morning, for instance, the clock radio woke me with news of the fourth extreme heat alert so far this year, and it is only the first week of June. "Emergency Cool Down Centres" have been established in public buildings, where wanderers can collapse on to chilled marble floors until nightfall. The general citizenry has been advised not to go outside, not to allow the sun to touch its skin, not to move, not to breathe. These are empty warnings, of course, as people still have to work and, worse, *get* to work. After I've dropped Sam off at the daycare, I make my way back along Queen, lines of sweat trickling down my chest, glaring at the passengers on the stalled streetcar, all of them struck in poses of silent suffering.

From here I turn up toward College, past the semi-detached Victorians, each with their own knee-high fencing protecting front lawns so small you could mow them with a pair of tweezers. I stick to the shady reach of trees as best I can. But the heat isn't the only thing that slows my steps: I'm on my way to meet Angela.

The card she'd slipped into my hand at the Harbourfront book signing was blank aside from a scribbled cellphone number, and beneath it, a plaintive *Call Me.* I didn't want to. That is, I was aware that pursuing any further contact with a woman I had actionably wronged and who, if published reports were to be believed, was no longer among the living, could lead to nothing good.

Even now, my legs rubbery from the heat, zigzagging up the sidewalk like some midday boozer, I'm not sure why I called. It must have been the same impulse that had me press the Record button the first time I heard her read. The reason I kept going back to the circle's meetings when it was clear they were of no use. The ancient curse of the curious, the Nosey Parkers, the natural-born readers.

I needed to know.

We decided to meet at Kalendar, a café where we can sit outside. Now, selecting the one remaining table (only half covered by the awning's shade), I wish we'd opted for a cellar somewhere instead. I'm here first, so I take the darker chair. Later, when the sun slides to a new angle that allows it to fire lasers through the side of my head, and the chair across the table from mine is comfortably shielded, I will realize the error of my positioning. But for the time being, I order an intentionally fun-free soda water, believing I am still in control of the events barrelling my way.

At first, when a young woman arrives and, spotting me, comes over with a shy smile below her State Trooper shades, I assume it's a fan. Over the last few months, it has become not entirely uncommon for strangers to approach and offer a word about *The Sandman*. Some will stick around for more than this—the lonely, the tipsy, the crazy. And I'm trying to decide which this one is when she joins me at my table. I'm about to tell her I'm sorry, but I'm waiting for someone, when something in her face changes, a trembling strain at the tops of her cheeks, and I see that it's not a stranger at all.

"I guess we've never seen each other in the light of day," Angela says, studying me. It makes me wish I'd brought sunglasses of my own.

"You're right. We haven't."

"You look different."

"That's just heat stroke."

She looks at my soda water. "Are we having real drinks?"

"We are now."

Once a shot of vodka has been added to my drink and a glass of white wine placed next to Angela's hand, we talk a little about how she's spent the last few years. Following a period of clerical odd-jobbing, she decided she needed something more permanent. She went back to community college and came out with a certificate in legal administration, which landed her a position as an assistant at one of the Bay Street firms. It was this job she was stealing an extra hour away from, having told her boss she had a dental emergency.

"That's why I can afford to have a couple of these," she says, raising the glass of wine to her lips. "Laughing gas."

The waiter arrives to take our order. Angela asks for some kind of salad and I have what she's having (my nerves won't let me eat, only drink, so it doesn't much matter what prop is put in front of me). When he leaves, Angela looks at me. That same measuring gaze I caught her at a couple times in the circle. I don't get up and walk home, or turn my face away, or run to the men's room to hold my wrists under the cold water tap (all things I'd like to do). She knows too much already. My crime, of course. But other things as well. What had she whispered to me when she appeared out of nowhere, risen from the dead?

Something's happening.

Yet for a time the sun, the rare treat of dining outside in the middle of the day, the first edge-numbing blur of alcohol leaves us chatting like a pair on a blind date, one that has so far gone better than expected. In fact, Angela seems almost pleased to be here. It's as though she is a prison escapee who'd never guessed she'd have gotten as far as she has.

Our salads appear. Aggressively healthy-looking nests of radicchio, beets and chickpeas. Normally the sort of thing I'd lay a napkin over to not have to look at, let alone eat. But the illusion of immunity has given me a sudden appetite. I swing my fork down, and it's on its way mouthward as Angela speaks the words I thought we'd decided to leave alone.

"I read your book."

The fork drops. A chickpea makes a run for it.

"Well, yes. Of course you would have. And I suppose you saw that I . . . borrowed certain elements."

"You stole my story."

"That's debatable, to a point. I mean, the construction –"

"Patrick."

"– required a good deal of enhancement, not to mention the invention required in –"

"You *stole my story*."

Those sunglasses. They keep me from seeing how serious this is. Whether I am to now endure merely hissed accusations, or whatever wine is left in her glass thrown in my face, or worse. A knife impaling my hand to the table. The naming of lawyers.

"You're right. I stole your story."

I say this. I'm forced to. But I'm not forced to say what I say next. It comes with the unstoppable breakdown, the full impact of facing up to the person you've done injury to, sitting three feet away.

"I just wanted to write a book. But I didn't *have* a book. And then I heard you read at Conrad's and it wouldn't leave me alone. Your journal, novella, whatever—it became an obsession. It had been a while since my wife died—oh *Christ*, here we go—and I needed something. I needed *help*. So I started writing. Then,

when I found out about your car accident, I thought . . .
I thought it was more *ours* than just *yours*. But I was
wrong. I was wrong about all of it. So now . . . *now*?
Now I'm just sorry. I'm really, really sorry."

By now a few heads have turned our way. Watching
me blowing my nose on the napkin I steal from under
the next table's cutlery.

"You know something?" she says finally. "I rather
enjoyed it."

"*Enjoyed* it?"

"What it said. About you. It made you so much more
interesting than before."

"What I wrote."

"What you *did*."

My puzzled look nudges Angela further.

"In the circle, you were the only one without a story
to tell. Most people at least *think* they have stories. But
you assumed all along that there wasn't a character-
worthy bone in your body. And then what do you do?
You steal mine. Tack on an ending. Publish it. Then
regret all of it! That's almost *tragic*."

She takes the first bite of her salad. When the waiter
comes to check on us (a look of phony concern for me,
the messed-up guy with the already sunburning forehead) Angela orders another round for both of us. There
is no talk of retribution, settlements, public humiliation.
She just eats her salad and drinks her wine, as though
she has said all she needs to say about the matter.

When she's finished her meal she sits back and takes me
in anew. My presence seems to remind her of something.

"I guess it's your turn to get an explanation," she says.

"You don't have to tell me anything."

"I don't *have* to. But you probably deserve to know how it is that I'm not dead."

She tells me she heard about Conrad dying with a girl in a car accident, a girl believed to be her. Angela had been seeing him a bit at the time ("He was doing a close reading of my work") and left her purse in his car—which is how the authorities established their identification of the remains. The police didn't look into it much further than this, and had little reason to. The female body had been especially savaged in the crash, so there was no apparent inconsistency between it and the photos on Angela's ID. The accident was circumstantially odd, but there was no evidence of foul play. The presumed victim, Angela Whitmore, was known to have moved around a lot over the preceding years, job to job, coast to coast and back again, so that the authorities weren't surprised they couldn't discover her current address, as she likely didn't have one. Her relationship with Conrad White wasn't looked into either. The old man had a history of enjoying the company of much younger women. It was likely that Conrad and Angela had set out on some cross-country journey together, a sordid, *Lolita*-like odyssey, and hadn't made it through the first night on the winding highway through the Ontario bush.

After she has related all this to me, Angela's posture changes. Shields her face from the street, hiding behind her hair. The playful ease with which she'd introduced and then promptly dismissed the topic of my story-theft has been replaced with a stiffened back.

"So if it wasn't you, who was in the car with him?"

Angela's hands grip the table edges so tight her knuckles are pale buttons.

"Nobody's certain," she says. "But I'm pretty sure it was Evelyn."

"*Evelyn?*"

"They were hanging out together a lot around the time of the circle. And she was coming around to his apartment even after the meetings stopped."

"Were you *following* her?"

"If anything it was *her* following *me*." Angela lifts her wine glass but her shaking hand returns it to the table before taking a sip. "I was there too sometimes. For a while I liked the attention. Then it just got weird. I stopped going. But before I did, Evelyn would come by. I didn't stick around long whenever she showed up. It didn't feel like she was too happy to see me."

"Did you get a sense of why she was seeing him?"

"Not really. It felt like a secret, whatever it was. Like they were working on something together."

"And that's why you think it was her body in the car."

"I looked into it a bit more. After the initial report in the local paper –"

"The clipping you sent to me."

Angela cocks her head. "I didn't send you anything."

"Someone did. In the mail. Unsigned."

"That's how I first found out about it too."

I can't help wanting to know more on this point—if she didn't send the clipping, then who did?—but diverting her any further might shut her down completely. Already she's looking at her watch, wondering how much longer she has.

"Okay, so you followed up," I say.

"Because I thought it was Evelyn, but wasn't sure. And then, in one of the reports, it mentioned that the only distinguishing feature on the female victim's body was a tattoo. A raven tattoo."

"On the back of her wrist. I remember."

"I know I should have come forward. Evelyn probably has family who are still looking for her. They must think she's disappeared."

"So why didn't you?"

"At first, I think I saw it as a chance to just, I don't know, *lose* myself. Be erased. Start over. You know what I mean?"

"It's not too late. You could tell the police now. Straighten it all out."

"I can't do that."

"It's not like you did anything wrong."

"That's not why."

"I don't understand. Someone dies—an acquaintance of yours dies with your name on her toe tag, and you're letting the people who care about her live with the lie that she might still be out there? That Evelyn might be *alive*? I'm not taking any moral high ground here—you know I can't. But what you're doing is hurting others who've got nothing to do with you."

Angela takes off her sunglasses. Pupils darting from one peripheral to the other. Her voice had almost managed to disguise her panic. Now it's her eyes that give her away.

"After the accident, I took on different names," she says. "Changed where I lived, how I looked, my job. It was like I'd disappeared. And I *needed* to disappear."

"Why?"

"Because I was being *hunted*."

The waiter, who has been watching us from the opposite side of the patio for the past few minutes, drifts over to ask if he can bring us coffee or dessert.

"Just the cheque," Angela says, abruptly pulling open her purse.

"Please. This is on me," I say, waving her off, and the enormous understatement of the gesture, under the circumstances, brings a contrite laugh from my throat. But Angela is too agitated to join me in it.

"Listen, Patrick. I don't think I can see you again. So I better say what I came to say."

She blinks her eyes against the sun that is now cast equally on both of us. For a second I wonder if she has forgotten, now that she's come to it, what the point she wanted to deliver actually was. But this isn't what causes her to pause. She is only searching for the simplest way to put it.

"Be careful."

"Of what?"

"He was only watching before. But now . . . now it's *different*."

The waiter delivers the bill. Stands there long enough that I have to dig a credit card out of my wallet and drop it on the tray before he reluctantly moves away. In the meantime, Angela has gotten to her feet.

"Wait. Just *wait* a second. Who's 'he'?"

"Do you really think you're the only one?"

"What are you saying?"

"The Sandman," she says, and disappears behind her sunglasses once more. "He's come back."

19

The next morning I refuse to let my thoughts return to my lunch with Angela other than to remind myself that she has no apparent plans to sue me. This is *a good thing*. As for the other stuff—I do my best not to go there.

What's needed are rituals. New habits Sam and I can set about repeating so that they will blaze a trail to follow over the days to come. Starting with food. Instead of the improvised meals we have been surviving on— willy-nilly takeout, tins of corner-store glop, Fruit Loops—I set out with Sam to lay in proper stock.

We drive down to the supermarket by the harbour, where the warehouses and piers are being turned into nightclubs and condominiums. This is where we shop, or used to shop. It's been a while.

Yet here it all is, the pyramids of selected produce, the microwavable entrées, the aisles of sustenance for those who needn't look at price tags. Sam and I drop items in our basket as they glide by. The outrageous bounty of North American choice.

"This is why the rest of the world hates us," I tell

Sam. He looks up at me and nods, as though he were having precisely the same thought.

Later, down in the Crypt, our purchases stocked away, I sit at my desk and realize that I have no work to do. No freelance assignment, no novel-in-progress, no review deadline. There's still an hour to kill before lunch, and I click on the computer to indulge in a moment of virtual masturbation: I Google myself.

As always, the entry at the top of the list is my official website. The creation of my publisher's marketing department, www.patrickrush.com features a Comment section I sometimes visit. The correspondents generally represent one of two extremes: gushing fan or crap-taking critic. The latter favours the sort of spluttering, all-lower-case tirade that soils the screen for a few hours before the Webmaster gets around to striking it from the record. This morning, however, there's something waiting there of an altogether more disturbing nature.

Not an incoherent screed, not a copyedit nitpick, not a demand for money back. Just a single word of accusation.

Thief.

The correspondent's name is nowhere to be seen. There's only his or her *nom-de-blog*: **therealsandman**.

It could be only coincidence—the specificity of the allegation, the timing of Angela's belief that the Sandman has returned, the identity implied by the name—but I'm certain it's someone who *knows*.

I immediately write back in reply. This requires the creation of a blog identity of my own: **braindead29.**

Why are you afraid to use your real name?

Reading the question over, I see how it's too clear and benign for blogspeak. I make a go at translation.

why r assholes like u 2 afraid to use your reel name?????

Better.

I press Send. Lean back in my chair, confident **therealsandman** will shrink at this direct challenge. But my reply comes within seconds.

You don't know what afraid is yet.

Looking back on it, I wasn't all that surprised when Angela showed up at my book signing table, even though, being deceased, her appearance was an impossibility. Maybe this came from writing about a ghost so much over the preceding years. I've simply gotten used to seeing the dead.

Or maybe not.

This afternoon, while Sam is at his Summer Art Camp in Trinity-Bellwoods fingerpainting or rehearsing a play or writing a poem, I walk up to Bloor Street to buy a book. I may not be able to write any more, but that shouldn't stop me from reading. I'm thinking something non-fictional, a dinner-party talking point (in case I'm ever invited to a dinner party). The melting of the polar ice caps, say, or the emergence of nuclear rogue states. Something light.

I head into Book City with the idea that my earlier efforts at living a normal day may not have been entirely derailed by my encounter with **therealsandman**. The sheer hopefulness in the stacks of new releases and the customers opening the covers to taste the prose within fills me with a sense of fellowship. It is here, among the anonymous browsers, that I belong. And where I might be allowed to return, once I can slip back into being another bespectacled shuffler, instead of someone, like Angela, who believes they are being hunted.

I'm halfway to convincing myself when I see him.

I have sidestepped my way past New Fiction and headed straight for the Non-Fiction Everyone's Talking About! table at the back. When I pick up my first selection, I hide behind the cover and allow myself a furtive scan of the shop. Right away I notice a man with my book in his hands. In profile, backlit by a sun-bleached Bloor Street through the display windows. *The Sandman* open a hundred pages in, the man's face showing a grimace of disapproval. Conrad White. My writing instructor. Not at all happy with the published results of his worst student.

He turns his head.

An abrupt twist of the neck that allows his hollow eyes to find me instantly. His features shifting, forming deep creases over his ashen skin. A look of reproach so fierce it gives the impression of a snarling animal.

It takes a second to remember he's dead.

That's when my free hand pushes the books to the floor. A pile of travel guides tumbling over the table's edge. A flailing collapse that leaves me sprawled out, trying to push myself up from the slippery paperbacks.

"My God, are you okay?" a clerk asks, rushing out from behind the cash register.

"I'm fine. I just . . . sorry about . . . I'll pay if there's any . . ." I stammer, looking to where Conrad White was standing.

But there's nobody there now. The book he'd been reading left at a crooked angle atop its stack.

Once, having been recognized, I've declined the clerk's invitation to read his own novel-in-progress ("What I *really* need are *connections*, y'know?") I skulk out of the bookstore into the foul heat. The foreign students and Chardonnay hippies of the Annex pass me by as I stand there, disoriented, trying to figure my east from my west. In my hand, a bag carrying my guilt purchase: the first book I grabbed off the check-out counter, which turned out to be empty and untitled. A journal that the clerk guessed was meant to help with my next book.

"There won't *be* another book," I blurted.

Now, on the walk downtown to pick up Sam, I wonder again if my seeing ghosts is a symptom of a more serious condition. Untended sorrow allowed to turn into a full-blown psychotic break. Acute post-traumatic stress, perhaps (what is the loss of your wife, your career, and the defilement of your sole ambition, if not trauma?) Maybe I need help. Maybe it's too late.

Yet the old man had looked so *real*, just fifteen feet away, with none of the foggy edges or spectral floating attributed to most apparitions. It was Conrad White, dead and *looking* dead. But there nevertheless.

Once I've entered the relative cool of the trees in Trinity-Bellwoods, I've decided that if my sanity has to go, it's my job to keep its absence to myself. Sam has already lost one parent. He's got to be better off with a mad father looking over him than none at all.

I come to stand on the other side of the temporary fence the playground has put up around the kids' Art Camp, watching Sam read a book in the pilot's seat of a plane made of scrap wood. He raises his eyes from the page and looks my way. I wave, but he doesn't wave back. I'm sure he's seen me, and for a moment I wonder if I'm confused as to whether that's Sam in there or not. And then I remember: my son is entering the age when your parents are embarrassing. He doesn't want the other kids to see that's his dad over there, waving, clutching a goofy book bag.

But on the walk home he offers an alternative explanation. Sam hadn't waved because there was a strange man staring at him from the other side of the fence.

"That was me."

"Not *you*, Daddy. I saw *you*. The other man. *Behind* you."

"There wasn't anyone behind me."

"Did you look?"

"What do you want for dinner?"

"*Did* you? Did you see –"

"We've got chicken, lasagne, those tacos-in-a-box thingies. C'mon. Name your poison."

"Okay. Burgers. *Takeout* burgers."

"But we bought all those groceries this morning."

"You asked."

After dinner, I check the phone for messages. Three tele-marketers, a hang up, two complete strangers asking if I'd forward their manuscripts to my agent, and Tim Earheart wondering if the "great novelist" wanted to "come out and get shitfaced sometime." As well as Petra Dunn, the Rosedale divorcée from the circle. Saying she's sorry, she doesn't want to impose, but she thinks it's important we talk.

I take down her number but decide not to call back tonight. A retreat to bed is my best bet. Tuck Sam in, scan a few paragraphs of something and, if precedent holds, I'll be sent off to a dreamless nothing. Trouble is, I didn't end up buying a book to *read* this afternoon, but a book to *write* in.

This may be breaking a promise I've made to myself, but I figure there can't be much harm in just making notes. I take a pen and the journal under the sheets with me and start scribbling. Jotted points covering the events since Angela showed up at my book signing, and then jumping back to the beginning of the circle, my first encounter with the Sandman's story, and here and there over the period of time of the killings four years ago.

Not really writing at all, but a compiling of facts, impressions. If I have angered the gods for being a story thief, surely there can be no offence in this, the unadorned chronicling of my own life.

Even in this I'm wrong.

A sound from downstairs.

Something that awakens me from that in-between state of nodding off without being aware that this is what you're doing. A bang. Followed by a millisecond of reverberation, which confirms that whatever it was, it's of sufficient weight to rule out the usual bump-in-the-night suspects, *a creak of the floorboards* or *mice between the walls*. My first thought is it's a bird that's mistaken the clear surface of the sliding back doors for night. And it might have been a bird, if it weren't for the sound that follows. The cry of fingernails scraped over glass.

I slip on the boxers and T-shirt left in a pile next to the bed and check on Sam. Still asleep. I pull his door shut and shuffle to the top of the stairs. Only the usual peeps and sighs of an old house. Miles off, a low rumble of thunder.

Downstairs, there's no sign of disturbance. But why would there be? If someone has forced their way into our home with an intent to do us harm, there'd be little point in overturning a side table or shattering the hall mirror along the way. Still, there's a comfort in seeing Sam's playground sneakers sitting side by side on the mat, the stack of envelopes on the bottom step ready to be tossed in the mailbox in the morning. What evil could possibly be strong enough to pass these talismans?

At the base of the stairs, I move as quietly as I can toward the living room at the rear of the house. From here, I can see a sliver of the sliding glass doors that open on to the deck. The rain has started, slow and dense as oil. A soft drumming on the roof.

Then the rain turns to silver.

The motion-sensor lights I had put in last week activated by something in the yard. Not the rain (they're designed to ignore it), or moving branches (there is no wind). Something large enough to be spotted. Moving from one part of the property to the other. Something I can't see.

I run to the kitchen and pull a pair of scissors from the butcher's block, hold them out in front of me as I dash to the glass doors. The lights flick off before I get there. Just three seconds of brightness. Why had I told the guy who installed them to set the timer for *three seconds*? Not long enough to catch a raccoon's attention, let alone thwart a break-in. But I remember now: I hadn't wanted it to wake up the neighbours. That this is the very point of such devices must have been lost on me at the time.

I unlock the door and slide it open. Thrust the scissors out first, as though to sink the blades into the body of rain.

Once outside, the downpour instantly seals my T-shirt to my skin. I keep moving on to the deck. At its edge, I come into range of the motion sensors and the floodlights come on. The backyard suddenly ablaze, so that everything—the thirsty lawn, weed-ridden flower beds running along the fence, the leaning garden shed in the back corner—is translated from grey outlines to harsh specifics. Nothing else. Nothing out of place.

Three seconds later, the lights are off. The yard expanded by darkness.

Waving my arm over my head, I activate the sensor again. Everything as it was. The curtain of rainfall. The dim shape of neighbouring houses.

I have done my duty. Two a.m. and all's well. Time to go back inside, grab a towel and count sheep.

But I don't.

Absently this time, I lift my arm high, the scissors held skyward. And once more the lights come on.

To show someone standing in the yard.

A man with his back against the far fence, next to the garden shed. His face shielded by the overhanging branches of the neighbour's willow. Arms loose at his sides. And at the end of those arms, the creased gloves of his hands.

The lights flick off.

There is no way I could swing my arm up again if it weren't for Sam. My son, asleep in his bed upstairs. Counting on me to keep the bogeyman away. It's the thought of Sam that turns the lights on.

But the yard is empty. It's only the same sad square of real estate as before, a neglected garden and shed with cobwebs sprayed over its window. And no one standing by the back fence. If he was here at all, the terrible man who does terrible things is gone.

20

After seeing a ghost reading my book, after my lunch
with Angela, after glimpsing a monster in my own backyard, you'd think I'd be packing up and moving me and
Sam to a different time zone by now. But the events of
the past few days have instead provided the answer to an
age-old question: Why do characters in horror movies
go back into the haunted house one more time, even
when the audience is shouting *Run! Start driving and
keep driving!* at the screen? It's because you don't know
you're *in* a horror movie until it's too late. Even when
the rules that separate what is possible from what is not
start to give way, you don't believe you're going to
end up as just another contribution to the body count,
but that you're the hero, the one who's going to figure
out the puzzle and survive. Nobody lives their life as
though they've only been cast in a grisly cameo.

And besides, in my case it's not the house that's
haunted. It's me.

When I called Petra back she sounded as though she
couldn't remember who I was.

"Patrick Rush," I said again. "From the writing circle. *You* called *me*."

"Oh yes. I wonder if you could come around later this afternoon?"

"I wouldn't mind knowing what this is about."

"Say five o'clock?"

"Listen, I'm not sure I –"

"Great! See you then!"

And then she hung up.

I know the sound of someone pretending they're speaking to someone else on the phone (I'm friends with Tim Earheart, after all, surely one of the best multiple-affair managers in contemporary journalism). But what reason would Petra have to conceal my identity from whoever was in the room with her?

Coming out the doors of the Rosedale station I recall my conversation with Ivan in this same place. It makes me wonder if he is still driving trains underground, still writing about his imaginary metamorphosis, still alone. He might well have been behind the controls of the train that brought me here. The thought of it starts a shiver up my back in the hot sunshine. It's not necessarily the idea of Ivan himself that does it, but that if Angela and now Petra have come looking for me, how far behind could Ivan and Len be? And if these two wait for me down the line, why not William too?

"Patrick?"

I turn around to find Petra jogging in place. Brand-new trainers on her feet. Hair tied back under a Yankees cap.

"I should warn you, I'm not in the greatest shape."

"Sorry," she says, and stops hopping. "I usually go for a run around this time, so I figured I'd come meet you here instead of at the house."

"We're not going there?"

"It's best if we don't."

She gives me a pleading look, as though it's possible that I might not only deny her request, but take her forcibly by the arm and drag her home. I've seen versions of the expression on Petra's face before, though not among society divorcées but the bruised faces of women outside the shelters downtown. Women who have been conditioned to be pleading with all men, and to expect the worst anyway.

"Where would you like to go?"

"Down in the ravine. That's where I run," she says. "It's cooler in the shade."

"And more private."

"And more private. Yes."

I gesture for her to lead on, and she starts over the bridge that crosses the tracks. As she goes, she glances over her shoulder every few steps. We are exposed at every angle—to people exiting the station, the traffic on Yonge, as well as the tree-shrouded windows of the mansions that sit along the crest of the ravine. It makes Petra move fast.

When she pushes through the brush on the other side of the bridge and rustles down an overgrown trail, I lose her for a couple minutes. But when I break through the patches of wild raspberry at the bottom she's waiting for me.

"I forgot to thank you for coming," she says.

"You made it sound like I had no choice."

"It's not only for my benefit."

Petra walks further along the trail. We carry on like this until the trees become thicker where the ravine opens wide. When we've come along far enough that we can see there's no one for a couple hundred yards in either direction, Petra stops. Turns to me with an agitated expression, as though she hadn't expected to find me following her.

"I don't have a lot of time," she says. "My schedule is pretty much set. And people notice if I make any changes to it."

"People?"

"My personal life," she says vaguely.

Petra puts her hands on her waist and bends over slightly, taking deep breaths as though she's come to the end of her run and not the start of it.

"There's a man who's been watching me," she says finally.

"Do you know who it is?"

"The same person who's been watching all of us."

"Us?"

"The circle. Or some of the circle. Len, Ivan, Angela."

"You've *spoken* with them?"

"Len contacted me. He told me about the others."

The entirety of our conversation to this point has taken less than a minute but it feels much longer than that. It's the effort required in shielding my surprise from her.

"I'm guessing you think it's the Sandman," I say, trying to sound doubtful.

"It's occurred to me, yes."

"This is crazy."

"Are you saying you haven't seen him?"

"I'm saying I have. That's what's crazy."

Petra checks the trail again. I can see her figuring how much longer she has before she should be opening her door and wiping the sweat from her eyes.

"I suppose you've read my book," I say.

"*Your* book?"

"Okay. The book with my name on it."

"I've seen it. Picked it up in the store a couple times. But I don't want it anywhere near me."

Petra looks suddenly lost. It's my turn to say something to keep her here.

"Who was in the limo that picked you up from Grossman's that night?"

"I'm not sure that's any of your business."

"It wasn't. But that was before you told me we're being followed by the same person."

For a second I'm sure Petra is going to walk away. But instead, she comes to some decision in her head. One that brings her a step closer to me.

"My ex-husband's business required his involvement in things that weren't entirely conventional."

"Judging by your house up that hill, it seemed to be working for him."

"Still is."

"So was that him in the limo?"

"It was Roman. Roman Gaborek. My husband's business partner. *Former* business partner."

"A friend of yours."

"My boyfriend. Or something like that. He's who I left my husband for. But my husband doesn't know that. If Leonard knew that I was seeing Roman, it would be bad for everyone."

"Jealous type."

"Leonard *owns* people."

"So maybe he's the one who you've seen around your house."

"It might be. And sometimes it *has* been. But I don't think it's who we're talking about right now."

"Why not?"

"Because this man . . . he's not *right*."

From somewhere behind us there's the scurrying of something in the underbrush. The sound makes Petra jump back, hands raised in front of her. Even when she realizes there's nobody there, she remains coiled.

"If it is the Sandman, why *now*?" I say. "What brought him back?"

"What do you think?"

"My book."

"Yours. Hers. Whoever's."

Although responding to a signal only she can hear, Petra turns and starts off down the trail, deeper into the humid shade of the ravine. A light, prancing jog at first, then picking up the pace, her arms pumping. By the time she turns a corner and disappears she's running as fast as she can.

The orange sky of a smog-alert dusk has darkened into evening. An hour when most of the suits and skirts are safely locked in their air-conditioned condo boxes, and the others, averse to sunshine, spill out of the dumpster alleys and piss-stained corners. The last four blocks along Queen to my house are predominately populated by the troubled and addicted at the best of times, but tonight there are even more of them milling about. It's because they're *visitors*. Even homeless junkies can be summer tourists, checking to see what the big-city fuss is all about. One toothless beauty who staggers into me takes special offence when I refuse her request for change. "But I'm on *vacation!*" she protests.

That makes two of us. I'm certainly not working any more. After the author tour for *The Sandman* was completed, my plan went no further than a retreat from occupation, from doing. Perhaps this was a mistake. Perhaps the idleness of the past few weeks has left a space open for unwanted elements to enter. How else to explain the return of the Kensington Circle to my life?

Of course I do have a job. A single purpose I committed myself to after Tamara died: to bring up Sam. Be a good father. Share my few good points and try to hide the legion deficiencies.

And yet now, my single responsibility has turned from nurturing my son to protecting him. If there is something wretched that my wretched book has brought into the world, then the vacation is over. My job is now the same as the girl's in Angela's story who tried to keep a threat from the only ones she loved. To make sure that, if it comes for us, it touches only me, not him.

I make the turn on to Euclid and once more there's a sense that something isn't right. No police tape this time, no pursuer making me run for my front door. But there's a lightheaded pause nevertheless, a sudden churning of nausea. A sensation I'm beginning to associate with being close to him.

Where's Sam?

He's at home with Emmie. Sam is fine.

So why am I running? Why do I have the keys out of my pocket, the sharp ends poking out between the knuckles of my fist? Why, when my house comes into view, is there the outline of a man standing in the front window?

He sees me coming and stays where he is. Watches me slide the key in and open the door.

The front hallway is dark. He hadn't turned the lights on, hadn't needed to. He knew where he wanted to go.

I round the corner of the dining room where the front window looks on to the street. The room is empty. Nothing to hide behind. From here I step back into the hallway to check the rear of the house. The kitchen drawers closed, nothing unsettled on the counters. And the living room as it was left as well.

I'm about to make my way upstairs when a lick of breeze turns my attention to the sliding doors. Open. What I'd seen at first as glass now revealed as the intruder's means of entry.

But it doesn't mean he left by the same route. It doesn't mean he's not in the house.

"Sam?"

I take the stairs three at a time. Slapping at the wall as my feet skid out on the landing. My shoulder crashing into my son's bedroom door.

"*Sam!*"

Even before I look to see if he's in his bed, I check the window. *Blood tattooed on the curtains.* But it's closed, the curtains untouched. His bed made, just as he'd left it this morning.

Then I remember. He's over at his friend Joseph's across the street. A birthday party. Sam's not here because he's not *supposed* to be here.

I cross the hall and grab the phone. Joseph's mother answers.

"I just . . . the back door . . . could you *please* put Sam on?"

Half a minute passes. Something is wrong. All that's left is for Joseph's mother to come back on the line and say, *That's funny. He was here with the other kids the last time I checked.*

"Dad?"

"Sam?"

"What's going on?"

"Are you inside?"

"That's where the phone is."

"Right."

"Where are you?"

"At home. There was . . . I forgot to . . . Oh, *Jesus* . . ."

"Can I go now?"

"I'll come pick you up when the party's over, okay?"

"I'm across the *street*."

"I'll pick you up anyway."

"Sure."

"Bye, then."

"Bye."

Whoever was standing in the window had got the right house this time. But it was the *wrong night*.

Luck. Who'd have thought there'd be any left for me, after all my undeserved laurels, my devil deals? Yet Sam is alive. Eating cake and horsing around in my neighbour's basement.

It's time, however, to get some help. Not of the psychiatric variety (although this seems increasingly inevitable) but the law. There's no more room to wonder if the Sandman is real or not. There was someone in my *house*. And now it's time to bring in the guys with badges and guns.

But before I can pick up the phone, it starts to ring.

I look up to see that my bedroom curtains are drawn open. Left that way from this morning when I'd pulled them wide to let the light in. But now, at night and with the bedside lamp on, I would be visible to anyone on the street.

The phone keeps ringing.

If I'm about to speak to the terrible man who does terrible things, I can't help wondering what words he wants to share with me.

"Hello?"

"Mr. Rush?"

Some sort of accent.

"If this is about your goddamn manuscript, I can't help you. Now if you don't mind stuffing your precious –"

"I've got some bad news for you, Mr. Rush."

"Who *is* this? Because I know he's safe, alright? So if you're –"

"I think there's some confusion here –"

"– trying to threaten me, I'll call the police. You hearing me?"

"Mr. Rush—*Patrick*—please. This is Detective Ian Ramsay, Toronto Police Services. I'm calling about your friend, Petra Dunn."

A Scottish lilt. The giveaway of an immigrant who's been here for the better part of his life but still hasn't wholly lost the accent of the homeland. It distracts me for a moment, so that when he speaks his next words, I'm still trying to guess whether he'd more likely be from the Edinburgh or Glasgow side of things.

"We believe she's been murdered, Mr. Rush," he says.

21

The police, when they arrive, take the form of a single man, a tall plainclothesman with bright green eyes that suggest one needn't take him too seriously. A moustache that seems an afterthought, an obligatory accessory he'd be more comfortable without. I've never been around a real detective before, and I try to prepare myself to be at once cautious and relaxed. And yet his open features, along with finding myself a couple inches wider than he (I'd expected a broad slab of recrimination), instantly make me feel that no real harm can come from this man.

"I'm here about the murder," he says, with practiced regret, as someone in coveralls might arrive at the door to say *I'm here about the cockroaches.*

I extend my arm to invite him in and he brushes past, makes his way directly into the living room. It's the sort of familiar entrance an old friend might make, one comfortable enough to go straight for the bar and not say hello until the first gulp is down.

When I follow him in, however, Detective Ramsay hasn't helped himself to a drink, but is standing in the centre of the room, hands clasped behind his back. He gestures for me to sit—I take the arm of a ratty recliner—while remaining standing himself. Even being half-seated, however, concedes the weight advantage I'd briefly held. For what might be a minute, it seems I'm of little interest to him. He looks around the room as though every magazine and mantelpiece knick-knack were communicating directly to him, and he wants to give each of them the chance to speak.

"Are you a married man, Mr. Rush?"

"My wife passed away seven years ago."

"Sorry to hear that."

"Yourself?"

He raises his hand to show the gold band around his ring finger. "Twenty years in. I tell my wife a fellow does less time for manslaughter these days."

I try at a smile, but it doesn't seem that he's expecting one.

"Someone told me you're a writer."

"I'm out of it now," I say.

"Going into a new line of work, are you?"

"Not decided on that yet."

"Would've thought the writing life would be close to ideal. No boss, set your own hours. Just making things up. Not work at all, really."

"You make it sound easier than it is."

"What's the hard part?"

"All of it. *Especially* the making things up."

"It's a lot like lying, I imagine."

He steps over to the bookshelf, nodding at the titles but seemingly recognizing none of them.

"I'm a pretty avid reader myself," he says. "Just crime novels, really. Can't be bothered with all that Meaning of Life stuff." Detective Ramsay turns to look at me. His face folds into a disapproving frown. "Can I ask what you find so funny?"

"You're a detective who only reads detective novels."

"So?"

"It's ironic, I guess."

"It is?"

"Perhaps not."

He returns his attention to the shelves until he pulls out my book.

"What is it?" he says.

"I'm sorry?"

"What *kind* of book is it?"

"I'm never quite sure what to say to that."

"Why not?"

"It's tricky to categorize."

Detective Ramsay opens the back cover to look at the author's photo. Me, looking grumpy, contemplative, air-brushed.

"That title's quite a coincidence," he says.

"Yes?"

"The Sandman killings a few years ago. I was the lead investigator on that one."

"Really."

"Small world, isn't it?"

"I suppose, on some level, the title was inspired by those events."

"Inspired?"

"Not that what the murderer did was *inspirational*. I mean it only in the sense that it gave me the idea."

"What idea?"

"The *title*. That's all I was talking about."

His eyes move down and at first I wonder if there's a stain on my shirt. Then I realize he's looking at my hands. I resist the reflex to slip both of them in my pockets.

Ramsay brings his eyes up again. Repeatedly lifting and lowering my book as though judging its merits based on weight alone.

"Mind if I borrow this?"

"Keep it. There's plenty more in the basement."

"Oh? What else have you got down there?"

It's only the laugh he allows himself after a moment that indicates he's joking. In fact, everything he says in his half-submerged brogue could be taken as a dry joke. But now I'm not sure any of it is.

"I need to run through your day with Ms. Dunn," he says, putting my book down on a side table and producing a notebook from his jacket pocket.

"It wasn't a *day*. I was with her for twenty minutes at most."

"Your twenty minutes then. Let's start with those."

I tell him how Petra left a message with me the night before, asking to speak in person. The next morning I returned her call, and we arranged to meet at her house at five o'clock. On my way out of the subway she was there, wearing running attire and a Yankees cap. Reluctant to go to her house, she guided me into the ravine. She told me of her concerns about a man who seemed to be following her, someone she'd spotted outside her house at night. She was frightened, and wanted to know if I had noticed a shadow after me as well.

"And have you?" Detective Ramsay says.

There is a point in the telling of every story where the author becomes his own editor. Not *everything* is included in an accounting of events, no record the complete record. Even the adulterer who cannot live with his conscience excludes the smell of his mistress' perfume from his confession. Nations at war provide casualty numbers, but not a tally of missing arms versus legs. Deception, in the active sense of distorting the facts, may not be the cause of these absences. Most of the time it is a matter of providing the gist without inflicting undue pain. It's how one can be truthful and keep secrets at the same time.

This is how I later came to justify my telling Detective Ramsay, No, I haven't been followed, don't know what Petra was talking about in the ravine at all. Even as I take this path I'm aware it may be the wrong one. The police could be the only ones to keep me and Sam safe at this point. But there is something that makes me certain that such disclosure would only make me next. If I am being watched by the Sandman as closely as it feels I am, then I have every intention to play by his rules, not the law's.

Not to mention that I'm starting to get the feeling I may be a suspect in Petra's murder. Trust me on this: one's instinct, in such cases, is to withhold first, and figure out if this was a good idea later.

"So why'd she call you?"

"I suppose it was because of the writing circle we were in together. Years ago. She was trying to draw a connection between us, my book, the concerns she had about a stalker. It was rather vague."

"Vague," he says, pausing to reflect on the word. "Tell me about this circle."

So I do. Give him all the names, the little contact information I have. Again, I decide to leave a couple things out. My meeting with Angela, for instance.

"Just want to confirm the sequence of events with you," he says. "You met with Ms. Dunn around five o'clock. Is that right?"

"A couple minutes before five, yes."

"And you left her in the ravine twenty minutes later."

"Give or take."

"You walked home after this?"

"Yes."

"Did you talk to anyone? Stop anywhere?"

"I had a drink in Kensington Market."

"Where, exactly?"

"The Fukhouse. It's a punk bar."

"You don't look the part."

"It happened to be on my way."

"Would anyone recognize you from The Fukhouse?"

"The bartender might. Like you say, I don't look the part."

"When did you arrive home?"

"It was evening. Some time after nine, I guess."

"That's when you called over to the neighbour's to check on your son."

"Yes."

"Did you have any particular reason to be concerned for your son's safety?"

He was standing in my window.

"I'm a widower, Detective. Sam is the only family left to me. I'm never *not* concerned for his safety."

He blinks.

"That's a long walk," he says. "Even with a couple of drinks."

"I like to take my time."

"You might be interested to know that Ms. Dunn disappeared some time between your meeting with her and eight o'clock. Two and a half hours or so."

"Disappeared? I thought you said she was murdered."

"I said that's what we *believe*."

How could I have gotten this guy so wrong? The combination of Ramsay's leftover Scots accent and droll demeanour had me thinking that if they really suspected that I could have done whatever was done to Petra, they would have sent over one of their hard cases. But now I see that Ramsay *is* a hard case.

"Do you know of anyone who would have a motive to do this to your friend?" he asks absently. "Aside from her shadow?"

"I'm not her friend. *Wasn't.* I barely knew her."

"'Not friend'," he says, scribbling.

"As for motive, I have no idea. I mean, she mentioned her divorce, and how she was seeing her ex-husband's business partner. It seemed like a delicate situation."

"This is during your twenty minutes in the ravine?"

"It wasn't much more than a name."

"And what name would that be?"

"Roman. The boyfriend. Roman somebody. Petra was concerned that if her relationship with him came to her ex's attention, it would cause her some inconvenience."

"Roman Gaborek."

"That's him."

"Did your friend mention that Mr. Gaborek and Mr. Dunn are both leaders among the local organized crime community?"

"She alluded to it."

"Alluded. She *alluded* to it."

"That's right."

"It's a funny thing," he says, flipping his notebook closed. "Most of the time, people who hear about something like what you've just heard about ask how it was likely done. But you haven't asked me a thing."

"I don't have much of a stomach for violence."

"It's a good thing you didn't ask me then. Because Ms. Dunn, she met with *considerable* violence."

"I thought there was no body."

"But what the body *left behind*—well, it was indicative of certain *techniques*. Reminded me of four years ago. Remember?"

If one were to enter this room right now, one might mistake Detective Ramsay's expression as showing how much he enjoys moments like these. But I can see that it's not pleasure so much as rage. An anger he's managed to disguise, over the years, as something near its opposite.

"Well, that's it," he says. I rise and offer a hand to be shaken, and when he finally takes it, the grip is ruthless.

"Hope I was of some help."

"If you weren't, you might yet be."

Ramsay goes to the door to let himself out and I follow, suddenly desperate to hear the click of the bolt closing behind him.

"One last thing. The cap you say Ms. Dunn was wearing when she met you . . ."

"Yes?"

"What team was it again?"

"The Yankees. Why?"

"Nothing. They just never found a cap, Yankees or otherwise."

He opens the door and steps outside. Before he closes it, he shows me a smile. One he's saved right for the end.

The morning brings a funny thought: I'm about to be famous all over again. Whenever they come for me and I make the shackled walk from police cruiser to courtroom, cameras whirring, reporters begging for a quip from the Creep of the Day for the suppertime news.

Then the clock radio clicks on. And I have the same thought all over again.

It's the morning news telling the city that Petra Dunn, forty-five, was abducted yesterday in the Rosedale ravine. Evidence at the scene strongly supports foul play. Police are currently questioning a number of "persons of interest" in connection to the crime.

Person of interest, that's me. Yesterday morning I got out of bed an unemployed pseudo-novelist, and just twenty-four hours later I'm facing a new day as the prime suspect in a probable homicide. But it doesn't stop there. Because if Detective Ian Ramsay thinks I did in poor Petra Dunn, it follows that I did in Carol Ulrich, Ronald Pevencey and Jane Whirter four years ago too.

Angela may have been right. The Sandman's come back. And as far as best guesses go, it's me.

"Dad?"

Sam standing in my bedroom doorway.

"Just had a bad dream," I say.

"But you're *awake*."

He's right. I'm awake.

The first thing I do, once I've showered and shaved, is take Sam to stay with Stacey, Tamara's sister in St. Catharines. On the hour's drive there I do my best to explain why a policeman came to talk with me last night, and why it's best if the two of us are separated for a while. I tell him how sometimes people get caught up in things they have nothing to do with, but that they must nevertheless endure questions about.

"Process of elimination," Sam says.

"Kind of, yeah."

"But I thought it was 'innocent until proven guilty.'"

"That's only in courtrooms."

"Does this have to do with your book?"

"Indirectly, yes."

"I never liked your book."

Of *course* he's read it. Although forbidden to do so, how was he *not* going to read his father's one and only contribution to the bookshelf? I can't know how much of it he's able to understand—a gifted reader, but still only eight years old—yet it appears he's gathered the main point. The Sandman of *The Sandman* is real.

Once home, I leave a message on Angela's machine, asking her to get back to me as soon as possible.

Waiting for her return call, I consider how many in the circle have already been in contact with each other. After the night at Grossman's, I just assumed all of us went our separate ways. But there may have been relationships formed I had no inkling of at the time. Lovers, rivals, artists and their muses. The sort of passions that have been known to give rise to the most horrific actions.

To kill the time, I check back on the Comment page at www.patrick.rush.com. Once more, it mostly shows the same obsessives debating the finer points of *The Sandman*'s plotlines, unearthing inconsistencies, along with differing personal impressions of the author ("He signed my book and asked if I was a writer too. And I AM! It was like he READ MY MIND!!" vs "actually saw PR on queen street the other day, trying (but failing) to look like a 'normal guy,' walking with a <u>bag of groceries</u>(!?) pretentious twat!").

I'm about to log off when the cursor finds the day's most recent entry. Another bulletin from **therealsandman**:

One down.

Angela gets back to me. She has to work late tonight, but can meet me later on. For some reason I insist it be at her place (which she reluctantly agrees to). After she hangs up, I realize I need to see wherever she lives in order to make sure she's real.

I'm set to arrive at Angela's around eight, which gives me time to put in a call to the only number other than hers I have from the circle. Len.

"The police just left," he says, skipping over hello, as though only a day sits between now and our last conversation instead of years. "Did you hear what happened to Petra?"

"I heard. Was the man you spoke to named Ramsay?"

"I was too freaked to really listen. Kind of a funny guy."

"Yeah?"

"Like funny strange and funny ha-ha at the same time."

"That's him."

I would walk to Len's apartment in Parkdale but the heat wave has once again broken the temperature record it set the day before, so I head west along King in the Toyota with the windows down. I turn left toward the lake, into one of the blocks of stately family homes long since cut up into dilapidated rooming houses. Len's building looks even worse than the others. The paint peeling off the porch in long curls. The front windows obscured by pinned-up flags, tin foil and garbage bags in place of blinds.

Len has the attic flat. The side entrance is open as he

said it would be and I climb up the narrow stairs past the suffocating assaults of hash smoke and boiled soup bones and paint thinner seeping out from under the doors.

Rounding the corner to the last flight, I look up to see Len waiting at the top. The big doofus stooped in the door frame, spongy with sweat but otherwise looking relieved to see me.

"It's you," he says.

"Were you expecting somebody else?"

"The thought had crossed my mind."

Len's apartment is a single room. A small counter, hot plate and bar fridge in one corner, a bare mattress on the floor, and the only natural light coming from two windows the size of hardcover books, one facing the street and the other the yard. The severely sloped ceiling drops on either side from a beam that cuts the space in half, which allows Len to stand straight only when situated in the middle of the room. On the walls, movie posters bubbled with moisture. *The Exorcist*, *Suspiria*, *Night of the Living Dead*. The floor strewn with laundry that smells of a battle between deodorant and old socks.

"Have a seat," Len offers, scooping a pile of paperbacks off a folding chair. It leaves him to sit cross-legged on the floor. An over-heated kid ready for storytime.

"So, how have you been?"

"Okay. Not writing much. I haven't been able to think straight for a while now. It's hard to write spooky stuff when you're living spooky stuff."

Over Len's shoulder, stacked atop makeshift shelves made of milk crates, I notice my book. The cover tattered, the pages within fattened by greasy-fingered rereadings.

"I couldn't sleep for a week the first time I read it," Len says, following my gaze.

"Sorry."

"No need to be. The best parts weren't yours."

"No argument there."

Len glances at the door, as though to make sure it's locked. All at once the haggard, skittish look of him reveals he's been cooking away up here far longer than is healthy.

"When was the last time you went outside?"

"I don't like to go out much any more," he says. "It's like when you have a sense that you're being watched, but when you turn there's nothing there? I have that all the time now."

"Did you tell Ramsay about it?"

"No. It's a secret. A *secret agent* secret. You tell and you're dead."

"I know what you mean."

"He asked about you."

"What did he want to know?"

"If you had any relationship with Petra outside the circle. What I thought of you."

I keep my eyes on Len as he selects what to reveal. He doesn't seem the sort of man who can stand too much pressure, so I do my best to apply some in my stare.

"I told him you were my friend," he says finally.

"That's it?"

"I don't *know* anything else."

"Aside from the source for my book."

"Aside from that."

"And?"

"And I didn't tell him about it."

"Who else have you spoken to?"

"Petra called. Angela, too. She told me about Conrad's accident. Even Ivan came round just the day before yesterday. All of them scared shitless."

"Not William?"

"Are you kidding? The day that guy looks me up it's time to move."

All at once, the stifling heat in the room closes in on me. There isn't half enough air for two sets of lungs to live on, and Len is getting most of it anyway, panting like an overfed retriever.

"Angela told you about Conrad's accident?"

"I told you she did."

"But did she tell you that anyone *else* was in the car when he died?"

"*Was* there someone else?"

"No. No, there wasn't," I say, banging my head on the ceiling when I stand. "Sorry, but I'm late for another meeting."

"Who with?"

"Angela, actually."

"She must be pissed with you."

"Apparently she's decided to let it slide."

Len scratches the islands of beard along his jawline.

"I want to show you something," he says.

Len uncrosses his legs and rolls over the floor to the milk-crate shelves. His thick fingers plow through the piles of comics, digging down into the wreckage of toppled towers of books. By the time he finds what he's looking for his T-shirt is black with perspiration.

He scrambles over on hands and knees to where I'm standing and hands me a book. A literary journal I have heard of, *The Tarragon Review*. One of the dozens of obscure regional publications that print short stories and poems for readerships that number as high as the two figures.

"You in this?" I ask, expecting Len is trying to show off his first appearance in print.

"Check out the table of contents."

I read every title and author on the list. None of it rings a bell.

"Look again," Len urges. "The names."

The second time through I see it. A short story titled "The Subway Driver." Written by one Evelyn Sanderman.

"San-der-man. Sand-man. See?"

"Are you saying Evelyn wrote this?"

"At the back," Len says, excited now. "The Contributors' Notes."

The journal's last pages feature short biographies of the volume's writers, along with a black-and-white photo. At the entry for Evelyn Sanderman the following paragraph:

Evelyn is a traveller who is fascinated by other people's lives. "There is no better research for a

writer than to get close to a stranger," she tells us.
This is Evelyn's first published story.

Next to this, a photo of Angela.

"When was this published?"

"Last year."

"And why do you have it?"

"I subscribe to *everything*," he says. "I like to follow who's getting published and where. It feeds my jealousy, I guess. Some mornings it's the only thing that gets me out of bed."

Len is kneeling before me now, looking crazed with the heat, the rare visit of human contact. The sharing of a plot twist.

"Can I borrow this?"

"Go ahead. I kind of want it out of here anyway," Len says, eyes ablaze with the narcotic rush of fear.

"The Subway Driver" is good. The critic in me insists on getting this said upfront. A totally different voice from the one who told the story in Angela's journal. This time, the narrative tone is chillingly anesthetized, a man transported through a crowded urban environment, unnoticed and hazy as a phantom. But there are also moments of heartbreaking despair that cut through to the surface. Not Angela's voice at all, or any other strictly fictional creation. It's because the voice belongs to someone real. To Ivan.

As the title partly suggests, "The Subway Driver" is a day in the life of an unnamed man who speeds a train through the underground tunnels during the day, and scratches at chronically unfinished stories at night. What really takes me by surprise, though, the revelation that leaves me shaking in the front seat of the Toyota where I'm parked outside Len's rooming house, isn't this blatant borrowing from the biography Ivan presented to us during the Kensington Circle's meetings, but the private backstory, the tragic secret I assumed he had shared only with me.

At points in the main narrative, the Ivan-character reflects on the accidental (or not) fall of his niece down his sister's basement stairs. The same event he related to me standing at the urinals in the Zanzibar. Even some of the details, the very phrasings (as best as I recall them) make their way into Angela's text.

> *Her name was Pam . . . I watched her run off down the hall and start down the stairs and I thought* That's the last time you're ever going to see her alive *. . . One of the old kind, y'know? Like a comb except with metal teeth . . . That's how a life ends.* Two *lives. It just happens.*

She must have learned Ivan's secret on her own. He *told* her.

And she used it. Used him.

The address Angela gave me included a security code number for her condominium in one of the tall but otherwise nondescript towers of grey metal and glass that have weedishly cropped up around the baseball stadium.

I would never have known how to ring her otherwise, as her number isn't listed next to Angela Whitmore, but Pam Turgenov. The name of Ivan's dead niece.

Once she's buzzed me in I take the elevator up, each blinking floor number to the twenty-first ratcheting up the rage within me. Flashpoints bursting into flame.

She is a liar.

A threat to me.

To Sam.

And then:

It wasn't me. It wasn't my book. She has taken my old life away from me.

I've never felt this way before. This angry. Though anger seems to have little to do with what I'm feeling now. It's too soft, a mood among moods. This is *physical*: an electric charge crackling out from my chest. A clean division between a thinking self and an acting self.

Angela left her door open. I know because when I take a running kick at it, the handle crunches into the plaster of the interior wall.

The acting part of me lunges at her.

The thinking part takes note of the cheap furniture, the curtainless picture windows looking west over the lake, the rail lines, the city's sprawl to the horizon. The day's heat hanging over everything.

Angela might have said something before I slammed into her but it made no impression. No words escape her lips now, in any case. It's because I've taken her by the throat. My thumbs pressing down. Beneath her skin, something soft gives way.

Then I'm lifting her up and throwing her on to the sofa. Straddling her hips. Putting all my weight on to my locked arms so that they stop any sound coming from her.

Screaming into her with a voice not my own.

I don't know what you want. I don't know who you are. It doesn't matter. Because if I see whoever you've got tailing me anywhere near my house or my son again, I'll fucking kill you.

Her body spasms.

You getting this? I'll fucking kill you.

I keep my grip on her throat and feel Angela's body yield beneath me. I already *am* killing her. There is a curiosity in seeing how the end will show itself. A final seizure? A stillness?

It's you.

I'm letting her go. That is, I must have let her go, as she appears to be making an attempt to say something.

"I thought you were too . . . *simple*. But that's the kind of person who does this sort of thing, isn't it? The blank slate."

"It's not *me*."

"You didn't know what you were doing just now. You were a different person. Maybe that person is the one who killed Petra."

Angela struggles to stand. Moves away from me without taking her eyes off my hands.

"*I'm* the one being followed," I say.

"You nearly *strangled* me!"

"Because you're fucking with me. My son."

"Fuck you!"

The exhaustion hits us both at the same time. Our feet dance uncertainly under us, as though we are standing on a ship's deck in a storm.

"Just answer me this. If you're so innocent, why are you hiding behind someone else's name?"

"To stay away from him."

She tells me how she's seen him from time to time. Ever since the Kensington Circle stopped meeting. Someone who would appear across the street from the building where she worked, her different apartments over the years, watching through the window of a restaurant as she ate. Always in shadow. Faceless.

It was the Sandman who forced her into changing her name, her appearance and her job *before* she learned of Conrad White and Evelyn's accident. Afterward, it only let her disappear that much more easily.

"Did disappearing involve sending out stories under pseudonyms?"

"Pseudonyms?"

"Evelyn Sanderman. Pam Turgenov. Who else have you been?"

Angela crosses her arms. "'The Subway Driver.'"

"And very fine it is. Though not entirely yours."

"What you did, you did it to be recognized."

"That's not true."

"No?"

"I did it to have something that was mine."

"Even if it wasn't."

"Yes. Even if it wasn't."

"That's not what interests me."

"What does?"

"People," she says. "*People* are my interest."

It was Angela's belief that no matter how many times she changed her life—or sent her writing out under others' names—he will eventually find her. Most recently, on the same day she had lunch with me, she went to get into her car in an underground parking lot to find a message written on her windshield in lipstick. *Her* lipstick. Taken from where she left it in her bathroom.

"He's been *in* here?"

"And he wants me to know he has. That he can come back whenever he wants."

"What did it say? On your windshield?"

"*You are mine.*"

At first, she thought his surveillance was meant only to threaten her. There was, she supposed, a pleasure he took in knowing her life was shrinking into little more than the exercise of nerves, the fidgety survival instincts of vermin. Now, though, she thinks there is also a logical purpose to his reminders: the traces he leaves may one day work to implicate her. Eventually something of his will stick, and it will be taken as hers. Just as I have begun to think of myself as suspect instead of victim, so has she.

As if to confirm this very thought, I look past Angela's shoulder and notice something on the kitchen counter. Angela turns to look at it too.

"Where'd you get that?" I say.

"It was stuffed in my mailbox this morning."

"It's a Yankees cap."

"Another one of his messages, I guess. Though I can't

figure out what it means. Are you okay? You look like you're going to pass out."

I've got both my hands clenched to the back of a chair to hold myself up. The room, the city outside the window, all of it teeter-tottering.

"That cap," I say. "It's the same one Petra was wearing when she disappeared."

Angela looks at me. A wordless expression that proves her innocence more certainly than any denial she might make. Even the greatest actors' performances show signs of artifice at their edges—it's what makes drama dramatic. A little something extra to reach all the way to the cheap seats. But what Angela shows me is so confused, so without the possibility of consideration that it clears any residue of suspicion I held against her.

"It's going to be alright," I say, taking a step closer.

"Who is *doing* this?"

"I don't know."

"Why *us*?"

"I don't know."

Outside, the sky dulls as it begins its fading increments of dusk, and beneath it the city takes on an insistent specificity, the streets and rooftops and signage coming into greater focus. Both of us turn to take it in. And both of us thinking the same thing.

He's out there.

The grid patterns of skulking traffic, the creeping streetcars, the pedestrians who appear to be standing still.

He's one of them.

———

I wake in the night to the digital billboards along the lakeshore flashing blues and reds and yellows over the ceiling. Money lights.

Sitting up straight against the headboard, I watch Angela sleep, her body curled and still as a child's. I haven't been with another woman since Tamara died, and it's funny—perhaps the funniest of all the funny revelations of this day—that it is Angela whose hair I stroke back from her face as she sleeps.

I watch her for a time. Not as a lover watches his beloved in the night. I look down on her shape as a non-presence, a netherworld witness. A ghost.

But a ghost that needs to go to the bathroom. I fold back the sheet from my legs and slide to the bottom of the bed. Angela's bare feet hang over the side. Pale, blue-veined.

I'm about to lift myself from the mattress when something about these feet holds me still. Three missing toes. The littlest piggy and the two next to it nothing more than healed-over vacancies, an unnatural rounding of the foot that sends a shiver of revulsion down to where my own toes touch the floor.

Angela may go by any number of different names, but the absent digits of her foot tie her to an unmistakable identity. The little girl in her story. The one who lost the same toes to frostbite when she slept overnight in the barn when her foster father disappeared into the woods.

That girl, the one with an unspeakable secret.

This girl, sleeping next to me.

22

This may be hard to believe, to accept as something that a person in a real situation would do (as opposed to what I am unfortunately *not*: a character in a story), but the reason I don't ask Angela, having seen her diminished foot, if she is, in fact, the grown-up version of the little girl in her journal of horrors, is that I don't want her to think I am so unsophisticated a reader. To assume that missing toes prove that whatever happened to the Sandman's girl was autobiography and not fiction—a fiction that, like all fiction, is necessarily made of stitched-together bits of lived as well as invented experience—would reveal me as that most lowly drooler of the true-crime racks, the literal-minded rube who demands the promise of Based on a True Story! from his paperbacks and popcorn flicks: the *unimaginative*.

And why do I care if she held this impression? Pride, for one thing. I may be a charlatan author, but I'm still a *good reader*. Still on the endangered species list of those who know it is only foolish gossip to connect the dots between a writer's life and the lives she writes.

There is this, along with another reason I keep any questions of frostbitten piggies to myself as I step out of her bedroom to find Angela pouring me a cup of coffee: I'm lonely.

"Sleep all right?" she asks, sliding a World-Class Bitch mug over the counter toward me.

"Fine. Bad dreams, though."

"How bad?"

"The usual bad."

"Me too. It's why I'm up. That, and I have to be at work in less than an hour."

I'd forgotten she has a job. I'd forgotten *anyone* has a job. Another of the side effects of the writer's life. You start to think everybody can professionally justify shuffling around the house all day, waiting for the postman, pretending that staring out the window and wondering what to toss in the microwave for lunch is a form of meditation.

"About last night," I start. "I wanted to tell you how much –"

"I think you should talk to some of the others."

"The others?"

"From the circle."

Angela holds her coffee with both hands, warming them against the bracing chill of condo A/C.

"That's funny. I was going to say something about *us*. Something nice."

"I'm not too good at the morning-after thing, I guess."

"So you've had others. Other mornings."

"Yes, Patrick. I've had other mornings."

I take a suave gulp of scalding coffee. Once the burning in my throat has dulled to an excruciating throb, I ask why she wants me to speak to the others.

"To find out what they know. If they've been . . . involved the same way we have."

I nod at this, and keep nodding. It's the word she's just used. *Involved.* Said in the way Conrad White said it when I asked what he thought of Angela's story. *You want to know if someone else has been involved in the way you have been involved.*

"How did you come to leave your purse in Conrad's car?"

"I told you. We were seeing each other a little at the time."

"Seeing each other? Or *seeing* each other?"

"He was interested in who I was."

And who are *you?* I nearly ask, but stop it in time with another tonsil-scarring sip of coffee.

"Have you read his work?"

"*Jarvis and Wellesley*? Sure," she says. "Why?"

"I think he saw in you what the character in his book was looking for."

"His dead daughter."

"The perfect girl."

"He told you that?"

"So I'm right."

"You're not wrong."

Angela tells me that Conrad would drive her home sometimes after their get-togethers. At first, their topics were the usual literary matters such as favourite books

(*The Trial* for Conrad, *The Magus* for Angela), work habits, writer's block and how it might be overcome. Soon, though, Conrad would focus their discussion on where Angela's story came from. Her childhood, her friends growing up, where her parents were now. Something in the pointedness of his queries put Angela on the defensive, so that her replies became more intentionally vague the more he persevered. It made him angry.

"Like he wasn't just curious, but desperate," Angela says, slipping her cellphone and keys into her purse.

"Was he in love with you?"

"He might have been, in a way. More like a freaky fan than a lover, you know? But that wasn't what made him ask all those questions."

She stops. Not liking where this is taking her.

"I think he was scared," she says.

"Scared of what?"

"The same thing we're scared of."

"And he –"

"He thought it had to do with my story."

I'm following Angela to the door, slipping on watch and socks and shoes as I go.

"Did he have any contact with the Sandman— someone he *thought* was the Sandman? There were those killings back then. Maybe he was making connections in ways none of us had thought of."

"Maybe," Angela says. "Or maybe he was a messed-up shut-in who was driving himself crazy making something out of nothing."

In the elevator down, I ask who from the circle she thinks we should try to look up first.

"We?"

"I thought you said it might be useful to know what the others know."

"But I can't do the asking."

"Why not?"

"Who did he deliver the Yankees cap to?"

The elevator doors open. Outside, the heat bends the air into shimmering vapours.

"Can I call you?" I ask.

"Not for a while."

"Why not?"

"*You are mine.* Remember?" she says, opening the doors to the burning world. "I don't think he'd like it if he thought I was yours."

You wouldn't expect, being caught in a *web of intrigue* (who knew I would ever use this phrase so personally, irreplaceably?) that, in between the recorded scenes of revelation and confrontation, one could still have so much spare time. Unemployment can open yawning chasms in the middle of the most mentally preoccupied days, believe me. There are still the self-maintaining banalities to attend to: the belated meals, the bathroom dashes, the long showers. Still the mail, the erupting laundry hamper, the dental appointment. One can be a murder suspect, a serial killer's prey, and still have time to waste on the last sobbing half-hour of *Dr. Phil*.

There are a pair of activities over these melting July days, however, that are returned to with too great a frequency to note each time they occur. The first is my journal. I've graduated from stolen jottings at bedtime to carrying it around wherever I go, recollecting snatches of conversation, the wheres and whens of things. It is, in the rereading, an increasingly unstructured document. What begins as tidy pages of coherent points soon breaks down into messages to Sam, scribbled drawings of Petra, Detective Ramsay (though I don't attempt Angela, can't imagine where the first line would start), even a letter to the Sandman, asking that if he has to take me with him into the Kingdom of Not What It Seems that he leave my son behind. It occurs to me that later, when it's all over, this journal of mine may be the sort of thing that supports the contention that poor old Patrick had lost his way well before the shadow got him. After all, what is sanity other than guarding the border between the fiction and non-fiction sections?

My other habit is to give Sam a ring and see how he's doing. Most of the time he's out in the yard playing with Stacey's kids (they have a pool, an unthinkable suburban luxury for us city mice), or camping overnight (instead of the artsy-craftsy day school I've been sending him to), or one of any other number of healthy summer distractions I have long meant to get around to doing with him, but mostly never have, slipping him books or movie passes instead. In other words, even when I call I don't get to talk to him. But it gives me a chance to thank

Stacey yet again for what she's doing, to assure her that I'll collect Sam once I've "cleared the deck of a few things," to ask her to tell him that I called.

There you have it: even a man caught in a web of intrigue still fights against the inevitable with whatever's left to him. To hang on to the shape life used to take before he became trapped, and now can do little but wait for the spider to feel his struggle and decide enough, that's *enough* for this fly. It's time.

Since we parted in her condo's lobby, and despite her asking me not to, I have put in a handful of calls to Angela, and received some cursory excuses in return ("Work is really crazy this week," "I don't know, I'm just so tired."). I tell her I need to see her. That I miss her.

"I'm not sure I can do that," she says.

"We can just talk."

"What would we talk about?"

"It wouldn't have to be . . . bad things."

"But that's all there is."

She goes on to tell me how she's gotten a couple more signs from "him." When I ask what these indications are, she goes silent. Her breath clicking in her throat.

"Maybe, if we stay together, we could protect each other," I suggest.

"You don't believe that."

"I said *maybe*."

"I think he wants us apart. For each of us to have our own course."

"And if we don't play along –"

"– he'll separate us. Or worse. We've got to play this the way he wants."

And look how well that's turning out, I want to say. Along with another remark that comes to me too late: *What do we think he wants anyway?* If it is Patrick Rush feeling the profoundest regret for having used his name for the title of a ripped-off novel, then mission accomplished. *Mea culpa.* And if it's just random lives he wants to get back to taking, then I'm certainly not the one standing in his way.

Random lives.

This is the puzzle that fills the next hour. Buried away down here in the Crypt, mapping out the few connections I can make in my journal.

Carol Ulrich.

Ronald Pevencey.

Jane Whirter.

And now Petra Dunn.

Not a thing common between them. But in *his* mind, there must have been. For the Sandman, there was nothing random about them at all. All that's required is to think like a psychopath.

Well, I think. *I'm a retired writer. How hard could it be?*

Even in the four years since the Kensington Circle, the available venues for writers' groups have multiplied. Libraries, bookshops, coffee houses—but also rehab clinics, synagogues, yoga ashrams, Alcoholics Anonymous. There is no limit to the Self-Writing Seminars, (Her)story

Workshops, Focus Group Your Novel! round tables one might sign up for. And I sign up for them all. Or as many as I can. Not to learn, to exchange, to discover myself. But to retrace the steps that have delivered me here. The same journey all murderers of passion are obliged to make: a return to the scene of the crime.

With Sam safe at Stacey's, I am free to skip from one circle to another over the sweltering remainder of the week. As I expresswayed and subwayed to the various gatherings uptown, crosstown, and out-of-town, I asked the same question. And a couple of times I got answers.

"Do these names mean anything to you?" I would inquire of my fellow circlers, and offer to them the first names (and surnames if I knew them) of each member of the Kensington Circle. By the end of the week I had confirmed what I'd suspected.

In a basement in Little Italy, I learned that William had been a participant for a time several years ago, and was going to be asked to leave (the boyhood tales of an animal-skinning sociopath too much to take) before he abruptly stopped showing up all on his own. I heard much the same thing in a Coffee Time in Scarborough, a public library in Lawrence Park, a gay bar on Jarvis Street: big scary man with too-real horror story joins writers' club, then disappears.

And that's not all.

There were other names I mentioned in the circles. Names of those I had never met, but were of increasing significance to my situation, nevertheless. Carol Ulrich. Ronald Pevencey. (I left out Jane Whirter, as she had lived in Vancouver for over twenty years prior to her death.) Names that some of the people I asked had heard of before. But not only because Ulrich and Pevencey were among the Sandman's first round of victims. They were remembered because, at one time or another, both of them were participants in some of the city's writing circles.

This is what I have, and what, if newspaper reports are to be believed, the police don't: a connection between the Sandman's "random" victims. They were *writers*. And somehow it got them killed.

23

As I walk home through the city, I take out my cell and pretend to speak to someone at the other end. It's not the first time I've done this. You can be the only pedestrian *not* on the phone for so long before you start to feel yourself disappear. You need to *text*, to *touch base*, to *screen incoming*. We speed-dial, therefore we are.

This time, when I check my messages at home, I'm surprised to hear a voice I recognize. Ivan.

"I've had an . . . *encounter*."

A pause so long it's like he's forgotten to hang up. Then he remembers.

Click.

An encounter.

I call the number he gave me as I pass a group of gigglers standing outside the sex-shop window, tapping at the glass ("What *is* that, Brenda?" "I dunno. Must be something you put where the sun don't shine.").

Ivan picks up on the first ring.

"Patrick?"

"You left a message –"

"Museum station. Tomorrow. Southbound platform. Ten a.m."

Click.

Without looking for it, I'm now like everyone else, the millions streaming past on sidewalk and street. I've got plans for the weekend.

Moments after arriving home there's a knock at the door.

"Finished your book. Very interesting," Detective Ramsay says, once again walking past me into the living room as though the place is only nominally mine. Then, even more falsely: "Can't wait to read whatever you're doing next."

"I'm retired."

"Really?"

"Are you actually here to discuss my book?"

"It's an investigation. We have to have *something* to put in the files."

There's a point in every conversation structured around the exchange of accusation and rebuttal—meetings with tax auditors, neighbours disgruntled over the leaves your tree sheds in their yard—where the nasty turn can be either taken or avoided. This is the point Ramsay and I have reached. And I have decided I don't like the man.

"You know something?" I say. "I may have another book in me yet. In fact, you're inspiring a character for me right now."

"Oh? What's this character like?"

"Flawed, naturally. An intrusive investigator who's

smart but not as smart as he thinks. The secret about him is that he wants to be a writer. Detective stories—the only thing he reads. He likes to think if he wasn't so busy solving real crimes, he'd be making them up."

To say Ramsay darkens at this would be understatement. His limbs stiffening into the vocabulary of the thug, the backstreet pub brawler. Now I can see the clear answer to my earlier question about him. Definitely more Glasgow than Edinburgh.

"A comic figure," he says.

"I think he is."

"You'd be wrong then."

"You mean he's not funny?"

"I mean you'd be wrong to laugh at him."

He gives me a look that's rather hard to describe. One better grasped in its effects, chief of which is to make me want to make a run for the door.

"What do you say to wish a writer luck?" he says, moving past me. "Break a leg?"

"Usually it's just 'Don't let the bastards get you down.'"

"That applies to my line of work too."

There's the clunk of the door pulled shut. The house waits a full minute before resuming its sighs and ticks.

Later, when I ask myself why I didn't tell Ramsay what I learned about the Sandman's first round of victims all being circle members—not to mention William's appearance at some of the very same meetings—I decide that it wasn't because I don't like the guy, or even that it might put me at greater risk. I didn't tell him because a thought occurred to me at the same moment Ramsay offered a glimpse of his darker self.

It might be him.

This suspicion was born out of nothing more than a flare of intuition, but now that he's gone I'm able to back it up with a reasonable tallying of bits and pieces. The first of these is that he was the lead investigator on the previous Sandman killings. This would have allowed him access not only to the crime scenes and the potential manipulation of evidence, but to his fellow officers, the media. A nice way to clean up any mistakes he may have made (though these would undoubtedly have been few). Then there's his physical aspect: as tall as the Sandman, give or take. And no doubt strong enough to carry out the business of human butchering.

Then again, this may only be my own continued inching toward madness. Suspecting the *detective*?

You don't need to be hunted by a Sandman to see nothing but crime and criminals. All the things you've done, the decisions you made, the possibilities laid out before you—it used to be *your story*. Then the thieves show up to take it. And you're left asking the question that is so compulsive, so bestsellingly popular because it belongs to a universal language. The first utterance of fear. Of failure.

Whodunit?

This isn't the end of my Friday social calls. In fact, I end up going out for drinks with a friend—though this sounds a good deal more normal than it is. Because it's drinks with Len. And because he has asked me to come out in order to share a "totally twisted idea" about Angela.

We decide on The Paddock, an ancient vault south of Queen. When the bartender comes by I order a bourbon sour, and am surprised to hear Len ask for the same.

"I didn't know you started drinking."

"I haven't."

"You could've ordered a juice or something."

"I don't want to call attention to myself," he says, glancing over his shoulder. "And it's important that I talk to you in the kind of place I wouldn't normally go."

"Why?"

"So *she* won't see us."

Once the drinks arrive, he tells me how Angela came to his apartment some days ago. She looked around his attic room, inspecting the bookshelves. *The Sandman* caught her attention, though she made no mention of it. Len couldn't help noticing she was wearing a "nice—you know, *sexy* nice—perfume." And a blouse he felt was missing a couple of buttons.

"When was this exactly?"

"Wednesday. Why?"

"No reason."

Wednesday. Two days after Angela told me we shouldn't see each other again. And then she's calling on *Len*—prematurely balding, cardboard-smelling, man-boy Len. Only a moment's pondering of this and my glass is empty. I knock back Len's too and raise my hand to signal another round.

Len tells me that, at first, she just talked to him like she might have during the circle, if she ever *had* spoken to him during the circle. Writer stuff. Queries about what he's working on, where he'd sent material out to, recent books they'd read.

"Did you ask her about being published under a false name?"

"There wasn't time."

"I thought you were just sitting around talking?"

"We were. But then it got *weird*."

It got weird when she confessed to him, leaning forward to put her hand on his knee, that if she were ever to write a story about him, she knew what title she'd use.

"'The Virgin,'" Len says. "So I say 'Why would you call it that?' And she says 'Because you've never been with a girl, have you, Len?' Then she kissed me."

"Kissed you? Where?"

"On the *lips*."

"Then what?"

"I don't know. I *resisted*, I guess. Kind of pushed her away."

"Why?"

"Because she wasn't really kissing me. It was more like she was making fun of me."

"How did you know?"

"That's how it *felt*."

I press Len's glass into his hand, urge him to take a sip. And he does. A big one. Followed by a bigger one.

"Welcome to the wonderful world of alcohol therapy," I say.

"It's warm."

"It only gets warmer."

He wipes his eyes with the sleeve of his shirt. I would put a hand on his shoulder to steady him, but the truth is, even now, I don't want to touch him. I offer him time instead. And when he's ready, he says that once Angela was done laughing at him, she said he didn't have to kiss her back. He didn't have to do anything because it was too late. She already knew everything she needed to know.

"About what?"

"About *me*."

"What did she want to know about you?"

"Everything she needed to write her version of me."

"She was writing a story based on you? 'The Virgin'?"

"I think she's writing stories on all of us," Len says, then drifts his face closer. "But I'm next."

"Her subject."

"No. The next to die."

Len is not well. This fact is coming into sharp focus now. He's not just another comic-book-collecting oddball, not one of the half-invisibles, the sort of mouth breather you try to ignore peering over your shoulder at a bank machine. He's *ill*. Yet, now that we're here, in a place where more cocktails are available if things get hairy, I figure there's little harm in nudging him further.

"Then why not me? Why am I not next?"

"You were the only one without a story," Len answers, finishing his drink and unintentionally slamming the glass down on the bar.

"She said that to you?"

"It was kind of obvious."

Len puts his hand on my wrist, pressing it against the bar's varnished surface, and I let him. I also let him come in close once more to whisper into my cheek.

"She isn't what she appears to be," he says.

I try to pull my arm away, but he's got a stronger hold than I thought he was capable of.

"I'm not just saying she's psychotic," Len goes on, suddenly louder. Behind me, there's the chair squeaks and interrupted conversations of other drinkers stopping to hear the agitated guy in the corner. "I'm saying she's not *human*."

"For God's sake, Len."

"In medieval legend, there is a name for a female being that incrementally consumes other beings until their eventual exhaustion or death."

"A succubus."

"Exactly."

"Oh Christ."

"A witch who appears in the form of a temptress."

"Calm down. Here. Take another sip –"

"Usually the succubus' purpose is to steal the semen of sleeping men—their life force. But in this case, it's different. She steals stories."

"Are you saying we need to put a stake through her heart? Shoot her with a silver bullet?"

"I'm serious. And the sooner you get serious about it too, the longer you might live."

Len *is* serious. The whole bar can see it. And it watches him stand, the boldness that had possessed him for these past moments instantly slipping away.

"There are some desires so foul they are never satisfied," he says, and appears to search his mind for something more. But if there was something, it's gone now. *I'm done*, his drooped shoulders and hanging head say as he walks away. *That's all I can manage.*

My Friday winding down to its bourbon-softened end. But even with the assurance that Len's theories are as twisted as initially advertised, the day closes with an unsettling idea. For as the door closes behind him, I can't help thinking I will never see Len again.

24

I start out to my meeting with Ivan early enough, but the sun, already high and merciless by nine, ends up making me late. Twice I have to stop and sit in the shade to get a handle on the dizziness that comes with pushing myself through air not made for walking, or for anything really, other than euthanizing the old and promoting sales of asthma inhalers for the young. By the time I shuffle by the old facade of the Royal Ontario Museum I don't really care if Ivan awaits me underground or not. What I need is to get out of the sun and wait for October to come.

But it's not much better here. Down the stairs the air is almost as warm, the trains growling and screeching below. So what am I doing here, anyway? Why do I want to know what Ivan means by "an encounter?" The smart thing would be to turn back. And not just from my meeting with Ivan, but from everyone. Someone else can tease out the mystery of the Sandman and be rewarded as Carol Ulrich, Petra and the others were rewarded.

But I don't do the smart thing. And it's here, carried down on the sliding escalator stairs, that I figure why: I want to save the day. Dishonoured author, pink-slipped critic, rejected lover—yes to all. Yet there may still be an opportunity for forgiveness, a full pardon that would see me returned from observing the world to the world itself. This is how deep the faulty hopes of fiction have been engrained in me.

It's in the next moment that I notice the man coming up the escalator opposite me.

Both hands gripping the rubber handrails, the hood of his sweatshirt pulled down so that his face is obscured. He would be tall if he were standing straight. But he's not.

He slides past. And I continue down.

It's not the look of him that strikes me, but the smell he leaves in the air once he's passed. A brief taste of compost. The first whiff that meets you upon opening the door of an unplugged fridge.

I have been close enough to that skin to catch its odour before. I have tried to *describe* it before too.

Wood smoke. Sweat. Boiled meat.

William.

He's already disappearing around the corner at the top of the escalator when I turn. The door to the outside squeaking open and vacuuming shut.

I make a hopeless run against the descending steps— one down for every two up—and surrender halfway when a mother with a stroller comes to stand at the top, scowling at me. *Another lunatic*, her organic-only face says. *When is somebody going to clean this town up?*

It's at the ticket kiosk, waiting for the attendant to hand over my change, that I notice the first sign that something worse than a William appearance may be going on down here. The sound of incoherent exclamations—*Don't touch it! Somebody . . . somebody!*—coming from the platform at the bottom of the stairs. Children bursting into hysterical, echoing cries. A woman's scream.

I push my way through the turnstile at the same time the attendant picks up his phone and starts to wave me back. Ignoring him, I carry on walking backwards to see the woman with the stroller being told she can't enter, and her demanding to know why. The attendant tells her. Whatever it is, it turns her around, her heels tapping out a distress signal on the marble floor.

On the way down to the platform the voices I'd heard earlier have grown in volume. More adult shouts have joined the wailing infants, and there's one or two official order-givers now too—*Stand back! Straight line here, people!*—along with the increasingly panicked *Ohmygod*s of mothers who have brought their children to visit the museum, many of them, by the sounds of it, still disembarking from the train. Shoes sliding against shoes. The grunt and gasp of those jostling for position in shrinking space. Human cattle.

I reach the platform and join them. The only one coming down as everyone else takes their first frenzied steps toward the exits.

Then I see why.

The southbound train has stopped two-thirds of the way into the station. Its doors open, the cars now wholly emptied. Men in fluorescent orange vests push through the crowd to open the door to the control cabin at the front. A moment later the driver emerges, hands trembling at the sides of his face, his lips moving but nothing coming out.

An accident. One that's just happened. Given the way some of the kids break away from their mothers to look over the side of the platform and instantly turn back, it's obvious what sort. A jumper. And that's not all I correctly guess before I push sideways to look over the side for myself. I know who jumped.

One of the most common ways of reckoning individual experience is through the number of times a thing has been seen or done: how many people one has slept with, foreign countries visited, diseases suffered and survived. Along with the dead. How many have you viewed outside of open caskets and TV news? Before today, my count was childishly low: just two. Tamara, of course. And my grandmother, discovered on the floor of her retirement home kitchenette, looking up at me with the same expression of annoyance she'd worn in life.

But I've made up for that now. I peer over the platform's edge and that's it. I'm all caught up on the death front.

What's unforgettable about seeing Ivan's body on the tracks isn't that it's someone I know, nor that parts of him are still webbed over the front of the train, nor that his face, despite the rest of him, is remarkably untouched. It's that he's not dead yet. His jaw's hinging open and half-shut.

Ivan is saying something I can understand. Not that I can hear him. I can tell because he knows it is me standing above him. And that his gulping mouth wants me to know he was pushed.

He stops moving before a uniformed police officer pulls me away from the edge. At first I think I'm being arrested. An exchange takes place in my head so clearly I wait for it to begin with the officer's first words:

– Do you know this man?

– Yes.

– What is your relationship to him?

– We both wanted to be writers. And we were both being hunted.

– Hunted? *Steve! Get over here!* Hunted by who?

– He has a few names, actually. My personal favourite is The Terrible Man Who Does Terrible Things.

But the policeman says nothing but *Please step away, sir.* So I do. Make a tiptoed dash for the stairs.

Joining the other passengers on the ascending escalator, the only ones coming down are more police and a pair of paramedics whose relaxed chatter suggests they've already been told this call is a done deal.

At the exit turnstiles, a pair of plainclothes detectives are asking if anyone saw what happened, and one or two from the shaken crowd stop to give a statement. I keep walking. Up the last staircase to the street, where the blazing heat is almost welcome, an awakening discomfort.

I cut on to the university campus, into the shade of the trees along Philosopher's Walk. Consciously refusing to think of anything but getting home. But before I get there, it will require all I have to simply keep moving.

And I *do* keep moving: from the bourbon to the vodka tonics to the red wine that's meant to rouse an appetite for dinner, but in the end turns out to be dinner itself. A full afternoon of channel surfing and heavy drinking that only partly succeeds in holding the flashes of Ivan's final seconds at bay.

Despite my best efforts, some stark implications of the day's horrors batter through: if Ivan was pushed, and it was William who'd passed me going up the subway escalator, who else could have done the pushing other than him? Even if I'm wrong, and Ivan had jumped, it seems beyond coincidence that William had appeared at the scene at the same time. Then again, *I* had been there. Had Ivan called William to the same meeting he'd called me to? It's possible. Yet the surest bet remains that Ivan had been followed to the Museum station by whoever he wanted to tell me about, but my lateness had allowed his stalker to reach him first. If it was the Sandman, he'd likely noticed me on the escalator. Which means he knows I'm getting closer to him. To who he is.

The evening takes its first truly unfortunate turn, however, when I embark on a tasting tour of the single malts saved for a special occasion. Well, *today* has been special, hasn't it? Seeing Ivan's body on the rails every time I close my eyes, every time I blink. Imagining how it will feel when it's my turn.

What I need is some company. Which leads to my second poor decision: calling Angela. When I get her machine, I call again. A couple hours with the un-pronounceable bottles of Scotch laid out over my desk, my free hand speed-dialling Angela and, each time she fails to pick up, me offering new apologies for whatever I'd done, for whatever I am.

After the rain starts to fingertap the basement window, I decide to walk over to her place. Along Front Street and past the convention centre where a twisting line of several hundred kids sit huddled on the sidewalk, camping out overnight in order to be first in line for the morning's *Canadian MegaStar!* auditions. The rain has left them shivering and hairless as chihuahua pups. I shout encouragements as I pass ("Return to your homes! Abandon hope all ye who enter here!") and they moan back at me like injured soldiers, casualties left on the fame battlefield.

Down past Union station, I'm sheltered from the rain as I stumble through the tunnel that runs under the tracks. By the time I make it to the far end, however, the precipitation has turned into something stronger, as though Lake Ontario had been tipped up at the opposite end to drop its contents over the city. It leaves me blind, but I keep going, possibly on the sidewalk, possibly down the middle of the street. All I know is when the downpour finally pauses long enough for me to open my eyes, the first thing I see is the shadow of the Gardiner Expressway overpass ahead. And beneath it, the figure of a man taking shelter from the rain. Staring at me.

At first, when I start my run toward him, he doesn't move. Just watches me come as though curious to see what I have in mind. Or perhaps he *wants* me to come. There is something in his posture—slouching, arms crossed—I hadn't noticed in his previous appearances. His presence, conveying only black threat before, has softened.

At the same time I come into shouting distance, he starts running south toward the lake. His strides longer and surer than mine, but showing a sluggish fatigue that keeps him within view.

"It was you!"

This is me. Screaming. A drunken madman among the other drunken madmen who live under the express-way and watch me pass.

"It was *you!*"

The figure slows. A wheeling of arms that might turn him around to attack, to speak. But he decides against it. Starts away again with fresh speed, his boots smacking against the slick pavement at a pace I couldn't dream of matching.

As I bring myself to a stop, coughing the evidence of a sedentary life on to my shoes, I watch him slip around the corner of a condo tower across from the harbour. Or behind a row of parked cars in the lot across from it. Or perhaps into the churning water itself.

In any case, there's only me here now. Me and the rain.

Once I'm able to breathe and stand up straight at the same time, I carry on to Angela's building only a couple blocks away. I keep my thumb on her condo number until the super comes out and asks me to leave. When I refuse, he executes a nifty bouncer move. The classic, in my experience: grabs the back of my shirt with one fist and the belt of my pants with the other and, kicking the door open, chucks me out on to the patch of manicured lawn like an overstuffed bag of garbage.

It's still raining. I can tell from the way it washes the blood off my hands when I check to see if I've split my lip.

There is no more *doing* tonight. Now is the time to think. To determine the *underlying meaning* of things.

The trouble is, for the second time today, the implications of what I've witnessed seem to slip away, leaving me to walk home teasing out the possibilities aloud. Even the first question gives me problems: was it William who'd run from me? Did I attribute the odour of the man on the subway escalator and posture of the figure under the expressway to him because I actually recalled these aspects, or have I been thinking it's been William all along, and thus any presence I encountered would be seen as him?

Next, an even more dizzying consideration: if it *was* William I saw tonight, was he the same person standing in my living-room window, the murderer of unknown writers, the ghost villain from Angela's journal? Perhaps there is a different monster attached to each of these crimes. Maybe the Sandman is merely one of the names shared by all the agents of the uncanny. The Sandman, the bogeyman, the succubus, the devil.

I tell myself to limit my thoughts to what is known. But what *is* known? Ivan is dead. Petra is missing. Conrad White—and Evelyn, if Angela is to be believed—dead too.

And what connects us is the circle. Or perhaps something more fundamental than that. A shared playing field that, even here in a city of millions, is limited to only a few, the last of the storybook believers. The ones who have not only seen the Sandman standing at the edge of their lives, but invited him in.

The morning is as bad as you'd guess. Complicated not just by a hangover serious enough to share eight of the nine primary symptoms of toxic shock, nor by the afternoon trip to the emergency room to get an intern to pinch and stick and *Oh, damn, I'm sorry* his way to stitching my lip closed, but by the prevailing sense that if what has come before has been worrying, everything from here on in is going to show how justified that worry actually was. I might be paranoid. But there's nothing that says paranoids can't be right sometimes.

On the way back from the hospital, I stop by Angela's building again. Still no answer. An idea strikes me all at once. Whether it was William or someone else, whoever I saw last night had come from calling on Angela too.

I try her work number, and the receptionist informs me she hasn't been in all this week. Len's not answering his phone. These are all the leads I have. Along with the faith that, if Angela were able to, she would have checked in with me by now, if only to tell me to stop bothering her with my sad-sack messages.

She is hiding. She is with him now. She is dead.

No matter which is true, it leaves me to find her on my own.

Later that afternoon I drive out of the city checking the rear view to see if I'm being followed. But speeding west along the QEW in a suicidal crush, every car fighting and failing to gain an inch on the competition—there is no way *not* to be followed. Still, there is one vehicle that seems to stick to me more doggedly than the others. A black Lincoln Continental that won't let me steal away whenever a gap opens in the slower lane. Not that this proves anything other than he has the same ideas about getting ahead that I have. And though the slanting light of dusk won't let me get a look at the driver's face, the same could be said for almost every other car jostling for position behind me.

But the Continental is still there forty-five minutes later when the first exit for St. Catharines comes up. I wait until the last moment before veering off on to the ramp. At first, it seems the black sedan tries to follow, lurching from the passing to the middle lane. But as the ramp curves into the town's residential streets, I catch sight of the Continental already shrinking down the highway. If I was being followed, the most the driver will know is where I've got off, but not where I'm going.

And where I'm going is to see Sam.

He looks good. Tanned, knee scrapes from rough-housing. Somehow he's aged a year in the past week.

"Am I going back with you?" he asks when we're on our own in the living room, a Disney movie paused on the jumbo screen.

"Afraid not."

"Then when?"

"Another week. Maybe two."

"A *week?*"

"I thought you were having fun here."

"It's okay. It's just—I miss you."

"Any money says I miss you more."

"Then why can't I come home?"

"Because there's something going on that needs to be settled first. And I want you to be safe."

"Are *you* safe?"

"You have to trust me. Can you do that for the next little while?"

Sam nods. Just look at him: he *does* trust me. And though this shouldn't surprise me—I'm his *father*—the weight of it does. It's a gift when another gives you their trust like this. A gift that can be taken back at any time, and easily too. This is what I read as clearly as the banana bruise freckles across my son's cheeks: once it's gone you never get it back. You might think you can. But you can't.

Later that evening when I'm tucking Sam into his bed, I ask if he would like me to read to him from any of the books he'd brought with him. He shakes his head.

"You want me to get you some new stuff? Next time, we can go to the bookstore and go crazy."

"No."

"What's the problem? You too old to be read to?"

"I don't read *any* books any more."

There are a thousand declarations a child can make to a parent more painful than this. But there is a seriousness, even a cruelty in what has just been uttered here in the dark of a spare room that smells of another kid's smells.

"Why's that?"

"I don't like them."

"You don't like stories?"

"They're what you've left me here for. Right?"

I deny this. Tell him fiction can inform and influence and provoke, but can't actually hurt anyone. But what we both know, even as I kiss him goodnight and leave the door open an inch, is that he's right. It's the unreal that has stepped off the page to cloud our lives. And until it can be made to go back where it belongs Sam must stay here, awake in the nightlight's glow, preparing to keep his sleep free of all dreams but the one where his father returns to take him home.

After nightfall, I drive back to Toronto. Down here, where the highway hugs the southern shore of the lake, you can look through the gaps between the old motels and fenced-in orchards and catch glimpses of the city's skyline across the water. In the past, I would see it as glamorous, a sexual invitation in the embracing pillars of light. It was the suggestion of possibility, of danger that I liked, and took pride in being associated with, if only by shared address.

Tonight, the sight of the distant towers has a different effect. They are an alien army, moon-glinting beasts rising from a dark sea. Their lights powered by desire alone. Unrequited, insatiable. A terrible wanting that feeds on anything that will submit to being possessed.

I drive on through the winemaking villages, smaller bedroom towns, the conjoined suburbs along the north shore before the final turn into the light. This last framing of the city before you are consumed within it: there was a time I thought it was beautiful, saw in it the beautiful promise of success. And I still do. Though what I know now is that every promise can also be a lie, depending on how it's kept.

25

Tim Earheart rings me again for drinks.

"God, I'm sorry," I tell him, remembering the unanswered emails and phone messages he'd left with me. "Things have been a little messed up the past while. Maybe tomorrow –"

"This isn't exactly a *social* call, Patrick."

"What is it then? Business?"

"Yeah. It's *business*."

We meet at one of the bank tower bars Tim has been favouring since he'd been given a raise following his appointment to Special Investigative Reporter ("What were you before?" "I don't know. But definitely not *special*"), not to mention the income that's been freed up since his second wife "got some other schmuck to pay for all the crap to which she'd become accustomed." This place is the New Tim Earheart, he tells me. He likes all the leather, the halogen pot lights, the sweep of upward mobility evidenced in the twenty-dollar martinis. And then there's the pickup opportunities.

"Just *being* here signals you as successful," Tim tells

me, seductively rolling a bill and dropping it in the coat check girl's jar.

"Successful at what?"

"That's the beauty of it. It doesn't *matter*. The details can be worked out later."

As the first round is consumed, Tim tells me a couple tales of women from these premises with whom he *has* worked it out later. It's vintage Earheart, and it makes me miss him. Companionship. Where had that disappeared to? Nestled in the same basket with a living wife, a job—all of it pushed down the stream and round the bend.

As if to bring this illusion of two friends having a worry-free cocktail to an end, Tim clears his throat at the arrival of the second set of martinis, pulls a piece of paper out of his jacket pocket and slides it over the bar toward me.

"What's this?"

"Read it."

"You wrote this?"

"Just *read* it."

It's a sin, the church says, to do the things that I do
But how can I stop until I've done them to you?
Later, in hell, is where my bones will be burned
'Til then, let it be known: the Sandman's returned.

"Where did you get this?"

"It was sent to the paper. To *me*, as a matter of fact."

"You think it's him?"

"What do you think?"

"The style certainly fits."

"Not to mention the name."

Tim watches me. To see how this grim revelation is sinking in. Or to take an accounting of how many years I've aged since he last saw me. I know I don't look *good*. But having my clean-shaven, gym-going friend study me like a coroner studies a corpse—it can't help but make a fellow a little nervous.

"Are you going to run it?" I ask.

"I'd like to."

"But they won't let you."

"It's my decision this time."

"So?"

"So? There's no story."

"'The Sandman Returns.' Sounds like a headline to me."

"He's not claiming any particular homicides. Not much point in terrorizing the public if there's nothing to terrorize them with aside from a shabby limerick."

"It's not a limerick."

"You're the expert."

There *are* victims, of course. Conrad and Evelyn. Ivan an apparent suicide under what the crime hacks call "suspicious circumstances." Not to mention Petra—and now Angela too—gone missing. But the only thing that connects all of them is the Kensington Circle, and if Tim Earheart hasn't discovered this yet, I'm not about to tell him.

"You know, there *is* a context in which I'd run the

poem," Tim says, musing aloud. "It would require a reaction, naturally."

"A reaction?"

"From you. A comment on how an internationally bestselling novelist feels to have inspired copycat psychopaths with a work of fiction. *That* I could I go with."

"Are you kidding me?"

"Just thought it might be fun."

"Me taking credit for spawning a new generation of serial killers? Yes, that's definitely amusing. That would be a *giggle*."

I figure that's about it. Tim had come for a story, not gotten it, and all that's left is for the *National Star* to pick up the tab. We bring things to a close with some banter about the latest newsroom outrages and gossip. It's just killing time. But it makes me nostalgic for the days of journalistic sniping and complaint, when it would have been *me* telling *Tim* about the photo chief's cross-dressing weekends.

As it turns out, however, we're not quite done with the business that Tim called me here for.

"Off the record," he says as he raises his finger for the bill, "what do you make of the whole Sandman thing? Someone using the name of a bad guy in your novel, I mean."

"I don't feel responsible for anything, if that's what you're getting at."

"It isn't."

"Then what *are* you getting at?"

"What do you know?"

"Just what I read in the papers."

"Has he contacted you?"

"Nope."

"I bet you've got a theory."

"You know what, Tim?" I start, slipping off the bar stool and surprised to find myself unsteady on my feet. "Here's the thing: I wrote a book. And I *regret* it. I truly do."

Tim puts his hand out to steady me but I take a step back. What I should do now is leave. But seeing how Tim Earheart, my one-time journalistic equal, looks at me with pity in his eyes, makes me stick around for a few more words.

"I'm just trying to survive. Understand? So if you receive any more third-rate verse from psychos, don't come to me."

"Jesus, Patrick. I'm sorry."

"*Sorry?* No, that's *my* department. Sorry is my *thing*."

My hands are sliding into the arms of my jacket. The coat check girl, God bless her, appears out of nowhere to dress me against the evening's chill. Giving me a commiserating look, smoothing my collar against the back of my neck. A moment that proves there is still comfort in this world, though you may not know where it will come from. I could kiss her for it. Maybe Tim Earheart already has.

I take a cab home but get the driver to drop me off a couple blocks early so I can walk the rest of the way on my own. Continue tipsily homeward feeling my way around a thought: Maybe the shouters and shooters and moon howlers on the streets down here are versions of where all of us are headed. City in Fear. Yes. We've been right to be more and more afraid—we've just been afraid of the wrong thing. It won't be a cataclysmic nasty from Out There that will bring us down, not ozone depletion or impacting comet or dirty bomb, but the advance of madness. Why? There isn't enough room for sanity any more. Eventually, the asylum doors will be forced open. And it will be us who walk out.

Or maybe it will only be me. Because I am once again of the opinion I am being pursued. Somewhere between the sex shop and the other sex shop I pick up the heavy, thick-soled step of someone behind me.

Past the Prague Deli ("Czech Us Out!") and the used record shops he keeps up without changing the rhythm of his steps. I should start running now. A sudden break for it that might steal the few yards needed to give me a chance. But I'm suddenly too tired.

I round the corner on to the darker stretch of Euclid, straight to the patch of exposed tree roots that is my front yard. When I finally turn it's with the resignation of prey that cannot retreat any further.

"Got some news," Ramsay says, wearing a quarter-grin.

"You couldn't use the phone?"

"People say I'm better in person."

"Better at what?"

He takes a step forward. The streetlight can't reach him where he stands, so that all I can see are flashes of teeth.

"Len Innes has been reported missing."

"Missing? How?"

"That's the point with missing. You don't *know* how."

"Christ."

"When was the last time you spoke with him?"

"I don't know. A while ago."

"And what was the substance of your conversation?"

"Nothing much."

"Just a friendly chat then?"

"You think I killed Len?"

"I thought he was only missing."

"I don't know *anything*."

"Sure you do."

"Is this *fun* for you? This droll, Columbo, cat-and-mouse bullshit?"

"Everyone's a critic."

"Not everyone. I'm out of the critic business."

"Idle hands."

"Idle would be *nice*. But you keep coming around accusing me of murdering people. It's the kind of thing that can get in the way of a fellow's retirement plans."

"Here's some news: I don't give a fuck about your retirement plans."

"I don't think you believe I'm a killer, either."

"You might be wrong there."

"So arrest me. Do *something*. If not, get off my property."

Something changes in Detective Ramsay's face. Not in his expression—which remains jaw-clenched, bemused—but in his *face*. The skin pulled taut over the bone, showing the animal-thing beneath. Here is a creature free from the encumbrances of loyalty, of empathy, of seeing the human race as an enterprise that stands a chance over the long haul. All of which likely makes him a more than capable investigator of man's darkest actions. It may also enable him to carry out those actions himself.

"How's Sam?"

"I'm sorry?"

"Your *son*. How is he?"

"Fine."

"Daddy's out pretty late to leave a little guy like that on his own."

"You know he's not inside."

"I do?"

"Sam's safe."

"You sure? Because it's getting less and less safe everywhere you go."

I turn away, expecting him to launch a final remark my way, but I unlock the front door, step inside and close it behind me without another word from him.

Not that he's gone.

I peek out the window without turning on the lights. Ramsay stands under the dark bough of the front yard's maple. Unmoving as a statue and yet somehow undeniably alive, the air around him passing in and out of his lungs as though to be claimed as much as breathed. He belongs to the night world. The widening chasm between what you know is there and what can't be.

———

Ivan belongs to the night world too. And it is the next night that I see him in the food court of the Eaton Centre, making his way toward the entrance to the Dundas subway. All this is odd, as I hate malls, and hate mall food even more. I'm actually thinking this—It's odd that I'm here—when Ivan strolls by my table. Which is odder still, seeing as he's dead.

When I saw Conrad White thumbing through *The Sandman* in a bookstore when he was also among the no-longer-with-us, it gave me a chill. But as I watch Ivan lope through the crowd of tourists and locals like me with nowhere better to go, I'm instantly, paralytically afraid. It's because he's here for a purpose, and it's clear that I'm not going to like it. That's what Ivan tells me in his startling, unphantomly realness, the way he looks back over his shoulder at me, beckoning with hollow drill-holes for eyes. He's here to show me something.

And I follow him. Jumping the queue at the subway ticket booth, pushing through with understandable *fuck you*s fired at my back. Ivan may be dead, but he moves quicker than I ever saw him move in life. Sliding past the others making their way below. Scampering on to the escalator so that I have to take the stairs down two at a time to have a hope of catching him.

Once on the platform, I'm sure I've lost him. That is, I'm sure he wasn't there to begin with. This is what I try to tell myself: you haven't been sleeping, you're under stress, you're *seeing things*.

Ivan steps forward from the crowd at the far end of the platform as the train roars into the station. I start pushing my way toward him even as I expect this moment to play out as his last seconds of life played, with him jumping on to the tracks before the driver has a chance to lock the brakes.

But he doesn't jump. He looks my way.

His eyes find me instantly over the heads and ball caps and turbans. An expression of the same sort he wore to all the circle meetings, but now somehow intensified. It lets me see what's inside him, what may have been inside him all along. Longing. For someone to talk to. To be forgiven.

The train's doors open. All of us except Ivan step aside to let the passengers off, and they move around the space he takes. It lets him be the first one on. Then the crowd follows him, squeezing in shoulder to shoulder through doors not quite wide enough to accommodate them. By the time I am freed from Ivan's stare I'm left alone on the platform, the doors already closing. I make a dash to get on—a knocking at the glass that earns sneers from within—but I'm too late.

I step back to see if I can spot Ivan inside. And there he is, sitting face out in a window seat, finding me with a jealous glare. Except now he's not alone.

Conrad White sits across from him, knee to knee. Petra behind them. Evelyn a couple seats back. All the Kensington Circle's dead with their noses to the windows. Ovals of malice mixed with the indifferent passengers.

In the next second, as the train releases its brakes and picks up speed, their faces flatten and blur. The car they sit in swallowed into the tunnel's mouth. The faces of the Kensington Circle along with those of the living commuters, good luck awaiters, furious strivers.

If I didn't know who was who, I might say all of them were dead.

26

In the morning, I wake to find William sitting at the end of my bed.

His body shaped in the hunched, head-cocked posture of a concerned friend sitting vigil. Even his face—still densely bearded as an oven brush—could be mistaken for sympathetic, his eyes looking down on me with a still intensity. Yet these are only first impressions. And they are wrong.

William's hands rise from the sheets. Fresh soil dropping off them in clumps. The nails ripped and weeping. Hands reaching for me.

I try to sit up. A weight on my legs prevents them from moving. The only action I'm capable of is watching.

His *hands* are going to kill me. *They* are about to do the most terrible things, not *him*. This is what his cracked lips seem to want to say. He is an instrument of death, but also dead himself.

I make a note of this—my first fright of the day—in my journal which I have taken to keeping by my bed at night. A chronicle of actual events and dream diary all in one. I should likely have kept separate notebooks for each, but so many passways have opened between my waking and sleeping worlds it doesn't seem to make much difference.

Take the ball cap, for instance.

I'm plodding through my breakfast routine of coffee making and cereal pouring when I first see it. Even then, it takes a few seconds to understand what it means. A Yankees cap. Sitting on the coffee table in the living room.

I pick it up and bring it to my nose—Petra's shampoo, still clinging to the cotton. The sliding glass doors are closed. But unlocked. And the curtains I was sure to have pulled closed the night before stand open.

I can see you.

Once I've closed the curtains and locked the doors, then gone round the basement and main floor to check the other doors and windows, I return to Petra's cap, studying it as though a clue has been stitched into its fabric.

Petra wore it, now she's thought to be dead. It was left with Angela, now she's disappeared. And now it's with me.

It could be you.

Ramsay already thinks (and with some good reason) that I'm involved in Petra's death and perhaps the others from before. If he found out her ball cap was in my possession, it would be more than enough to arrest me. The first piece of hard evidence connecting me to one of the murders. The Sandman wants me to hold it in my hands and know how it feels. To know what can be done to me without ever touching me.

It's a sin, the church says, to do the things that I do
But how can I stop until I've done them to you?

The Yankees cap is a promise of things to come, a show of power, a signature. But it's also a *game*.

Tag. I'm it.

The next thing I know I'm being asked to leave the offices of the *National Star*. The lobby, to be precise. It's as far as I get before I'm stopped trying to tiptoe by reception without a pass. When asked my intended business—Patrick Rush, here for a surprise visit to my old friend Tim Earheart—the guy behind the security desk punches my name into his terminal and a flag pops up. Quite a few flags, judging by his reddened cheeks and phone at his ear, a digit shy of completing his 911 call.

"Just tell Earheart I'm downstairs," I tell the security guy, whose tortured face shows that while I'm in no position to be making deals, he might get into some serious trouble if he has to use his flashlight on me.

"Do as he says," a female voice says behind me. I turn to find the Managing Editor smiling one of her death smiles. Except now she's no longer the Managing Editor but the youngest Editor-in-Chief in the paper's history. "Let him say hello and be on his way."

She keeps smiling. If it were real, I'd be halfway to falling in love. But there's absolutely no mistaking the Editor-in-Chief's expression as warmth. As it is I'm backing away with every step she takes closer.

"Always nice to see an ex-employee going out the door," she says.

I'm spinning out into the heat as I glimpse Tim Earheart rushing past the Editor-in-Chief. *It won't happen again* on his lips.

"You can't get fired twice, you know. Or are you trying to get *me* fired?" Tim says as he takes me by the arm and hauls me away from the building. Through the glass doors I can see the Editor-in-Chief still there, her hands on her slim, treadmilled hips.

I follow Tim across Front Street to stand on the narrow edge of grass between the pavement and the fence that keeps pedestrians from the tracks leading in and out of Union station below.

"I'm working," Tim says. "We're not all *novelists* you know."

"I'll make this short."

"The shorter the better."

"Can you get access to government agency databases?"

"Depends which one."

"Children's Aid. Foster care. Whoever does permanent guardianships."

He puts a cigarette in his mouth but makes no move to light it. "Who's asking?"

"I'm looking for someone."

"Someone you know?"

"I know her. Not well, but I know her."

"A kid?"

"She's grown up now."

"So why not give her a call?"

"I don't know where she is."

Tim Earheart reads me closely for the first time, and I sense that what I say next will decide how the rest of this exchange is going to go. I want Tim involved, but not *involved*.

"Are you going to light that thing?"

He pulls the unlit cigarette out of his lips and flicks it over the fence. "What's her name?"

"Angela Whitmore. But that might only be her adoptive parents' surname. Or probably not. I mean, that's the name I know her by, but it may not be real."

"Tracking down an adoption without the kid's name—it's not going to happen."

"I don't think it was a voluntary adoption."

"How's that?"

"She was taken from her natural parents. State intervention. I don't know the specifics. One of those situations where they *had* to."

"That's something."

I tell him whatever other details I have that might be of help, which aren't all that many. Angela's approximate age (late twenties to early thirties), job experience (legal secretary), possible educational background (liberal arts most likely). I end up leaving out more than I give him: her fictional journal and my thieving of its essential contents, our night together and the discovery of missing toes. Maybe later, I tell myself. Maybe, if this all turns out well, I'll fill him in on the whole thing.

"One question," Tim says as I shake his hand in thanks and check both ways along Front Street for a taxi.

"You want to know why I need to find this out."

"No. I want to know what's in it for me."

"Nothing. Aside from a story."

"A newspaper kind of story, or a funny-thing-happened-the-other-day kind of story?"

"Just a girl-trouble kind of story," I tell him, with an embarrassed shake of the head. A gesture I know Tim Earheart will understand without going into the details.

Below us, another train pumps commuters and shoppers and ball game ticket holders into the city. Tim and I look down and try to pick out individual faces in the windows. But they're a little too far away, moving a little too fast, to see anything but a long row of silhouettes.

"I better get back," Tim says, starting across Front Street.

"Me too," I say in reply, and though the question occurs to both of us—Back to *what*?—he's considerate enough to keep it to himself.

The first email on the Comment board at www.patrickrush.com is from **therealsandman**.

Hope you liked the gift.

To cheer things up, Detective Ramsay rings with the news that he's discovered Evelyn has not been seen by family or friends for over four years.

"Starting to add up to a lot of missing people from that group of yours," he says. "Does that concern you?"

Is it illegal to hang up on a homicide investigator when he's addressing you directly? If so, Ramsay can add it to the list of charges he's tallying against me.

The phone rings again.

"This is harassment."

"Are you not taking your pills again?"

"Tim. Thought it was someone else."

"More girl trouble?"

"That would be nice. But no."

"Your heart belongs to Angela Whitmore. Is that it?"

In the background, the sound of shuffled papers.

"You've found her," I say.

"Not the person. But an interesting chunk of background. For one thing, turns out you were right about Children's Aid taking her from her birth parents. 'Acute neglect' is how the file puts it. Malnutrition, lack of basic hygiene. 'Indications of physical and emotional abuse.' Something beyond your standard junkie-mom scenario."

"The mother was an addict?"

"Lots of court-ordered rehab. Surprise, surprise: none of it worked."

"You got a name?"

"Mom is Michelle Carruthers. Which makes Whitmore either an assumed name, or maybe the name of her eventual adoptive parents."

"What about Dad?"

"No father on the scene at all, as far as the files show."

"And I'm guessing Michelle Carruthers is six feet under."

"Not as of a year ago. That was when she made an application to have Angela's adoptive parents' identities disclosed to her. They denied her, naturally."

"No kidding."

"Twenty-five years later and she wakes up in a trailer park on Lake Huron and goes, 'Hey, where'd my kid go?'"

"Does your file say where Angela ended up?"

"The adoptive parents' records are kept separate from the ones I could get my hands on. They're very particular about it."

"So you don't know."

"I still have a *job*, Patrick."

"Sorry."

"You want me to stay on this? Who knows, if I grease a few more wheels –"

"No, no. This is all I was really curious about anyway. Thanks."

"Listen, I don't usually put my nose into friends' personal stuff, but, given her pedigree, I'd say this Angela of yours might not be an ideal reintroduction to romance."

"Guess I've never known what's good for me."

"Tamara was good for you."

"Yes, she was," I say, the mention of my wife's name forcing something up my throat I don't want him to hear. "I'll let you go now, Tim. And thanks again."

I hang up. But before I pour myself a bourbon in a coffee mug (the glasses all look too small), before I even begin to digest the news of Angela's fatherless past, it strikes me that if Tim Earheart is as worried about me as he sounds, I'm in worse shape than I thought.

———

Of course I look up Michelle Carruthers. Of course I find her after a few Google searches and process-of elimination calls—a unit address in Hilly Haven, a "mobile home estate" on Lake Huron. And of course I make the drive to see her the same day without an idea as to what I want from her, or how it could help even if I did.

Hilly Haven isn't hilly, and what the few spindly poplars and collapsed snow fence around its perimeter might offer haven from would be hard to guess. The whole place has the appearance of an uncorrected accident: a couple dozen mobile homes arranged in rows, some sidled close, others aloof in weedy double lots, all with their backsides facing the lake.

Michelle Carruthers' place is the smallest. A camper trailer of the kind one used to see hitched to station wagons thirty years ago. Now, knocking on its side door and hearing the muffled greeting within ("*Who* the fuck?"), I wonder if Angela's mother can be convinced to step outside. It doesn't seem possible for there to be enough room for both of us inside.

When the door opens, however, I see that the odds of the woman hunched in its frame coming outside are slight. Her papery skin. An oxygen mask attached to her face, a tank on wheels by her side.

"Sorry to disturb you. My name is Patrick Rush," I say, putting out my hand, which her cold fingers weigh more than shake. "I'm looking for Angela."

"Angela?"

"Your daughter, ma'am."

"I know who she goddamn is."

"I was just –"

"Are you her husband or something? She run away on you?"

"I'm a friend. I think she may be in trouble. That's why I'm here. If I can find her, there's a chance I can help her."

After what may be a full minute's consideration, she pushes the trailer door open wide. Pulls the oxygen mask off and lets it necklace her throat.

"You might as well come in out of the sun," she says.

But it's hotter inside than out. And no larger than I'd feared. A stand-up kitchen smelling of canned spaghetti. A living room crowded by a giant TV in one corner and old combination radio-record player in the other. And at the rear, behind a half-drawn curtain, the tousled bunk where she sleeps. The only ventilation a rotating fan sitting atop a stack of LPs, though with all the windows closed, the best it can do is whisper hot air in my face.

"Have a seat," she says, collapsing into her recliner and leaving me to crouch on to a folding chair that, even pushed against the wall, forces my knees to graze hers.

"What I'm interested in learning is any background information that might –"

"Hold on. Just hold *on*," she says, putting her hands behind her head, a manoeuvre which offers me an unfortunate view of her armpits. "How'd you find me?"

"I'm a reporter. *Was* a reporter. We have access to information others don't have."

"They fire you, or you quit?"

"Pardon me?"

"You said you was a reporter. That's the past tense, am I right?"

"They fired me. But it was for the best."

"It's *all* for the best."

"I understand that Angela was put into the foster system when she was a child," I continue.

"You mean was she taken from me? Yes."

"That must have been difficult."

"I can hardly remember it. My life was . . . *busy* then."

"Nevertheless, I'm aware that of late you have made some efforts to locate her."

She shows her teeth. A stretching of lips that appears more like the response to a dentist's command than a smile.

"I'm not as old as I look," she says. "But that doesn't mean I've got much time left. So, you start looking back, and thinking, 'Well, nothing I can do about that shit now.'"

"And did you manage to contact her?"

"Nah. I'm out of the picture. Which I *get*, you know?"

She sits forward enough that her face slides into the light of the reading lamp behind her. All premature lines and poison spots.

"What was she like?" I say. "When she was young?"

Her hand crawls up her chest to grip the oxygen mask hanging there. "She was innocent."

"Aren't all children?"

"That's what I'm saying. She was just like any other child."

"That's the past tense."

She fits the mask to her face and takes a breath. The mist against the plastic obscures all her features but her eyes. And they blink at me, clouding over.

"She suffered," she says.

"How?"

"Loneliness. She was left *alone*. I sure as hell weren't in any shape to be taking care of her."

"She liked to read."

"She liked to *write*. Diaries. Piles and piles of stuff."

"What were they about?"

"How do I know? I was just glad she had *something*."

She pulls the oxygen mask from her face and I can see that she won't hold up much longer. Just sitting and remembering draws fresh sweat to her cheeks.

"Angela's father," I say, glancing at the door.

"I haven't spoken to that sonofabitch in twenty-seven years."

"Do you know where he is?"

"Look in the penitentiaries. Least that's where I *hope* he is."

"What did he do?"

"What *didn't* he do?"

"Was he violent?"

"Something he couldn't control, then didn't *want* to control. You know what I'm sayin'?"

"Tell me."

"What he done . . . what he . . . with his *own* –" she

says, coughing for air it will take the rest of the day to catch. "It's a thing I don't even want to talk about."

"It's important."

"How could *anything* to do with that man ever be important?"

"It might help me find your daughter."

She looks up at me and I can see that there's no strength left in her. But she's still a mother. Even in her, even now, there's the useless wish for everything to have been different.

"Killing," she says, teeth clenched so hard I can hear the chalky scrape of bone against bone. "Little children. *Girls*. He killed little *girls*."

Before I left Michelle Carruthers' trailer and stumbled, sun blind, to my Toyota, she had given me Angela's father's name. Raymond Mull. Which rang a bell the moment she said it, though specifically from where, and specifically for what, it took until I was able to get back to Toronto and start working my computer in the Crypt to discover.

Angela's mother was right. Raymond Mull was a killer of little girls. He was charged for the murders of two of them, in fact, a pair of thirteen-year-olds who went missing almost two decades ago. Roughly the same age that Angela, if she is thirty today, would have been then.

What follows from this? Nothing, perhaps. Or possibly everything.

If Angela was a thirteen-year-old contemporary of the murdered girls, it supports the interpretation (along with her missing toes) that she actually was the narrator of her fictionalized journal. Further, given Raymond Mull's relationship to her, it's probably true that he was the direct inspiration for the Sandman. In her story, she even had Jacob, her foster parent, suspect as much when he stated he believed it was the girl's father who was selecting victims. In the real world, odds are that Raymond Mull was the original terrible man who did terrible things.

What I discover next, however, suggests I wasn't the first member of the Kensington Circle to figure this much out.

A search on the media database I still have a password for left over from my *National Star* days finds dozens of stories on Raymond Mull's trial. There's photos of him too: bearded, eyes set too close together, but otherwise his face absent of expression. He doesn't look like Angela, but they share this. A half-thereness.

Judging from the initial reports covering Raymond Mull's trial, his conviction was viewed as a foregone conclusion. The Crown's evidence included work tools—saws, drills, hunting blades—found in his motel room. And he was identified by witnesses as being in the area over the preceding weeks, following students home from school, standing outside the convenience store where kids stopped for candy. His long list of previous convictions said little of worth about his character.

And yet none of this could prevent the case ending in an acquittal. The tools could render no blood samples from which to make positive DNA matches with the victims. The police argued this was only because Mull had been careful in cleaning them, and that even without blood, there was enough to connect him to the crimes. On this, the court disagreed. Without calling a single witness, the defence filed a motion to dismiss the charges on the grounds that the Crown failed in making a *prima facie* case. All that was left to the prosecution was to nail Mull for previous parole violations, which they did. His sentence was nine months.

Which means that, barring no other subsequent incarceration over the last eighteen years, Raymond Mull is a free man.

But what strikes me even more than this is the location where the murders took place. Whitley, Ontario. The same place where Conrad White and Evelyn drove their car off the highway.

It could just be coincidence. But I don't believe that it was. Evelyn and Conrad White's shared curiosity over Angela's story had led them to Raymond Mull, to Whitley. That's what they had been up to all the time I'd come to assume them to be having a May-December, teacher-student affair. They were searching.

If I'm right in this, the possibility that Conrad and Evelyn's accident was in fact accidental becomes considerably harder to accept. They drove into a cliff wall. But what made them turn? At that speed, what were they driving *from?* Even the police found the crash "puzzling." One solution would be if it was a double murder. If their killer was Raymond Mull.

Angela's father. The original Sandman.

27

Sam calls me.

I've been sitting in the Crypt all day, intermittently writing in my journal and trying Angela's number over and over, as though persistence is all that's required to bring back the dead. I even try Len, whose answering machine's message is the creepy piano soundtrack from *Halloween*.

All of them gone, or missing. Me too. It's why the ringing of the phone takes me by surprise.

"Dad?"

"What's up?"

"Are you coming to visit today?"

"Not today."

"What are you scared of, Dad?"

"I'm not scared."

"What are you *scared* of?"

"I don't want you to get hurt for something I did," I say finally. "You're *it*. You're all I have. There's nothing more important to me than making sure I don't screw up again."

"What did you do?"

"I stole something."

"Can't you give it back?"

"It's too late."

"Like a . . . perishable item."

"That's right. Just like that."

If you take another's past and use it as your own it can't be returned. It's bruised. Perishable. You take someone else's story and chances are even they won't want it back.

That evening, I know something's wrong even before I park the Toyota behind the house. The door to the yard is ajar. The one I'd remembered to padlock over a week ago. It keeps me in the front seat a couple minutes longer, hands on the wheel. A lick of breeze nudges the door open another foot. Even in the dark, I can see the pale cuts in the wood where a crowbar has wrenched it free of the bolt.

It's rage that starts me running two houses down, through the side alley to the street. Unlocking the door and kicking it open with an underwater rush of blood in my ears.

Upstairs. Making my way down the hallway, stepping blind into each room, not bothering to hide my steps or even turn on the lights.

No sign of anything taken or touched. Nothing left behind.

The same goes for downstairs. Every door locked, every window intact. Whoever went to the trouble of ripping the back gate apart was apparently interrupted on his way to the house. That, or the house wasn't his destination in the first place.

I pull back the curtains in the living room and look out the sliding glass doors. The light from a single hanging bulb illuminates the inside of the lopsided garden shed. A surprise. First, because it's been so long since I've been out there at night I didn't even know it had a bulb that still worked. And second, because the light wasn't on when I parked the car no more than four minutes ago.

I go down to the basement. Rummage through the neglected corner of sports equipment and find what I'm looking for at the bottom of the pile. A baseball bat. A Louisville Slugger that feels right in my hands, heavy but capable of decisive speed in the first swing. After that, if it works, I can take my time.

I'm opening the sliding door and shuffling through the uncut grass. The shed's door left open a foot in invitation.

The shed's window is small, maybe two feet square, the glass murky with cobwebs. I try to look in. At the angle I stand at, there are only the shelves and wall hooks that store ignored tools and unopened hardware gifts. A museum of the failed handyman.

I go to the door and bring the bat even with my shoulders.

For a moment, the traffic and air-conditioning thrum of the city is quieted. There is only me. A man standing in his backyard. Holding a baseball bat. Raising his foot to kick in a shed door.

It flies open. Hits the wall. Swings closed again.

Yet there is time enough to peekaboo what's inside. The old rotary lawnmower I've yet to take out this year. The 1999 Sunshine Girl calendar Tim Earheart gave me. Red paint dotted over the floor. Petra.

Then: not red paint, but blood.

Not Petra. Petra's body.

What did he use?

This is my first thought upon seeing what remains of Petra on my shed floor. Would a knife do that? A drill? Could you do it on your own?

Did he keep her in a freezer? I think this too. *She looks fresh enough.*

But this is shock talking. This isn't me.

I stare at her. The unfamiliar pinks and coiled blues that normally lie inside a person. I sit on a can of paint and do the same thing I did after finding her Yankees cap once it made its way from Angela's condo to my living-room coffee table. I just *looked* at it. Long enough for the morning to slip into afternoon, for a thunderstorm to come and go. And the whole time I was stuck on the same question as I am now: What do you do with evidence planted in your home that could put you in prison for the rest of your life?

There's going to the police and telling them the whole story, an expensive lawyer by your side, hoping they'll see it your way. Unavailable in my case, however. Not with all the connections that have even me wondering if I did it.

Next there's enlisting help. Calling a friend for advice, a drive across the border. But who would I call? Tim

Earheart? Hard to believe he could resist the temptation to print the transcript of my call on tomorrow's front page.

In the end, you might do as I did: put on gardening gloves, wipe the Yankees cap for prints using a wet tea towel, cut the thing into ribbons and stick it in the trash.

Which is the same thing I do with Petra's body.

Yet not right away. Not until after a couple hours of taking deep breaths with my head between my knees. Smoking a cigarette from the emergency pack I keep in the flour jar. A round of dry heaves into the compost bin. It's not easy coming to a decision like that. But that's still nothing. Deciding to do it is a breeze compared with the doing of it.

Not to mention getting *ready* to do it.

Here, finally, is some use for what I learned over the hundreds of hours of prime-time forensic cop TV I studied as the Couch Potato: How to best cover your tracks in the disposal of a body.

I begin by stripping myself naked (later burning the clothes I wore when I entered the shed, just to be sure). After the cutting, I wrap each smaller part in several garbage bags. Dry, air-tight. Place the resulting packages in a larger bag used for yard waste.

Once I'm finished, I cut nails, hair, shave. Shower. Scour every inch of skin with cleansers reserved for kitchen use only. Bleach the bathroom.

Then do it all again. And again.

What do I remember now, only minutes after it's done? Bits and pieces. So to speak. The protective walls already going up in my brain. They won't hold, of course. Not forever, and not entirely. But you'd be surprised. You keep the worst of it at bay and you can still pour yourself a drink, look in the mirror and recall your own name.

Let's just say that cutting up a ball cap and doing the same to a woman's body are two different things. The tools required, the time, what it leaves behind. It's just *different*.

And after the mopping, the bleaching, the wiping for toe prints on the concrete floor, I'm still left with six yard-waste bags.

I smoke the rest of the pack.

Today is recycling day. The truck arrives early on my street, usually just after eight. A little over an hour from now. The collectors who work this neighbourhood are used to the sight of me dashing out at their approach, barefoot and in boxer shorts, frantically hauling out the compost I'd forgotten to take to the curb the night before. Every time, they let me apologize for the delay and watch as I insist on swinging the bags into the back myself. Once I'm done, they pull the switch that compacts the load into the truck's hold. Then they're gone.

And today, they'll be taking Petra with them.

28

I suppose it's the guilt over what I did out back in the shed, the ratcheting worry of it being discovered—whatever the reason, I end up staying in all the next day punishing myself. A steady infliction of the most hideous domestic torture: I watch TV.

Not that I don't try reading first. Sniffing at the opening of the latest Philip Roth (too sharp), sampling a random page of Borges (too fanciful), then a re-taste of Patricia Highsmith (too much like real life, or at least *my* real life). It seems likely I will never read again. I feel like the Burgess Meredith bookworm character in that *Twilight Zone* episode who, finding himself the last man alive on earth and prepared to finally savour all the works of literature he'd yet to get around to, sits down on the library steps only to have his specs fall off and shatter into a thousand pieces. That's one nerd's version of hell for you. And here is mine.

Not since I was paid to do so have I settled in for a full day with the early-morning Born Agains, followed by the afternoon Chatty Cathys, the prime-time autopsies, all capped off with the soulless hours of miracle diet pills, phone sex lines, get-rich-quick infomercials. This, I realize now, was likely my true vocation all along. Not the life of one who writes or even writes *about* books, but a malingering lowbrow who wrongly thinks he deserves better. No wonder, when his life decides to assume the shape of literature, it isn't a novel of ideas, but a chronicle of murder and suspicion. The kind of thing I always felt I was too good to actually read, but am now being forced to live. A bloody page-turner.

On the positive side, it appears I've gotten away with it. No phone calls from the city's sanitation department inquiring about blue limbs punched out the side of compost bags, no neighbours coming by to complain about my screeching away with a rotary saw in the middle of the night. Petra will turn up some day, she'll have to. But it wasn't yesterday, and it wasn't today. And even when she does show herself, a week, a year, half a lifetime from now, there's no evidence to connect her to me. I likely won't be around for it anyway. If the Sandman's goal is to kill off everyone in the Kensington Circle one by one, he's almost finished. I'd put my money on me being the only one left alive. And he's already made it clear he knows where I live.

So now I wait for him down here in the Crypt, glancing up at any movement outside the basement windows, thinking every skulking cat or fast-food wrapper blown down the walkway are his boots passing by. He is waiting for me to come outside, and if I refuse, he will come for me here. I won't hear him enter. He'll find me in this very chair, the remote clutched in my hand. And he'll do what he'll do.

I wonder if he'll let me see who he is before he does.

All at once there's a collision of noise: the ringing of the doorbell, the sock-hop opening theme of *Happy Days*, the journal I'd been scratching in leaping to the floor. It's morning. A sandy light spills into the basement through the storm-drain windows.

I *must* be awake. Can you smell how bad you smell in your sleep?

The doorbell rings again. I'm tucking in my shirt as I climb the stairs, all the while wondering why I'm bothering to make myself presentable to the Sandman. For *this* is how he's decided to make his entrance. Not at night, but on a listless July morning with the clouds holding the heat over the city like a vast canopy of wool.

There's the shape of a man, tall and long-armed, standing on the other side of the front door's side windows. And I'm going to the door with no further prompting than another musical push of the bell—*Shave and a haircut, five cents!*—clicking the bolt lock open and turning the handle.

Ramsay offers one of his vaguely cruel, ironic smiles. He's in a good mood.

"You want some coffee?"

"I'm trying to cut down," he says. "But you know, I think I will."

I give him his coffee and warn him it's hot. But he

wraps his hand around the sides of the mug and takes a thirsty gulp.

"Can't get hot enough for me," he says.

By now Ramsay has walked over to the sliding doors and is looking out at the day. Then, so deliberately I can only assume he wants me to notice, he lowers his eyes from the sky to the shed in the backyard.

"So are you going to put the cuffs on, or do we just walk out of here?" I say, slapping both hands on the counter.

"You think I'm here to arrest you?"

"Yes."

"I thought we were friends."

"What *are* you doing here? Because I've got some important *Beverly Hillbillies* reruns to get back to."

When he puts his mug down on the counter I see that it's empty, while mine, still steaming, sits next to his.

"I'm here to tell you we found him," he says.

"Found him?"

"Arrested him this morning."

"I'm not following you."

"The Sandman," Ramsay says. "The fellow who killed your writing circle friends. He's *ours*."

By now I'm leaning against the fridge door to remain standing.

"Who is it?"

"You don't know?"

"I've thought it was everyone. Even you."

"In my experience, the first choice is usually the right one."

"William."

"Congratulations."

"And now you have him?"

"He'll be arraigned later this morning. It's why I have to run in a minute. Always like to be there for the reading of the charges."

I suppose I must ask Ramsay other questions after this, because he's telling me things. About the evidence they have on William. His background, criminal record, his aliases. The blood-spotted tools in his rented room. His membership not only in the Kensington Circle, but the ones before, the ones that Carol Ulrich and Ronald Pevencey and Jane Whirter had been a part of. How the police will keep searching for Angela and Petra and Len, and they'll find them too, their remains anyway, because Ramsay hates nothing more than an incomplete file.

"I never *really* thought it was you," Ramsay is saying now. "But you were in that circle. And you were the one with the novel with the same title as the killer's handle. It was *odd*. But the evidence speaks for itself. And besides, you were just using him for material, weren't you? A parasite—if you'll excuse the term. But that's *you*. That's the kind of fellow you *are*."

Ramsay checks his watch. He's still early for court—the kitchen clock has just gone a quarter to nine—but he pretends he's running late. The fun's over at the Rush household.

He strides to the door and I follow him. And though he moves with the self-assurance of a man who has once again been proved right, I realize, with an itchy thrill, that the triumph is actually mine. Nobody's found Petra. Even if they do, they'll attribute my handiwork to William. And Ramsay has done me the favour of catching the Sandman before he had the chance to visit me.

He's halfway down the front walk before he turns.

"You better hope we get a conviction," he says.

I knew it was William. That is, it could only have been him. And yet, almost from the very beginning, I had believed that the Sandman wasn't just a killer's pseudonym but an actual being for whom no real name exists. Separate from humanity not just in deed but composition. A monster.

Such was the charm of Angela's story.

As a psychological profile, William's a classic. A kid who lost his parents in swift succession when he was only six—the mother to MS, the father to a stroke—and spent the rest of his youth being traded around from one aunt or uncle to another, from prairie town to prairie town. "Nobody looking out for him," as Ramsay put it. "That, or they were trying to look the other way."

The fact is, little Will was a friendless bully as early as school counsellors started files on him. A teacher beater, window smasher, playground torturer. Followed by the emergence of more explicitly criminal talents. The dismemberment of neighbourhood pets. Thefts, break-and-enters, assaults. A graduation of offences from the petty to the brutal.

Then, a couple years out of high school, William went off the grid. No new charges, no known address.

As far as the police could tell, he spent the better part of his twenties rolling between the rougher parts of towns out west, renting rooms in the most forgotten quarters of Winnipeg, Portland, Lethbridge, Spokane. Odd-jobbing for money. Spending his free time on far darker pursuits.

Where William went, missing people followed. A seemingly arbitrary string of men and women with no shared characteristics or backgrounds, all cold cases with little in common other than a tall, bearded man who kept to himself, had spent some time in their towns around the time they disappeared. "Only circumstantial," Ramsay conceded. "But I don't believe it for a second. Not after what we found."

And what had the police found at William's apartment over a bankrupted butcher's shop in the east end? The tools of the trade for a new butcher's shop. Cleavers, saws, meat-cutting wires. Most of it encrusted with human blood. All of it off to the lab for DNA testing. But given some of the other personal items found in William's bathtub, kitchen cabinets, even lying at the end of his bed—Carol Ulrich's purse, Ronald Pevencey's diary—it's certain that the results will prove that his tools were what he used to dispose of them all.

There were also the storybooks. Do-it-yourself editions with cardboard covers. Inside, pages relating the disconnected tales of a shadow that drifted through the night, periodically stopping to carve up complete strangers who caught his eye. Written in William's hand. And the protagonist's name?

"Let me guess," I'd interrupted Ramsay. "The Sandman?"

"Isn't that copyright infringement?"

"Titles can't be owned. Only the contents."

"That's too bad. I thought I might have another charge to lay against our friend."

The police have their man. And their man *is* a man. Nothing supernatural about him, aside from the black magic that enables one to kill for no reason other than pleasure in the doing of it. The Sandman is a creation of fantasy. But the fantastical is not required here, it never is. All that's needed is your off-the-rack dismemberment artist: the unloved child, the world hater, the remorseless sociopath. Check the back pages of any newspaper. There's plenty of them.

I should be relieved. And I am. Sam can come home again. We can start on the business of making new lives.

But there is still the lone survivor's question: Why me? Someone has to tell the story, I suppose.

And this time, it isn't Angela's, it's not stolen. It's mine.

The next day is William's bail hearing, and though I want to go straight down to St. Catharines and pick Sam up, I prevent myself with a sobering dose of fear. If the lawyer for the one they call the Sandman somehow manages to loose him on the streets this afternoon, I know where he's most likely to visit first. Sam is safe now. One more day apart is the price for keeping him that way.

Still, the moment seems to call for some kind of celebration.

What I need to do is get out of the house.

A drive in the country.

The sign for Hilly Haven sprouts up from the horizon as a lone interruption of the flat fields. I turn in at the gate and wonder how I'm going to tell Angela's mother that her daughter is likely dead. I suppose I don't have to worry too much about the precise wording. Michelle Carruthers is used to receiving bad news. She'll know before I'm halfway to telling her.

I park on the gravel lane outside her trailer, thankful for the cloud cover that veils some of Hilly Haven's more dispiriting details. Its unwheeled tricycles, scalped dolls. The stained underwear swinging on the clotheslines.

"Nobody home."

I turn before knocking on the trailer's door to find a woman too old for the pig-tails that reach down to the two chocolate-smeared children at the ends of her hands. None wearing T-shirts of sufficient size to cover the bellies that peek out from over the waists of their sweatpants.

"Will Michelle be back soon?"

"Not soon."

"Is she well?"

"You a friend of hers?"

A cop. That's what I'd look like to her. Hilly Haven must get its share of plainclothes banging on its tin doors.

"My name is Patrick Rush. I was a friend of her daughter's. She's come into some trouble, I'm afraid."

"Trouble?" the woman says, releasing the hands of the chocolatey kids.

"It's a private matter."

"You mean she's dead too?"

"I'm sorry?"

"Michelle. She passed on last week."

"Oh. I see."

"The doctors didn't know exactly what got her. But with her, it could have been *anything*."

There is nothing more to say than this. Yet simply walking past the three of them to the car and driving off without another word doesn't seem possible either. If it weren't for the blackened tongue that the smaller of the two kids sticks out at me, I might not have come up with a question.

"Has there been a funeral already?"

"Two days after she died. A few round here were the only ones who showed up. As well as the son."

"The son?"

"It's who we all figured it was anyway."

"What was his name?"

"Never asked."

"What did he look like?"

"A big guy, I guess. Wasn't the kind who seemed to like you looking at him all that much. Like he wanted to be there, but not have anybody else know it."

I step down off the cement steps at the trailer's door. The midday sun unveils itself from behind a bank of clouds.

"When was the funeral?"

"Last week. I told you."

"Which *day*?"

"Thursday, I think."

Thursday. Two days *before* William's arrest. *A big guy*.

"I better be getting back," I say. But as I try to pass the woman, she stops me with a hand on my arm.

"I suppose someone should look that son of hers up if his sister's passed on."

"I'll let him know."

"So you *know* him? We was right? He was Michelle's boy?"

"You know families," I say vaguely, but the woman seems to understand. She gives me a nod that takes in her own children, Angela's mother's trailer, the blazing sun, all of Hilly Haven.

"Oh yeah," she says. "Full of surprises."

When I get home there's a message from Tim Earheart. He wants to get together, see how I am. But I know even as I return his call and arrange to meet at a bar near his new house in Cabbagetown that he's heard about William's arrest and wants to find out what I know about it. This has been Tim's assignment from the start. And now that the final act is beginning—the public cleansing ritual that is every high-profile criminal proceeding—he wants to milk every advantage he has over the competition.

Tim thinks I know something. And unless something juicier presents itself, he'll keep asking what it is. And yet I still cling to the possibility that I can escape disclosure. It's true that if William does end up going to a full trial, I'll be called as a witness. But if the prosecution ends up not having to probe that far, or, better yet, if William pleads guilty, no one need ever know that the author of *The Sandman* was once in a writing class with the Sandman. I still have a chance. So long as Tim can be discouraged from digging further into the Patrick Rush angle.

"How're you liking the new place?" I ask him as the first round arrives.

"It's an investment. Besides, I'm thinking of settling down pretty soon."

"Stop it. You're killing me."

"I just need to meet someone."

"Haven't you met enough someones?"

"She's out there. Just like your Angela person."

I nod, trying to read Tim to see if he knows something about Angela's disappearance that I don't.

"Must be strange," Tim muses. "Being so close to this William Feld business."

"I wasn't so close to it."

"Your book could have been the guy's biography."

"That's an exaggeration."

"The whole title thing. It's kind of hard to accept as coincidence."

"The police didn't think it was so hard."

"They've talked to you?"

"A detective came round to ask some questions."

"Ramsay."

"I think that's the guy."

"And what did you tell him?"

"What I'm telling you. It's a *novel*. It's all made up. I'm just glad it's over."

Tim chokes on the sip he's taking from his bottle. "Over? Not for me. This is my story. I'm going to be filing on Mr. Feld's trial for the next several months. Which could turn out to be a real bitch if I can't come at it through a side door."

He looks at me straight now, hands flat on the bar.

"I wish I could help you," I say, blowing him back an inch with an exhaled belch. "But there's not a goddamn thing I know about William Feld that anybody who read your story in today's paper doesn't know."

I'll never know if Tim believes me or not. But whether out of a sense that what I've said is true, or some last tug of friendship, he lets me go.

"Working on anything new?"

"I was thinking of returning to newspapering. I'd be prepared to try something new. The horoscopes, classifieds, crossword puzzles," I say. "You think the Editor-in-Chief would have me back?"

Oh yes. We both have a good laugh over that one.

In the morning I drive down to St. Catharines. I've brought all sorts of presents with me (a plasma screen TV for Stacey and her husband, iPods and a Tolkien collector's set for their kids) but nothing, intentionally, for Sam. Our gift to each other is the reunion itself. It will be up to Sam how he wants to spend the rest of the summer. We will work our way back to what we used to be at our own pace, and with only ourselves to tell us how it is to be done.

On the drive home I make a point of not overdoing

how difficult the last weeks have been without him. And
for the first hour or so, he offers anecdotes involving his
numbskulled cousins, how good a swimmer he's become.
He's going easy on me, too.

Then, somewhere around Oakville, flying past the
low-rise head offices and steakhouse franchises, Sam
decides I'm able to take his coming to the point.

"You have to tell me, Dad."

"I know."

"It doesn't have to be now."

"Okay."

"But sometime."

"I owe you that much."

"It's not about *owing*."

Sam turns in his seat. And there's not an eight-year-old
looking back at me but a young man who is surprised at
how his father can't appreciate what should be obvious.

"If you don't tell me, you'll be the only one who
knows," he says.

August decides to behave, with afternoon breezes off the
lake nudging the smog northward to reveal the city it
had shrouded in orange for the month before. To honour
this change, Sam and I go for long walks. Lunching out
in T-shirts and flip-flops, biking along the trails in the Don
Valley, sliding our hands over the Henry Moore sculptures
at the gallery when the security guards aren't looking.
We've even started reading again. Bookish picnics in
Trinity-Bellwoods swallowing *Robinson Crusoe* (Sam)
and *Atonement* (me) in the shade.

But even these happy days are not free of ghosts.

The first arrives in the form of a voice. A phone call near midnight that sounds like it's coming from a bar.

"Patrick?"

"Who is this?"

"It's *Len*."

"Where are you?"

"The Fukhouse."

"Why?"

"I'm not too sure. I guess it's got some sentimental value."

"This is going to sound stupid, but I have to ask," I say, squeezing my eyes shut against the bedside lamp I click on. "You're not dead, are you?"

"No," Len says after a moment's thought. "I don't think so."

"Where have you been?"

"I just kind of left everything behind and rented places all over town. It was pretty screwed up for a while there."

"It was."

"They got him now though."

"Yeah. They got him."

He sighs into the receiver. A wet-lipped whistle that tells me that until I just confirmed it for him, Len wasn't sure if it was over or not.

"You know what's funny?" he goes on. "I was about to say that maybe I can go home now, but I don't have a clue where that is. My old landlord threw all my books and comics out at my old place."

"You can always start again."

"Start what?"

"Collecting."

"Yeah. Sure."

In the background, someone smashes what sounds like a shot glass against the wall.

"Busy night down there?"

"It's okay," Len says nervously. "Hey, you doing anything right now?"

"I was getting ready for bed, actually."

"Is it that late? I was going to ask if you wanted to come out and meet me. To celebrate."

"Not tonight."

"Another time."

This seems to be it. But Len lingers, the loneliness travelling down the line like an invisible weight.

"I guess we're the only ones left," he says finally.

"What about Angela?"

"You think she could still be alive?"

"No."

"Neither do I."

"Well, here's to us, Len. To the living."

"To the living," Len says, sounding less than certain about who that might be.

The other phantom of August isn't dead either, but might as well be.

I see him walking back from the corner store one afternoon, Sam gripping my thumb with one hand, and screwing a popsicle into his mouth with the other.

A father and son holding hands on a neighbourhood street in summertime. One version of freedom.

We're passing by the punky hair salon on the corner—the place where Ronald Pevencey once cut and coloured—when a black panel van pulls over against the curb twenty feet ahead of us. Although this part of Queen Street has delivery trucks stopping and starting outside throughout the day, something about it draws my attention. Not any detail, but its utter *lack* of detail: no business name painted on the doors, no stickers, no rear licence plate. Even the black paint is of an age that has dulled its finish to an old chalkboard.

I slow our pace as the distance between us and the van shrinks to a couple of strides. Neither driver nor passenger doors have opened, and the angle of the side mirrors doesn't let me see who sits up front. But it's the back of the van that radiates trouble. The two rear windows webbed with dust, along with streaks of something else. Dried smears running from the top of the glass to the bottom. Rain. Or solvent rubbed off of work gloves. Or bare hands split open in an effort to scratch through the glass.

"Why are we stopping, Dad?"

I'm thinking of an answer—*It's such a nice day, I just want to turn around and go home the long way*—when I see him. William's face against the van's back window.

I pull Sam against me. His popsicle drops to the sidewalk.

Nobody sees William but me.

And even *I'm* not seeing William. He's in a solitary

confinement cell somewhere, awaiting sentencing. Because there will be no trial. Not now. Not after he pleaded guilty and agreed to sign a written confession just days ago. All that's left to be determined is how many consecutive life sentences he will serve.

So it's not William whose lips are stretched into an oval, his tongue pressed white against the glass in a silent scream. But this doesn't stop me from scuffling backwards to slam my shoulders against the hair salon windows.

This is what terrifies me about the van: not William, but what horrors have taken place within it. The sort of things that would frighten even William. And there's his face to prove it. Never before showing anything but veiled threat—coal-eyed, beard-shrouded—yet now stretched with panic.

The van spews exhaust. When it clears, William isn't there. But the wet circle his tongue cleared on the glass still is. Was there to begin with.

With a lurch, the van re-enters the lane of moving traffic. A half-block on, it makes a turn and is gone.

Sam kicks the melted pool of popsicle goo against the wall. Takes my hand to lead me home. He doesn't ask what I think I saw. He doesn't have to. As with the bad man who lives in the bedroom closet, if you can just hold on to what you know is real, he can't hurt you.

29

The summer ends with a string of identically perfect days, as though in apology for its earlier abuses. A lulling, blue-skied week of becalmed downtown traffic and evenings of clear air flavoured by barbecue smoke. All the uncertainties and worries of what has come before—not just for the especially beleaguered Rushes, but for all who wander, grinning, down the city's streets—are put into more manageable perspectives. Everyone wishing for this to go on forever.

And then, abruptly, it's Labour Day weekend. Overnight, there's an autumnal coolness in the air, the leaves trade half their green for gold. *Now's the time.* The chalky taste of Back to School days tells us this. *If there's something fun you've been meaning to get around to, do it now.*

It's how Sam and I decide to go to the Mustang Drive-in dusk-'til-dawn. The last show of the season at a place Tamara and I used to make the trip to, sneaking in a bottle of white wine under the seat and making out like teenagers. For Sam, the attraction is seeing what he, despite my repeated corrections, calls "My dad's movie."

"North," Sam says, his nose to the glass, as I turn off the concession road and join the line of traffic inching toward the admission booth.

I didn't know my son could tell directions from the stars.

"Look," I tell him, pointing to the back of the screen up the slope. The cowboy riding the bucking bronco atop the marquee, the fields of harvest corn beyond. Sam reads aloud the lettering announcing tonight's feature presentation.

"*The Sandman*," he says.

I've already seen it. Sam may not be old enough to handle some of the more "mature" subject matter (this is the opinion of the censor board, whose rating fussily warns of "Violence, and Suggestions of Improper Sexual Interest"). But if the guy in the ticket booth is prepared to take my money for two adults, then for tonight, that's what we are.

We park off to the side in front of the concession stand, haul folding chairs out of the Toyota's trunk. Throw a sleeping bag over our knees to guard against the chill.

Although *The Sandman* is based on my novel, my involvement in its being made has been limited to the guilty acceptance of a production-fee cheque. I was invited to the premiere in Los Angeles a couple weeks ago but declined. The studio publicists called to plead their case that my non-attendance might be misconstrued as my having "creative reservations about the project." I assured them I had no creativity with which to hold reservations. In return for my assurance of silence, they sent me champagne and an advance copy of the DVD.

Just the other day I popped it in, uncorked the bubbly, and for the next hour and a half sat myself down in the Crypt and drank straight from the bottle. It wasn't bad. The champagne, I mean. As for the movie, I suppose it possesses a certain propulsiveness, fuelled mainly by chop-chop editing and a techno soundtrack that makes the city in which the film was shot (Toronto, as a matter of fact, though Toronto as intended to look like New York) feel jacked on meth.

What's funny about the movie, what slightly bothers me about it, isn't its quality one way or the other, but how divergent it is from the real thing. From Angela. Her voice. That's what is utterly missing from the Hollywood version, through no fault of its screenwriters and actors and producers. How could they know what it was like to sit in Conrad White's candlelit apartment, the snow scratching at the windows, and listen to Angela reading from the doodle-margined pages of her journal? Even if they *had* been there, would it have changed anything? A movie tells a story, but its world is static. Every set and gesture and image carefully determined, the narrative hermetically sealed. A movie doesn't let you create what you see within yourself. But that's what Angela's voice did. It invited you inside.

"It's starting!" Sam announces as the floodlights cut out.

The rest you know.

You know from where all this started, deep in the middle of things. The story of the Man Who Lost His Son at the Movies. I say "lost" because that's how the police and newspapers referred to it, as though Sam was a dropped wallet. The media releases are careful to point out that no evidence of foul play was found at the scene. I don't know whether they said this as a matter of general policy or whether they simply didn't accept my account of chasing a shadow through the corn rows.

You already know how this Labour Day turns out for me. But when you start in the middle, there are certain angles that are left out, shades of meaning that wouldn't have made sense the first time around. Consider, for instance, the troubling effect that watching *The Sandman* on a towering screen under the night's stars had on me. How something in the oversized action tried to tell me to *Take your son and leave.* Tried to warn me.

What are you talking about?

The thing that lives under your bed. The eyes in your closet at night, watching you. The dark. Whatever frightens you the most . . .

I can only watch the screen for a few seconds at a time. The actors delivering their lines directly to me, their faces looking down with ironic masks of "fear," "determination," "worry." I was wrong about movies being fixed worlds. *These* characters, the action on *this* screen—all of it wants *out*.

"You want anything?" I ask Sam. "Tater tots?"

And he takes my hand. Lets it go only when the cashier takes too long to ring us in.

Then I'm running between the lines of parked cars, trying to tell myself what I know is happening isn't happening. It doesn't work. Because the Sandman is *here*. Not William, who is miles away, sitting in a cell. Not Ramsay. Not Len or Conrad White. Not Raymond Mull.

It's the Sandman who runs into the corn field, letting me catch a glimpse of him so I can follow. This is what he wanted me to do. It gave him the time he needed to disappear, to ensure I was headed in the opposite direction from where Sam was being kept in the trunk of one of the back row cars. Or maybe my son was in the car next to mine the whole time.

I was chasing the Sandman. But he never had Sam to begin with.

By the time I reach the abandoned farmhouse on the far side of the field it's over. I can only stand there, staring back at the Mustang's screen in the distance.

The terrible man who does terrible things isn't William. It isn't even a man. It's a girl. The one whose face is on the drive-in screen, the one who read from her journal in Conrad White's apartment, the one with toes missing from frostbite. A girl who has grown up to assume different names. Steal different lives.

My mistake was to assume that the villain of my story was the same as the villain in hers. But the monster who has taken the only thing left to me isn't the Sandman. It's the one who created him.

Part Four

The Terrible Man
Who Does Terrible Things

30

There is a search. You can imagine. A father loses his son at the movies, the boy snatched away in the time it takes to buy hot dogs and onion rings—it's a summer weekend news editor's dream come true. In the early morning of that Sunday—before the dawn of the cancelled dusk-'til-dawn—one of the networks awakens a "missing person expert" and tapes an interview in which we are reminded that "The first twelve hours are crucial in cases of this kind." Even the police supervisors behind the microphones at the first news conference of the day aren't immune to the excitement of a race against time, especially where there's a kid involved. It's like something on TV. It is on TV.

Look: there's the Chief of the OPP staring directly into the cameras and vowing to put all available resources into locating "little Sam," and until they do, "I can tell you there won't be sleep for any of us." There's the shots of local volunteers marching through the Mustang's neighbouring fields of corn, searching for clues, for body parts. And there's the father, his skin speckled and spongy as oatmeal, robotically pleading for his boy's safe return. *So*, thinks the readership of the Couch Potato, *that's what a novelist looks like.*

He looks suspicious. Even to me. An unconvincing performance of parental concern—not enough panic, the voice emptied, as though he's already made the turn toward grief. I watch a repeated loop of myself on the all-news channel down in the Crypt in disbelief. That's not how I *feel*. That's not even me. Here: this fellow sobbing into his hands, throwing a rock glass against the panelled wall to avoid pouring anything into it, and a minute later cutting his feet on the shards when he gets up to check with the police for the fifth time this hour. I'm your man.

It appears the police might think so too. They're coming around to "go over things" again, and though they once more offer the services of a "family crisis counsellor," I can tell their initial sympathy is already starting to dry up. There are fewer questions about the figure I'd seen at the back of the drive-in's lot, and more about my emotional condition over the last few years. First, there was the loss of my wife to cancer. Then the messy business of the William Feld murders, which, as one investigator puts it, "We had you on the longlist for the whole kaboodle." Plus all the other layers: my son taken at the screening of a movie based on my own book, a book in which a shadowy figure takes the lives of children. "I mean, you can't *write* that kind of stuff," another cop tells me, shaking his head. "But then again, you did."

By Sunday evening, they're suggesting I call a lawyer. When I tell them there's no need, they look at me as though that's just the sort of thing a guilty bastard would say. Out there in the night a search for my son is still under way, but in here, at the father's house on Euclid Street, they've already found the guy they're looking for, and all there's left to do is wait for him to break. In time, the ones like me always do.

With my permission, they're listening in on every phone call. They say it's in case a ransom demand comes in, but I can tell it's more likely evidence collection. A message from an accomplice. A midnight confession.

And I don't blame them. In such cases, the parent is always the prime suspect. Statistically speaking, shadows are merely shadows. Harm tends to come from the ones you know best.

There are always exceptions, however. There's always a Sandman. And when he strikes, don't be surprised when you're the only one who believes it was him.

For the first twenty-four hours, there isn't time to suffer. There's only the same answers to the same questions, showing complete strangers where everything's kept around the house, letting a nice woman straighten your collar and wipe toothpaste from the corner of your mouth before the press conference.

In the end, however, these distractions only make everything worse. In my case this comes on day two, upon awakening from a sleeping-pill nap and collapsing to the bedroom floor—one pant leg on, the other off—under the weight of facts. *Struck by the truth*. I'd never realized how literally this cliché could be taken. It's the truth that leaves me splayed out over the hardwood, blinking at the dust bunnies under the bed, both hands reaching around to the back of my skull to check for blood.

Sam is gone.

They're not going to find him.

I'm the only one who stands a chance of getting him back.

If it weren't for this last thought I'm not at all sure if, an hour later, I would have been able to finish getting dressed. A good thing, seeing as there is the press to be dealt with. Take a peek out the curtains: a pair of TV news vans, their hairsprayed correspondents practicing their serious faces, along with a gaggle of beat writers from the papers, sharing dirty jokes and flicking cigarette butts into my neighbour's garden. If life is to be carried on with—even whatever brittle simulation of a life that might be available to me—they will all have to be satisfied enough to leave me alone at least until their next deadline.

I decide the best way to proceed is to grant an exclusive. It's a reflex that prompts me to choose the *National Star*. And who does the police's media relations person bring in but the kid from Swift Current.

"So you're in hard news now?" I ask him, and despite the wilfully clenched jaw, he allows a grin at my recognizing him.

"No future in arts."

"You're right there."

"Guess they promoted me."

"The Editor-in-Chief knows talent when she sees it."

"This must be a very difficult time," he starts. It's how all of them start. The cops, the counsellors, the well-wishers, the hacks. Thank God for TV.

I follow with some televisual dialogue of my own. About remaining optimistic, asking whoever might know something about my son to come forward. Then the Swift Current kid asks the inevitable follow-up.

"What do you make of the overlap between all this and your novel?"

"I don't make anything of it."

"But isn't it striking how –"

"We're done."

"Sorry?"

I reach over and click off his recorder. "Interview's over. And remind the other vultures outside that you're the only one to get any roadkill today."

It works. Within a couple of hours, the vans have cleared off along with the shivering journos who will be forced to quote from the *National Star*'s piece if they want any comment from Patrick Rush. Even the police have honoured my request for a little privacy. They send over a social worker to sit vigil just in case Sam walks in the door. It allows me to go out.

I head up to Dundas Street and turn east on to the ever-lengthening tentacle of Chinatown. Before I know it was where I was headed I end up outside The Fukhouse. Anarchists. Evelyn told me this is where they met on the night I first saw her. Now it makes me wonder: *Can anarchists hold meetings and still be anarchists?* Then again, if the lawless can't be flexible with the rules, who can?

A light goes on in Conrad White's old apartment. Behind the gauzy curtains a pair of shadows move about in what is likely some domestic chore but, from out here, appears as a ballroom dance. The two figures circling, holding hands for a moment before casting off to the opposite sides of the room.

The bulb flicks off. The room lit for so short a time I doubt the shadows were ever there at all. More ghosts. Evelyn and Conrad glimpsed in an afterlife waltz.

But I'm still alive. My son too. He has to be. There's no point in seeing ghosts any more. They have nothing to tell me other than what has come before. All that remains for the living is to pick up the mystery where the dead left off.

"So this really is your local," a voice behind me declares. I turn to find Ramsay grinning at me through The Fukhouse's gloom. "Would have pegged you for something a bit more tweedy."

"The drinks are cheap."

"They ought to be," he says, surveying the room. "Let me buy you one?"

"Buy me two."

Ramsay orders bourbon with beer chasers. We get the former inside us as soon as they arrive.

"Just dropped by your house," he says.

"And I wasn't there."

"Went out for a stroll, did you?"

"You would know. You followed me here."

"I'm a cop," Ramsay shrugs. "Old habits."

We sit looking straight ahead for a time. Our heads floating in the greasy mirror behind the gins, whiskies and rums.

"A terrible thing," Ramsay says finally. "Your boy."

I try to measure the sincerity in his voice, the regretful shake of his head. Seems real to me. Then again, I've gotten Ramsay wrong before. I may have never gotten him right.

"I'm told your best men are on the case," I say.

"Then I'm sure they'll find him."

"I feel like I should be helping them look."

"Why aren't you?"

"They told me to stay at home."

"That's a hard order to follow if you think he's out there."

"I know he is."

"You *know*?"

"Sam is alive. And I'm going to be the one who finds him."

"Sounds like you're on to something."

"If I was, would I tell you?"

"You might. If you wanted to be clear."

"Clear?"

"A show of goodwill. Without it, people can start down wrong paths."

He had me. For a second, I thought now that Ramsay had William in his cell, there was a chance he would actually be sympathetic with a father who'd lost his boy. But suspicion is Ramsay's default position. It's where he lives.

"I would never hurt Sam."

"Nobody says you have."

"Nobody has *said* so, no. So if they're not being honest with me, why should I be honest with them?"

"Like I said. You could make this clear."

"It's clear enough for me."

I start toward the exit. A bit off balance from the bourbon, the rush that comes with the speaking of privately held revelations. But when Ramsay opens his mouth to say something as I go, I'm still able to beat him to it.

"You've found your Sandman," I shout as both palms slap the door wide open. "Now it's my turn."

Ramsay may still be following me, but I don't care. I'm not doing anything wrong. Only walking. And whispering questions out loud. Questions that, over a long night's wander east, lead me out of the fog of shock.

First up is how whoever took Sam knew we were planning to be at the Mustang on that particular night. As far as I can recall, I hadn't spoken of it to anyone. Had Sam? Perhaps. An overheard playground boast ("My dad's taking me to see *his* movie tonight!"), or something let slip to his friend Joseph. Still, these are unlikely scenarios, as Sam doesn't usually gossip with his gang of kids at the park, none of them do, all of them boys of an age where their primary communication is the role play of machine-gunning soldiers or robots with laser beams firing out from their eye sockets.

The far greater probability is that we were followed.

A black van. Changing lanes to keep me in view as we headed out of the city.

So why not take this to the police? I've come close to telling them about Angela a couple of times, but held back for reasons both rational and intuitive. On the rational side, I have no proof that it was her. More than this, "Angela" is dead. I've got Petra's disposal to keep hidden. And I'm currently the prime suspect in Sam's disappearance. Now that I think of it, Angela likely had something on everyone in the circle that they didn't want out in the open. It's how she's kept under the radar all along.

But what really prevents me from mentioning her name is the gut certainty that I'm not *meant* to. If Angela—or whoever it is who has my son—gets the idea that I'm telling the police everything I know, it's over. The only way to Sam is through following the story to the end.

Before I know it the sun is plucking stars from the sky. I've made it all the way out to the Beaches, turned down one of its side streets to the boardwalk. No one out but the few pre-dawn joggers and picnic-table snoozers, the lonely and haunted like me. With shoes off, the sand is cool under my feet. Yet when I step into the first timid waves the water is body temperature, having been simmered over the course of a heatwaved summer. It may never freeze again.

Something touches my hand—a fly, a candy wrapper lifted from the beach on a gust of wind—and I look down expecting Sam to be there. The fact that he is missing is always at the front of my mind, and yet the illusion of his presence comes to me several times every waking hour. He's not here. But he *should* be. Taking my hand and stepping out into the water. Asking if he can go all the way in. Telling me not to be afraid.

The morning brings an ugly specificity to the flatscreen billboards and construction cranes to the west. It turns my eyes back out over the water. But the lake is just as likely an industrial product, its surface wrinkly and thin as aluminum foil.

Here's what I'm thinking as I start back: there is nowhere to go any more that has not been modified, re-invented, enhanced. Places don't *exist* as they once did, simply and convincingly. Virtual reality is the only reality left.

And so what? If I can just have Sam back, the rest of the world can keep its recycled myths, its well-crafted fakery. I don't need anything to be real any more. I just need him.

31

To find Sam, I have to find Angela. But to search for someone who doesn't exist: not the best task for an out-of-work TV critic. So what would Tim Earheart or Ramsay do in my shoes? Start with what's on the table. Not much. There's Angela's name (false), her age (within a decade range), her published work (lifted from others' autobiographical accounts). There's also what I know of her appearance (especially susceptible to the whimsies of shadow and light, so that she was one thing reading from her journal on the opposite side of Conrad White's rug, and another the night she cupped her hands over my ears to muffle the sounds she made in her bed, as though it was me and not her neighbours she needed to save from distraction). For someone who has come to play such a cruelly important role in my life, Angela has done all the taking and in return left next to nothing of herself behind.

One thread I still have of hers takes me to the condo where, eighteen floors above, I had seen and touched parts of her that now, in recollection, fall in favour of the argument that Angela has never been anything but a creation of fantasy. My effort to return my hands to her skin renders only the most generic impression, a softcore going through the motions. The naked Angela comes to me now from too great a distance, implausibly flawless and blue-lit.

If this is the case—if I never was with Angela on what I thought was our only night together—then perhaps Angela isn't to blame. Perhaps *I'm* the psychotic. There *is* no Angela because there never *was* an Angela. Which would mean she isn't the one who has done something terrible to Sam. I am.

Only the building's superintendent throwing me against the wall puts these dark considerations aside.

"You," the man says. The same one who'd given me the heave-ho the last time. Now, however, he's giving me the clinical stare of a physician checking for signs of jaundice. "Tell me. Just between us. Whisper it in my ear if you'd like."

"Yes?"

"What is your *problem*?"

"I'm looking for someone."

"You've found him."

"Not you. A tenant."

"They're not tenants when they own the unit."

"What are they then?"

"They're *unit owners*."

"I'm looking for a unit owner."

"Buzz them."

"They're not here. Or not answering."

"If I'd known it was you down here, I wouldn't have answered either."

His hands have loosened their grip on his belt. It's his calmness that makes it certain he's going to hit me. In my experience, there's always a moment before taking a shot to the face when you see it coming, but don't quite believe it. *Here it comes*, you think. Then *No, he wouldn't*. And then he does.

"She has my son."

The super looks down at me over pockmarked cheeks. "Divorce?"

"Something like that."

"Call your lawyer like everyone else."

"It's not a lawyer kind of thing. If you know what I mean."

Apparently he does. One fist returns to his side, and the other fishes in his pockets for his keys.

"I'll tell you what the building's records show," he says, ushering me through the lobby and into a small office where the Christmas tree is stored. "But I see you in here again and I'll stuff you down the garbage chute."

I tell the super to look up the account under the name Pam Turgenov.

"Thought you said her name was Angela."

"She lies."

"Most of them do."

He pulls up the file on Angela/Pam's financial status with the condominium corporation. The mortgage and purchase agreement solely under Pam Turgenov's name, though the account has recently come under arrears. Unit 1808 hasn't paid its maintenance fee for three months, and the bank has frozen the accounts.

"We're looking for this one," the super says. "But from what I can tell, she hasn't been here for a while. Not since the break-in."

"There was a burglary?"

"Took some crap jewelry, personal stuff. But left the TV."

Personal stuff. Like Petra's Yankees cap. So it could find its way to my house.

"I'm changing the locks this week," the super says.

"It won't matter. She's not coming back."

"All her junk is still up there."

"Trust me."

"But she's got your kid."

"I'll find her."

I must sound convincing. The super gives me a soldierly nod. "When you speak to her," he says as he walks me to the door, "tell her I'm keeping the TV."

From the condo I walk straight up Bay Street toward the gold and silver office towers on the far side of the rail tracks. It takes a while. I'm occupied with working through what shouldn't come as a surprise, but has nevertheless: Angela not only failed to report to the authorities that it was Evelyn behind the wheel of the car she drove into a cliffside with Conrad White, but she likely had a hand in bringing about the crash in the first place. It was Angela who lured them north with breadcrumb clues. More than this, she must have been there. To make sure the job was done. And to replace Evelyn's purse with her own.

This is how Angela managed to live so completely off the grid: she made herself disappear *and* become someone else. And when the debts started to come due under Pam Turgenov's increasingly bad name she was gone again.

There's more support for this suspicion at the offices of the law firm where Angela claimed to work as a legal secretary. This time, I assume a cover—her jilted lover, which I suppose I am, among other things. It buys me enough sympathy with the girl at reception to find out that there was a Pam Turgenov working there for a time, not as a legal secretary but as a temp.

"Never got to really know her," the receptionist says sadly, as though this was her life's main regret. "Always had her nose in a book. Like, *Stay away, I'm into this.*"

"Do you remember what she was reading?"

The receptionist looks at her nails for an answer. "Actually, now that I think of it, she wasn't reading. She was *writing*."

"How long ago did she leave?"

"A while. Like, *months*. She was probably only here for a couple weeks."

"Do you know where she went after she left? Another firm maybe?"

"It's why they're called temps." The receptionist shrugs. "They come and go."

When I give her the flowers I'd brought with me ("Is Pam here today? I have something for her birthday.") I'm rewarded with a blushing thank you.

"If I happen to bump into her, who can I say came calling?" she asks as I start toward the elevators.

"Try Conrad. Or Len. Or Ivan."

It's only as the elevator doors are almost closed that the receptionist raises her narrowing eyes from writing each of these names down.

Dusk. That pinkish light over the city that is the occasionally beautiful by-product of pollution. The chill that comes within seconds of the sun dropping behind the rooftops. I'm headed east for no good reason. Or no better reason than to avoid what I know awaits me at home: messages from the police reporting how they haven't come up with anything yet. Maybe even the kid from the *National Star* camped out in my yard, a copy of *The Sandman* in his knapsack, the pages furry with Post-It Notes. Better to keep drifting through the darkening streets than face that.

Yet it's at this time of day, in this kind of light, that you see things. Twilight illusions.

Like the black van that slowly drives past me. A shadow behind the wheel. The outlined head and gloved hands that belong to whatever I chased into the corn rows at the Mustang.

As I start after it—noting again how the model name has been removed from the rear doors, a caking of dried mud obscuring the licence plate—the van picks up speed and chugs around the next corner.

I cross blind against the traffic. A station wagon screeches to a stop. Kisses its grille to my hip. The contact sends me spinning against a panel truck, but my feet continue to slap the pavement, righting my course on the sidewalk. There is honking and *Hey! Hey!*s behind me but I take the same corner the van took and all sound is gulped away. A man my age and in my shape can't run like this more than a hundred yards without his breathing becoming the only thing he can hear. And his heart. His untested heart.

The van is gone. I keep running.

And then he's there.

Up ahead, the shadow slides along the walls. Takes another turn into the grounds of the old Gooderham & Worts distillery. A few clustered blocks of Dickens' London shoehorned between the expressway and condo construction sites. Long, Victorian brick barracks with smokestacks at their ends like exclamation points.

The past slows me down. It's the cobblestone streets that turn anything faster than a walk into a tiptoed dance. During daylight hours, the doors on either side open into galleries and cafés, but they are locked now. No one else in the pedestrian-only lanes but me and the one who's led me here.

And there he is. Slipping into a narrow alley. But slowly. As though waiting for me to catch up.

There are no lights between two of the vacant buildings, so that all I can see of the figure ahead is the rise and fall of its head against the dim brick. And then he stops altogether.

A bit further, the body language of his cocked head says. *You're almost there.*

I come at him in what I intend as a rush, but there is little rush left in me. When I reach the point where he'd been standing I nearly trip over something on the ground. Heavy but with a liquid give. A bag of sand.

It gives him more than enough time. The black van is waiting for him in the parking lot. The extinguished brake lights turning my raised hands from red to pink as it shifts into drive and slides away.

Starting back, I nearly fall over the bag of sand a second time. Except now I have the time to see that it isn't a bag of sand at all.

A body, more or less. No: less.

Propped against the wall like a sleeping drunk. *Legless*. Also armless, noseless, eyeless. A man dissembled into disparate parts laid out over the cobblestones. A human anthology.

It makes me grateful for the dark. Still, I can see enough. And what I can't see my mind fills in with what it remembers from the night in the shed with Petra.

Time to go. Someone else will discover this by morning. There is nothing to be gained by lingering here aside from being seen.

And yet I stay where I am a minute longer. Partly because all the air has been sucked out of the world. Partly because the man scattered at my feet was once a friend.

We were the last ones. This is how I know it's Len even before I use the toe of my shoe to open the wallet next to the body's cupped hand and squint to read his name on the driver's licence inside. If you didn't know what I know, there would be no way of connecting the grinning face in the wallet's ID to his corpse—there is no identity left in him, all of the features that mark someone for who they are cut away. This has likely been Angela's lesson all along: you take a person's story and what remains is nothing more than skin and blood. The body is worthless. What counts is what it does. The lies and truths it tells.

I'm on the news in the morning. Once again they've used my taped statement from the first day of Sam's disappearance. Since then, I have continued to refuse the cameras, as it isn't doing me any favours on the suspicion front. Not to mention that pleading for Sam's safe return isn't going to make any impact on the person I know has him now.

A couple of the investigators come by to give me an update on the search efforts, but their eyes now openly betray their doubts. In the name of thoroughness they ask again if I've told them everything. Even after I repeat the same details, they wait for me to go on. *It's alright*, their seen-it-all faces urge me. *Just tell us what you did. We won't judge you.*

I start packing the moment the door closes behind them.

Before I go, I put in a call to Tim Earheart at a payphone around the corner. It strikes me that he's the only person in the world I have to say goodbye to. But I'm denied even this. He's not home, so I'm left to stutter some nonsense into his answering machine. All I remember is attempting a joke ("You know you don't get out enough when you've only got one name on your speed dial") and asking him to "Look out for Sam if I—if it turns out Sam needs looking out for." The kind of tight-throated message you wish you could erase as soon as you put the receiver down.

I stop off at home one last time after that, trying to think of anything else that needs to be accounted for. I look at the rows of children's books Sam is too old to read any more and think *A father and son used to live here.* But that past tense takes all the life out of it. People used to live in every empty house you've ever stood in, and this makes them no less empty.

32

Whitley, Ontario, is one of the stubborn towns along the two lanes that ride the hump of Lake Superior. Today it is known, to the extent it is known at all, as a stop to fill the tank or, perhaps, find a damp-smelling motel room to sit out a snowstorm. A half-day's drive past the last cottages anyone is willing to drive to, this is the land most can locate only through the abstract—on maps or in the imagination. A door that opens on to one of the last Nothings on the planet.

It's a drive that tortures the Toyota's four cylinders. North of the Soo, the Trans-Canada loses its nerve, coiling into endless aversions to every swamp, hillock and inlet, so that the four hundred miles to Thunder Bay requires an athletic slapping of wheel and stomping of brake. But it's not the wheezing ascents that are so troubling, it's the freefalls that follow, sending the car shuddering helplessly cliffward every five minutes, and each time the turn is made—with a yank at the gearshift and a whispered *Shit, oh shit*—it's a close call.

Not that the driver behind me has the same problems.

Over the afternoon's last hours of light, on the rare straightaways, I glimpse a black sedan in the distance. It could be the Continental I spotted on the way to my visit to Sam in St. Catharines. Every time I slow to get a better look, it must slow as well, or pull off to the side altogether—I never catch sight of it unless I'm moving. Later, when the dark forest leans over the road to block out any hint of a slivered moon, it's still there. Winks of headlight.

It was on this road, coming into one of these curves, that Evelyn and Conrad White met their end. And it was probably a car following them like the one following me that forced them into the turn too fast. It may have been the very same Continental. The same driver.

Whoever is behind the wheel doesn't seem to want me dead just yet, in any case. They want to see that I'm going in the right direction. Up here, there are only two choices: forward or back. One of which is no choice at all.

I roll into Whitley some time after midnight. The town itself sits behind a stand of trees, hidden from the highway as though ashamed of itself. A bowling alley. Two "Pre-Owned!" car lots. A tavern with squares of plywood where the windows used to be. Nothing appears to be open. Even the streetlights have been turned off for the night. Or were never turned on.

The TV in the Sportsman Motel's office is working just fine, however. It's how I decide on it over the competition: the sad glow that signals there may be someone else awake in Whitley aside from me. (When was the last time, I wonder, that the manager had to flick on the NO in front of VACANCY on the sign featuring a hunter with a rifle in one hand and a dead goose in the other?)

The guy behind the desk is watching *Canadian MegaStar!* Shaking his head at a girl from Saskatoon mangling a Barry Manilow tune.

"Can you *believe* these people?" he says, handing over the room keys without taking his eyes off the screen. "What are they *thinking*?"

"They want to be famous."

"Oh, this one here's going to be famous, alright. Famous for having a fat ass and a voice like a choked chicken."

He shakes his head at the TV, snorts, folds his arms over his chest, makes his chair squeak. But he doesn't turn the channel.

The room smells of rum and used rubbers. I pour the shampoo from one of the bathroom's little bottles on to the carpet to freshen things up. I'm lathering the floor with my shoes when I think I spot the Continental slide past through the window.

It's already reversing by the time I get the door open. Outside, the cold is a fist to the chest. It holds me there, my breath a grey halo over my head. Not that there would be any point in running after the car, now accelerating back toward the highway.

Whether it was him in the car or not, I know he's here. There is a taste that comes with the Sandman's presence that I'm spitting on to the Sportsman's pavement. He's *here*. Which means that Angela is too.

Aside from what remains of yesterday's donut batch at
the Hugga Mugga, the only breakfast in Whitley is to be
found at the Lucky Seven Chinese BBQ. The eggs taste
of egg rolls, the toast of won ton, but I'm hungry enough
to get it down. And when I look up from my plate, Sam
is sitting across from me. Looking worried. Not for
himself, but for me.

*You're not a ghost. This is just me missing you. You're
alive.*

"More coffee?"

I raise my eyes to the waitress. When I look again,
Sam's chair is empty.

On the sidewalk, I peer down Whitley's main street
and imagine Angela's father walking its length, searching
for her. Just as I am. Raymond Mull is my sole connection to whatever traces she left behind here. What I need
is to find the farm where he came to visit her, and to do
that, I'll have to find Edra, Angela's foster mother. And
if her surname was Stark in her journal, chances are she
went by something else in the real world.

I decide to start at the offices of the *Whitley Register*.
Although the sign on the door says they open at nine,
the place remains locked at a quarter to ten, which forces
me to sit on the front steps wishing I'd bought cigarettes
at the Lucky Seven. Faces in passing pick-ups openly
stare as they pass. I pretend not to notice. Pull the collar
up on my overcoat against the stiffening breeze.

Autumn is a month further along up here, so that the
trees have already surrendered their colours. A back-to-
school litter clogs the storm drains: orange leaves and

Red Bull cans. Garbage soon to be buried by snow only to emerge, fermented and soft, in the spring. Just as Jacob Stark's body had shown itself after he'd taken his bootless run into the woods.

When a woman in a plaid hunting jacket pulls up I wonder if she's going to ask me to leave. There is a down-turn to her mouth and thickness in her shoulders that suggests expertise at this sort of thing. But when she stands with her hands on her hips and inquires as to what she can do for me, I end up coming right out with it.

"I'm doing some research. Hoping you could help."

"Research? Into what? The history of the Whitley Whippers?"

"Sorry?"

"You're speaking to the *Register*'s sports editor, not the archivist. If we *had* an archivist."

"Maybe there's someone in news I could speak to?"

"I'm news too. And entertainment, business, garden-ing tips. Some ad sales thrown in when I have the time."

She extends a gloved hand, and I at first shake it, then use it to help pull me to my feet.

"Patrick Rush," I say.

"Jane Tanner. *Acting* Editor-in-Chief. The *real* editor having passed on."

"Sorry to hear that."

"Don't be. It was three years ago. And he was a foul son of a bitch."

Jane Tanner opens the door and lets me in. Offers me coffee from a pot that's been left to stew on its hot plate overnight.

"So what would you be researching in Whitley? I'm thinking mines or crime."

"Why would you say that?"

"That's all we've got up here. A few bad people and some holes in the ground."

"Well you're right, as a matter of fact. I'm looking into the Raymond Mull killings of a few years ago."

Jane Tanner lowers her mug. "Eighteen years."

"I was wondering if I could go through the papers from that time. Your back issues aren't available online yet."

"Yet. I like that. *Yet.*"

I'm expecting questions—a stranger shows up asking about the worst thing to ever happen in a neither-here-nor-there town—but Jane Tanner just shows me down into the earth-walled basement where mouldering stacks of *Register*s threaten to bury anyone who gets too close.

"Have fun," she says, and starts back up the stairs.

Eighteen years. I start sorting through the papers at the garden tools and work back toward the broken typewriters. The issues from autumn 1989 are to be found next to the furnace, so that I have to dig out copies while being careful not to burn myself. When I've collected an armload, I clear the rat droppings from an empty milk crate, sit down and start reading.

He was here alright. Over Raymond Mull's child-stealing spree the *Whitley Register* was a weekly memorial issue, with grieving family members and news of the unsuccessful police investigation, along with outraged editorials calling for the return of the death penalty. But it's the smiling school photos of the victims that make what he did unthinkable. Laney Pelle first. Then Tess Warner. And finally Ursula Lyle, the one they never found because, if Angela's journal is to be believed, she did such a good job burying her in the Stark farm's woods.

After they caught him at a roadside motel twenty miles north and discovered—as they'd discovered at William's—the pickaxes and hacksaws and gloves, Raymond Mull had nothing to say. The one picture of him in the *Register* shows a man in the grey work pants and matching zip-up jacket of a mechanic, eyes lifeless but with an uncertain grin on his face, as though surprised to find he was the only one to see the dry humour in all this.

I track back over the weeks prior to Mull's arrest, searching for stories of Jacob Stark's mysterious death and his traumatized adopted daughter found nearly frozen to death in the barn, but when I do find mention of the incident, there are notable distinctions from the account in Angela's journal. The name, for one thing. Jacob Stark was actually David Percy. And while his body was found under the unusual circumstances Angela described—buried in the first blizzard of the season, the flesh slashed and torn by a frenzied run into the trees— there is no Angela, no daughter, no girl who refused to share her secret. Along with something else. David Percy was legally blind.

Among the other missing pieces in the *Register* is the specific location of the Percy farm. In fact, it isn't described as a farm at all, only the "Percy residence outside Whitley". No good checking the phone book now, either. Marion (not Edra) Percy would almost certainly be dead now too. There's no way of knowing who currently lives on that property, if anyone.

I drop the last *Register* on to the pile and think *Maybe this is it*. Maybe this is where it ends, in a cobwebbed basement with a man wiping his eyes at his flawed instincts and stupid mistakes.

Sam isn't here. He never was. And in the time I've wasted, she could be anywhere. With him.

This very moment may have been Angela's punchline all along: to make me think that all would be answered in Whitley, only to find that she had never lived here, never buried another girl her age, never been beckoned by the Sandman from her window. It was a story, nothing more.

"Sorry to say so," Jane Tanner says, appearing at the bottom of the stairs, "but seems to me you found what you were looking for."

"As a matter of fact I didn't."

"I can say with some regret that I've lived here all my life. Maybe I can help you."

"David Percy."

"Thought it was Mull you were researching."

"I had an idea they might be connected."

"You wouldn't have been alone in that. At the time, every missing cat and lost car key was being blamed on Raymond Mull."

"Did he have a child? Percy, I mean."

"There was a girl."

"The Percys'?"

"Adopted. Nobody knew her much because she lived outside town and wasn't here long."

"Why didn't you mention her in the paper?"

"To protect her."

"From what?"

"Whatever had come looking for her."

"So they thought it was Mull who'd driven the old man into the woods."

"Who else? Everyone figured it had to be him."

"And that he wanted Percy's daughter."

"She was the right age. And she'd obviously been through something traumatic."

"Hiding from him. In the barn."

Jane Tanner comes to stand directly under one of the basement's hanging bulbs.

"How do you know that?"

"It was just a story I heard."

"You mean just a story you wrote."

"You read my book?"

"Of course. Journalist turns successful novelist. Lucky bastard. You were one of *us*."

She goes on to ask if I'm here to uncover the truth behind the bits and pieces of the Percy case I'd used for *The Sandman*, and I encourage her misunderstanding as best I can. Tell her I'm working on a magazine article. A behind-the-scenes exploration of where fiction comes from.

"Anything else I can help you with?" she offers, though unconvincingly, her body gesturing for me to lead the way up the stairs.

"Probably not. It looks like I can't go much further than this."

"That's the thing about the past. Most of the time, it doesn't *want* to be known."

I'm about to step around her when Jane Tanner surprises me by putting a hand on my arm.

"Sorry about your boy," she says.

"Thank you."

"He's not why you came to Whitley, is he?"

"I told you why I'm here."

"Yes, you did."

She remains standing in the basement even when I make it to the top of the stairs.

"Guess you've already spoken to her?" she calls up at me.

I turn. *This woman knows Angela?*

"She's *here?*"

"Still alive, as far as I know. Up the road a bit. A nursing home called Spruce Lodge."

"I don't understand."

"Marion Percy. She might be able to tell you how wrong or right the story you heard is."

As is often the case with nursing homes, there is little nursing in evidence among the residents of Spruce Lodge. No one checks me in at the front door, and the halls appear empty of all but a couple wheelchairs and their head-slumped passengers, as though paused midway toward a destination they could no longer put a name to.

Things are even more disheartening in the Recreation

Lounge. Fluorescent tubes ablaze over a dozen or so jigsaw puzzlers and chin tremblers, nothing on the walls but a taped-up notice on how to perform the Heimlich manoeuvre. The only one who notices my entrance is a fellow standing by the water fountain with his arm down his pants. Spotting me, he releases his grip long enough to take his hand out and offer a welcoming wave.

"You belong to someone here?" a nurse asks after I've been standing in the doorway five minutes or more.

"Marion Percy."

"Family?"

"No."

"Then the church must have sent you."

"Is Mrs. Percy here?"

The nurse was just warming up—she looks about as lonely as any other Spruce Lodger—but she can tell I'm not in the mood. She points out a woman sitting on her own next to the room's only window. "That's Maid Marion, right over there."

Who knows how old she is. Marion Percy has reached that post-octogenarian stage of life where any numerical expression of age doesn't do justice to the amazing fact that she is still here, still a blinking, Kleenex-clutching being. A living denial of odds who is at the moment staring out at the tangled woods that surround the rear of Spruce Lodge's lot.

"Mrs. Percy?"

I'm not sure she's heard me at first. It's the turning of her head. A twitch that takes a while to become something more intentional.

"You're new," she says.

"I'm a visitor."

"Not a doctor?"

"No."

"Too bad. They could *use* a new doctor."

She might be smiling. I can see her teeth, anyway.

"I know your daughter," I say, watching for whatever effect this announcement has on her, but nothing changes in her face. A waxy stiffness that might be a reaction in itself.

"Oh?" she says finally.

"We were friends."

"But not any more."

"We haven't seen each other in a while."

"Well she isn't here, if that's what you're thinking."

"*Was* she here?"

The smile—if it was a smile—is gone.

"Are you a policeman?" she says.

"Just a friend."

"So you said."

"I don't mean to pry."

"You haven't. But you're about to, would be my guess."

"I'm here to ask about what happened to your husband."

She looks at me like she hasn't heard what I just said. It forces me to speak again, louder this time.

"His accident."

"Accident?" She reaches out to touch my hand. "Would you *accidentally* run four miles half-naked into a snowstorm?"

Her hand returns to her lap. I step between her and the window. She looks through me anyway. Studying the small square of world outside the window she's come to memorize in such detail she needn't look at it to see it.

"Do you believe he was driven into those woods? Mrs. Percy? Please?"

"I'm old. Why are you asking me this?"

"I know your daughter, ma'am. I was just interested –"

"But this isn't about her. Is it?"

"No."

"Then what?"

"My son."

"Your son?"

"He's missing."

Maybe it's the sound I make trying to sniff back my show of emotion—a reddening, moistening attack that strikes within seconds—but she sits up straight. Her knuckles white and hard as quartz.

"You're looking for *him*."

"Yes."

She nods. Sucks her bottom lip into her mouth. "What were you asking me?"

"Your husband. Have you thought that perhaps he was pursued into the woods?"

"He wouldn't have left her alone like that. Not unless he thought he was trying to save her."

"Angela."

"Your friend," she says, her eyes clouding over. "Our daughter."

Mrs. Percy tells me how in the days before her husband died—and before she went into hospital to have her gallbladder removed—he confessed to hearing voices. David Percy believed someone was coming into the house and tormenting him, nicking him with knife cuts, moving the furniture so that he would trip over it. And a presence he felt, outside but looking in. Waiting. He wondered if he was losing his mind. By the time Marion made it home, her husband was gone. And Angela wasn't talking.

"Do you think it could have been her?"

"Beg pardon?"

"Whatever drove your husband into the woods. Could it have been your daughter?"

The old woman wrinkles her nose. "She was only a child."

"Still, who else could –"

"*Our* child."

Marion Percy may be old, but she is clearly more than able to hold the line. In this case, it's the question of her adopted daughter's involvement in the events of the night that changed everything for her. She has *ideas* of what happened. But that doesn't mean she's about to share them.

"Does she ever come to visit?"

Mrs. Percy squints at me through the smudged lenses of her bifocals. "Who *are* you?"

"My name is Patrick Rush."

"And you say you know our girl?"

"Yes, ma'am. I do."

She nods at this, and I'm expecting her to inquire as to Angela's whereabouts, the events of her intervening years, her health. But she only returns to staring out the window.

"What happened to your farm?" I ask. "After you retired?"

"The land took it back. Not that we ever made much of a claim on it. No good for growing more than rocks and trees. Potato mud, David called it."

"Who owns it now?"

"She does."

"Angela?"

"That's the thing about children. Without them, there's no one to say you were ever even here."

33

I start out toward the Percy farm directly from Spruce Lodge, the afternoon light already showing signs of giving up. Although described by Marion Percy as only "a few miles—a dozen, or maybe a baker's dozen— outside town," there are moments when I wonder if the old woman has intentionally led me astray. Her directions are free of road names or numbers, and involve only landmarks ("right at the stone church") and subjective distances ("a bit of a ways," "straight for a good while"). After an hour, I crumple the page of notes I'd made from her telling of the route and toss them into the back seat.

It leaves me to make every turn on instinct. Eventually I'm headed down a private lane with branches scratching to get in on either side. "You won't see a farm, or a house, or anything to make you think anyone ever lived in there," is how Marion Percy described the entrance to her place. Well, *this* certainly qualifies.

It is by now the beginning of that stretched period of a northern autumn day that lingers in *almost darkness*. Almost, *almost*—and then it suddenly is. I turn on the headlights but it makes little difference, the snarled trees ahead flashing orange before clipping off the Toyota's mirror. The lane continues, but does not yield to any sign of habitation. No fence, no gate, no rusting equipment enfolded in the forest's weeds. I'm wrong: this isn't a lane at all, and it doesn't lead to anything. But it's too tight to turn around, and too boggy to risk trying to reverse the whole way. The sole hope is that there is an exit on to some other road at the end.

I turn on the radio. Right away I get the weather forecast: the first storm of the season is coming in. Snow squall warnings overnight for the whole county, with accumulation of up to forty centimetres. Overnight lows of minus twenty. Road closures anticipated. If travel outside the home is not strictly necessary, all are advised to stay indoors for the duration.

Too late for me.

The cold licks in around the windows and brings with it new imaginings of where Sam might be. Inside or out? Tied up, hooded? Have they given him food? Can he see any light? Is he cold?

Is he still alive?

No. I won't allow this one.

My attention must remain on the *doing* of things. Going forward—this alone might bring me to Sam. Or, in my case, going backwards. Because now I'm taking my foot off the gas, slapping the gear shift into reverse, turning around in my seat to see how I might slither out the way I've come –

An opening ahead. There just as I turn my head to start an inching reverse.

I shift back into drive, taking a run at the last branches drooped over the lane. There's a thud as one hits the front windshield, splintering a web of cracks through the glass. I keep my foot down and the car fishtails sideways into the mud. The tires glued a foot into the earth.

Not that it matters now. Because I'm here.

A square, red-brick farmhouse barnacled with leafless vines. A lopsided barn off to the side. Beyond these structures, an open space that was once a cultivated field but would now go by the name of meadow, or whatever one calls land midway in its return to chaos.

I step out of the car and take in the farmyard as though a location from my own memory. It is not exactly as I imagined it while listening to Angela read, but this doesn't stop it from being instantly recognizable. The wrought-iron weather vane atop the farmhouse roof, the buckled swing set in the yard, the partial log fence unsuccessful in holding the brush back from a onetime vegetable garden.

I start toward the house. The first flakes falling slow and straight as ash. I hold my arms out in front of me and there is already a thin layer of white over my coat, my shoes. Ghosting me.

An electric thrum travels up my legs from the earth. Is there an opposite to sacred ground? I suppose certain fields and farmyards in Poland and France store this kind of energy, the memory of horror held within the soil. I know it's only my own apprehensions—however this is going to turn out, it's going to happen here and now—but as I lift my feet up the farmhouse's front steps the history of this place rushes to possess me.

I look skyward. Tongue out, eating snow like a child. But it's to see if anyone stands in the upstairs window to the right. The window where the young Angela once stood, looking down at her father.

The door is open a crack. Something prevents me from touching the handle with bare skin, so that I enter by shouldering it wide enough for me to slip through. The new air rolls dead leaves and vermin droppings over the floor. It's still not enough to hold back the rank odour of the place. Backed-up plumbing. Along with something sweeter, animal.

A smell that soldiers and surgeons would recognize.

"Sam?"

My voice silences the house. It was quiet as I came in, but now some previously unnoticed activity has been stopped. The plaster and floorboards held in the tension of a held breath.

I try to leave the front door open but the angle of the frame eases it almost shut each time. Although it is not yet dark outside and the curtains that remain are limp ribbons over the glass, the interior holds pockets of shadow in the corners, around every door and down the length of its hall. It is hard to imagine as a building that sunlight ever freely passed through. Bad things happened here because they were always meant to.

The main floor is arranged as rooms that open off a narrow central hallway that leads straight into the kitchen at the rear. A few feet in, the living room opens on the left, the dining room on the right. Both slightly too small for their functions, even now, unpeopled and with most of the furniture missing. In the living room, signs of a stayover: a trio of wooden chairs, a broken whisky bottle on the floor between them. The fireplace and the brick around it black with soot, charred logs too big for its hearth still teepeed on the grate. I bend to touch them. Cold as the snow collecting on the sill.

The house has darkened further still when I return to the hallway, so that I proceed half-blind down its length, hands sliding over the walls. David Percy must have negotiated this route in much the same way on the last night of his life. Old, his sight gone. Tormented by what he believed to be some demonic intruder.

I turn to see the front door standing open. As the gust from outside loses its force, the door retracts once more. *Only the wind.* But David Percy would have had such thoughts too. Explanations that didn't quite hold all of his mind together.

The smell is stronger on the way upstairs. Warmer, humid. It makes each step a fight against being sick.

Something happened here.

And not just eighteen years ago.

Something happened here today.

At the landing I see that I'm right.

Blood. A line of dime-sized circles leading to the room at the front of the house. Angela's room.

And a book.

Lying face down on the landing, its spine broken as

though to bookmark the page. I know the title before I'm close enough to read the text on the cover. I know what it means before I lift the brittle paper to my eyes and see that it is a paperback from my own bookshelf, a hand-me-down that Sam had chosen for his nightstand pile. *Robinson Crusoe.* The book he brought with him to the Mustang Drive-in the night he disappeared.

"Sam?" I try again, and will his voice to answer. But there's only the squeak of the floor as it makes note of the book dropped from my hands, my shuffled steps toward the front room's partly open door.

My boot kicks the door open wide. It lets the smell out.

A single bed with Beatrix Potter rabbits painted on the headboard. A wooden school desk. Animal stickers—a smirking skunk, a giggling giraffe—on the cracked dresser mirror. And blood on all of it. Thin lines crosshatched over the room, as though squeezed from a condiment bottle. Not so much that it is evidence of a butchering, but of a struggle. Something half-done and then interrupted. Or half-done to be finished elsewhere.

And then I notice the chains laid out on the mattress. Four links attached to each of the bedposts with metal loops at the end. Shackles.

I'm not sure what I do in these next moments. They may not be moments at all. All I know is that I'm tracing the lines of blood and looping a finger through a rusted link of chain. Everything still. Everything falling away.

That's when I hear it.

Faint but unmistakable in the distance. From some-where within the woods beyond the fields.

A voice calling for me.

The snow has gained weight over the last hour. The wind throwing it into my eyes. Dusk a black umbrella opened against the sky. My legs seem to know where to go. Out of the farmhouse yard and into the frozen ruts of the abandoned field.

Sam doesn't call out for me again as I make my way toward the woods. It doesn't stop me from hearing him.

Daddy!

Daddy, not Dad. His name for me when he was little, the second syllable dropped a couple years ago in favour of the more grown-up short form. The reversion only happens now when he's been hurt. Or when he's scared.

The trees close in. Nightfall arrives at the same time as the bare limbs overhead deny what little moonlight there might be. The relatively even earth allows me greater speed here than over the furrows, but there is also more to hold me back. Interlocked branches. Stumps rising out of the gathering snow to crack my shins. Buried stones.

A hand swiped across my eyes comes away wet. Cut.

The weather forecast was right. Not just about the squall, but the cold. The temperature has dropped to whatever level it is that freezes your nostrils closed. Tightens the skin over your cheeks until it feels like the bone could rip through.

I stop and try to tell myself I'm determining which

course to take, that it's not the cold and the panic that has freeze-dried all oxygen out of the air. Which way is north? If Sam is out here, this is where he'd be. And only Sam would know how to get out again. He could read the stars. Through momentary pauses of the snowfall I can make out some of the brightest constellations, but I didn't listen when Sam tried to explain how they could show you the way. The thought that I may never have the chance to let my son teach me this doubles me over. Puking a stain into a creamy drift.

Sam's shouted name is lost in the blizzard. A new inch of snow on the ground with every count to twenty in my head. In the creek beds it's already up past my knees.

The struggle now isn't against the cold but my desire to lean against the nearest pine and go to sleep. Forty winks. It would be a nap of the forever kind, I know. But it's how David Percy exited the world. Who's to say I have any greater reason to live than he had? A pair of fools who thought good intentions alone might find them a way through.

I'm bending down to curl into a nice spot when I see him. A human form against a tree in a clearing ahead.

"Sam."

A whisper this time. Louder than any of my shouts.

But as I get closer I see that the figure is too large to be Sam. And that whoever it is, he has long since frozen. Not that freezing was how he died. Iced blood pooled in his lap. Stiff hands plugging the wounds. Lashed to the trunk with wire that has sliced deep through his last struggles to free himself.

The man's chin slumped against his chest. I lift his head so that his lifeless eyes, still open, look up.

It's strange to see Ramsay's face showing anything but his wry cockiness. There is nothing of the kind about it now. A mask of terror waxed over the self-certainty he maintained over all the preceding years of his life.

Whatever was done to him in Angela's room took some time. And then he was brought out here. Aware of what was coming, but clinging to the possibility of escape nevertheless. Isn't that what the detectives in his detective novels did? Wait for a last-minute opportunity just when things looked their worst?

I regain my feet. Ramsay already halfway to buried. In half an hour, you would never know he's here.

There isn't a reason I keep walking but I do. Sam isn't out here, if he ever was. It's more probable that what I heard came from within my own head, or was Ramsay himself, instructed to find the right pitch with the assistance of the wire around his throat. It doesn't matter. The point is what it's always been: the determination of beginnings, middles and ends. Stories like symmetry, and my fate is to act out David Percy's concluding moments. I carry on now only to see the place they'll find me whenever they do.

Maybe it will be here. Out in the open of the Percys' field. An unintended circling back to where I started.

A single light appears through the snow. The bulb over the farmhouse porch.

Someone's home.

I fall to my knees. Across the field, a looming shadow

takes its time coming to me. A darkness on its way to swallow me whole. Behind it, emerging from the house, what may be a smaller figure looking on.

Something about the two of them suggests they have always been here. Not just today, but forever. They have all the time in the world.

34

Do shadows cast shadows?

Firelight over a cracked plaster ceiling. Gradations of darkness nudging each other aside. Peeling paint lent a sinister animation. Hooked fingers reaching down for me.

Random connections, mini-hallucinations. I'm aware that this is all they are. Hospital room thoughts.

Except I'm not in a hospital.

No, don't ask. Just leave it alone—watch the shadows make shadows. Don't *ask*.

Where am I?

Now I've done it. You can't deny a query like that once it's out. It's the first information we insist upon when we wake.

Which means I am awake.

Which means I'm here.

Out and in again.

There was a gap, anyway, that only blacking out can explain. While away, the timid fire in the hearth has been stoked. The blizzard quieted to the suspended feathers that follow a pillow fight. And though it was unthinkably cold before, just beyond the range of the fire's heat—where my blue left hand rests, as opposed to the pinkish right—it has dropped a few more degrees.

For a moment or two I entertain the possibility that this could be another abandoned farmhouse altogether, another empty living room with windows that look out into a night dark and confining as a mine shaft. But there's the broken whisky bottle at my feet. And the chair I'm seated in feels like the one I noticed when I looked into the Percys' living room. Splintery but solid, its legs firmly planted.

And me firmly planted in it.

Chains looped around my wrists, holding both arms flat to the armrests. Tying ankle to ankle. A bruising yoke around my neck. I can't see what fixes the chair to the floor but given how it won't move no matter how I shift my weight, it must be screwed in.

I'm clothed but coatless. Only socks on my feet. I suppose this was done to get a good fit around my chest and legs, but the side effect is an even greater vulnerability to the cold. Without the fire I won't last long. Even with it, I can feel the sweat turning to frost on my upper lip. The hard air stinging my eyes.

My strength is gone. I never had much to begin with. And there are the tingly black dots of unconsciousness dancing around my peripheral vision, waiting for the chance to bury me.

But I have to try. There's nothing else to do but try.

I figure the best way to test the chains is to pull on each limb one at a time, seeing if there's some give anywhere. The concentration required in this—turn *this* wrist, lift *that* foot, now *that* foot—proves that my mind has weakened as much as the rest of me. And while I'm able to twist some parts an inch or two, there is no indication that anything might be slid out if teased a bit more. If I'm to get out of this chair, it won't be gently.

So I try the hard way.

A crazed spasm. Lunging forward and back, trying to topple the chair. Kicks and punches that don't go anywhere.

When I'm done I'm still here. Except now I've left the door open to the black dots. A nauseous sleep rolling in like fog.

My eyes won't open. That, or I'm blind. But there is movement somewhere within the house. The sense of vibrations more than the sounds themselves. Hearing as the deaf hear.

A heavy footfall along the upstairs hallway. And something lighter, metallic. A clattering of pots and cutlery in the kitchen.

I try to stand again. It doesn't work. And this time it hurts.

"Who's there?" I shout, or attempt to shout, but it's nothing more than a dry ripple of air. The turning of a newspaper page.

Yet there's a pause in the sounds. Was I heard? The black dots gathering round again.

Where's my son?

This finds a way out. A broken cry that carries through the bones of the house.

A minute passes after the echo of it has faded. Nothing other than knuckles of wind against the glass.

And then it resumes. Boots clumping through the floorboards above, the noise of cooking. But no voices in reply. No recognition that there is a man freezing to death in the front room. A father whose only wish is to know if his son is here and could hear him if he could find the breath to speak his name.

A figure beyond the doorframe. Standing in the hallway holding a candle in a teacup. A frantic play of the dim light. Glimpses of fur-topped boots, a knitted toque, the ridged tendons down a white neck.

She doesn't come forward. Holds the candle to the side so that it won't illuminate her face directly. A pose struck by the subject of a gothic portrait.

Don't hurt him.

When my tongue refuses to form the words I try to send this to her through the silence. But she has been pleaded to before. She knows the things people ask for at the end.

Don't.

A fight for air. And by the time I find it, the hallway is empty.

She is there again when I next wake.

In the room with me, standing in the corner. Still huddled in the deeper darkness, as though shy. But it's not that. She simply prefers to watch than be watched.

I jump toward her—but the chains restrain the motion to a hiccup jolt.

A small fire flickering its last sparks in the hearth. Outside there is the black clarity that comes with the deepest dives below zero.

"Where is he?" My voice a dry crinkle. The peeling of an onion. "Where's Sam?"

"Not here."

"Bring him to me."

"He's not *here*."

"Is he alive?"

The question passes through her.

I make another attempt to rise from the chair. A snake wriggle. It makes the bindings even tighter than before.

"Let me go."

"You *know* you're never getting out of here."

"I wish I'd fucked you in the ass."

"This is out of character."

"I'm not a character."

"Depends on the perspective."

"Ask my perspective. You? You're an empty, talentless bitch. You're *nothing*."

"That won't do you any good either."

"Am I hurting your feelings?"

"It's going to be a long night. Anger takes up so much energy."

"Then how are you still standing?"

"Me?" she says. "*I'm* not angry."

Angela steps toward me. The floor groaning as if

accommodating the weight of a giant. As she passes, the disturbance of the air creates a feathering breeze against my face.

"They're going to find you," I say.

"Really?"

"The police. They'll come after me. After Ramsay. They know where we went."

She has bent to the fire. Placing fresh logs, nothing more than thick branches really, atop one another. The flames hiss at the ice under the bark.

"No one is coming here," she says.

The only part of her exposed from here is the back of her neck. Hair up, with just the downy strands beneath curling against the collar of her parka. I stare at this one point and will it closer. If she allowed herself just one incautious approach, I could rip through her spine from back to front with my teeth.

What is required first is for her not to leave.

"That's how David Percy died, wasn't it? You did to him what you did to me."

"What did I do?"

"Had him believe that you were out there. A blind man who thought he'd lost his child. He wasn't chased by a ghost, or a Sandman. He ran into the woods to look for *you*."

"Maybe that's how you should have ended your novel."

"But it's what happened."

"You're blinder than that old man ever was."

"What part am I wrong about?"

"It's not the killing. Not for *me*, anyway."

"Tell me."

Angela puts down the crowbar she was using to arrange the fire. Stands facing me.

"It's getting into someone else's head, right at the point when everything is laid bare," she says.

"You think this is *research?*"

"It's more than that. It's material. You and I have more in common than you'd guess. Trouble making things up out of nothing, for one thing."

"I don't understand."

"We both wanted to write *books*. And this is mine. The life I'm living. The lives I'm taking. It's all going into my novel. A novel that's not *really* a novel, because, in a way, it's all true."

"An autobiography."

"Not exactly. The point-of-view won't be mine. I'm not sure whose yet. I need to find the right voice."

"So you're stealing your book as much as I did."

"I'm not stealing. I'm assembling."

"You have a title?"

"*The Killing Circle*. Like it?"

"Can't say I do. But I suppose I'm biased. Given that you're going to kill me just so you can end a chapter. Just like you killed the others."

Angela comes at me with surprising speed. Instead of meeting her with whatever fury is left in me, I reflexively rear back. She grabs my hair. The fused seams of the chains audibly tearing the skin.

"*I* never killed *anyone*," she says.

Another waking. Another recognition that my believing myself bound to a chair in a haunted house isn't a dream.

She has Sam.

I will die after the fire goes out.

I cannot leave this place.

The hope that I will be released because I am the teller of this tale, and the teller never dies in his own tale: another falsehood.

I close my eyes. Try to let sleep return. But whatever it is that comes to smother my next breath isn't sleep at all.

She is sitting in a chair ten feet away. It may be further. There being nothing else to look at, no furniture or picture on the wall within range of the diminishing firelight, she looms where she might otherwise shrink. I've never thought of her as large. But she is. She's all there is.

She looks out the window. Taps her heels against the floor. A schoolgirl growing impatient at the bus stop.

"No wonder you're so fucked up. Having someone like Raymond Mull for your father."

Angela turns her eyes to me. A dull sheen of interest over the black pupils.

"What do you know about him?"

"That he hurt you. How did that make you feel?"

"How did that make you feel?"

"It would explain a lot."

"How I was such a bad girl at such a young age? How I drove a blind old man to the point he ran into the woods in a snowstorm?"

"Why you have no self."

"I have plenty of selves."

She stands. Peers out at a particular point on the night's horizon.

"You know something? I almost feel sorry for you."

"Artists enjoy certain privileges," she says. "They also endure certain sacrifices."

"Sounds like something Conrad White would say."

"I think he *did* say it."

"Was this while he was telling you how you were his perfect girl? His dead daughter returned?"

"People see in me what they wish to see."

"A mirror."

"Sometimes. Or sometimes it's someone else. A twin. A lover. Someone they lost. Or would like to be."

"What did I see?"

"You? That's easy. You saw your muse."

Angela goes to the fire. Places a pair of spindly branches on to the flames.

"Not much of a wood pile," I say.

"It's enough."

"Not staying long?"

She ignores this.

"How did you do it on your own?" I try again.

"Do what?"

"What was done to some of the bodies—that's some heavy lifting."

"You'd know."

I work to push aside the images of Petra in the shed as best I can. "You were watching me?"

"I was always watching. But *that*—that was un-expected."

"Was it William? Did you convince him to help you?"

"I urged him to study his fellow man."

"But he didn't kill the people from the circle. Or Carol Ulrich, Pevencey. The earlier ones."

"You forgot Jane Whirter."

"Yes. Why did she come to Toronto?"

"I invited her. She had suspicions. So I told her I did as well."

My chin falls against my chest. It awakens me with a gasp.

"You put the bloody tools in his apartment," I say. "William's."

"The police needed to catch a monster. Now they have one."

"Not the right one."

"Do you hear him protesting his innocence?"

"Why isn't he?"

"I convinced him otherwise."

Angela backs away from the fire and walks to the far side of the room. Her shoulders folded in, her hair greasy from a few days without water. The girl has been busy. And she *is* a girl again. Through her fatigue, the years that had been added since she first opened her journal in Conrad White's apartment have fallen away to reveal someone a little lost, uncertain of where she is and what has brought her here. It's an illusion, of course. Another mistake that leads to more mistakes. This is what she is as much as anything else: a collection of misreadings.

"Why Ramsay?" I say, and she half turns.

"What I do—it requires improvisation."

"They'll come looking for him."

"They won't."

"Why?"

"I spoke to him. And he—he *assured* me that he came here on his own time. No one knew where he was headed, because he was tracking you."

"You don't think he was bullshitting you?"

"He was in a position where lying would be unlikely."

"You're not clever, you know," I find myself coughing as she drifts toward the hallway. "You might *think* you're some kind of artist. But you're not. You're shit."

Angela stops. Out of the range of firelight, so that she's a shadow that surprises with its ability to speak.

"You're a *plagiarist*, Patrick," she says. "At least what I do is original."

I flinch awake at what I think at first is a sound, but it isn't. It's light. Two white pins pushing through the darkness outside. Growing brighter, surrounded by a widening penumbra of snow.

Angela is here with me. Standing by the window, rolling back on her heels.

"Who's that?"

"A harder question to answer than you'd guess," she says.

"The Sandman."

"But he could be anyone."

"Not anyone. He killed Petra and Len. The one who drove Conrad and Evelyn off the road. The hands that pushed Ivan on to the tracks."

"That's not really a guess."

She turns from the window. Outside, the headlights swing around and point away, exposing the side of the vehicle. A black van. The one I'd seen on Queen Street. The one that drove off from where I'd found Len's body.

"I suppose I'll be meeting him soon enough," I say.

"You'd *like* to?"

"I'd enjoy nothing more than to meet the man of your dreams."

Angela giggles in fake embarrassment. "It's not like that."

The child's sound of her voice reminds me that, whatever she is now, happened when she was young. It's why her age is so hard to guess, how even in her bed she was play-acting at being an adult. Part of her belongs to the past because part of her died there.

"Whatever your father is making you do, it's not your fault."

"Thank you. My burden has been lifted."

"If you let me go, I could help you."

"Help me?"

"Show me where Sam is, and we could all go away together. Or go our separate ways. But I'd make it so that your father couldn't touch us ever again. We'd be safe."

"I am safe."

"Angela, please. You don't have to keep doing this. Not for him."

"I could be with you instead? Your replacement bride? Your co-author?"

The van door swings shut. A workman's vehicle's screech of neglect. After a moment, there's the heavy footsteps coming up on to the porch.

I am the ground beneath your feet . . .

The door opens. Snow being stomped off his boots. Then the few steps along the hallway it takes to stand in the archway, looking in.

A giant's shadow. The same one I'd seen coming for me before collapsing in the field outside. But somehow familiar now that it is indoors. The shape of a man I've seen before.

"I'd like you to meet my brother," she says.

The figure steps forward to the edge of the firelight. Tentative, gloved hands crossed over his stomach. Grinning in a trembly, rubber-lipped way that suggests he's trying not to, but can't help himself.

"Len?"

"That's how you knew him," Angela says, sliding close to him but carefully. Without touching. "Virgin Len. But he, like me, has gone by a number of different names over the years. Different *incarnations*."

"But I *saw* you. In the alley."

"You saw what you thought you saw," Len says, his grin widening. "We counted on that. We've *always* counted on that."

"Oh Christ."

"You alright?"

"Oh *Christ*."

The room is swimming. No, not the room—*I'm* swimming. Fits of motion through the nearly solid air. A fish finning through a tank.

"I'm going to take a look around upstairs," Angela says to him.

Len nods. When she moves past him into the hallway she brushes against his nylon jacket and the sound is like a knife rendering tin foil.

"That was you," I say. "At Michelle Carruthers' funeral. Mull was your father too."

"As far as we know."

"And you were taken into foster care just like your sister."

"Shared experience can bind people in powerful ways."

"So you decided to take other people's lives to replace your own."

"Too simple. *Way* too simple."

Len spits on the floor. The white foam of it on the hardwood holds his attention, and in his stare I can see the emptiness in him, the sterile indifference.

"You're a good actor."

"I'm not Len," he says, taking a predatory step into the room. "If that's what you mean."

"Len was somebody. It was a performance, but there was a personality there. You, on the other hand, are nobody."

"Are you trying to insult me?"

"It wouldn't work if I was. There's nothing in you to hurt. Just like your sister."

"Angela is an artist."

"And you're the king of the Kingdom of Not What It Seems."

"No."

"The Sandman."

"No."

"Who is?"

"Whoever scares you most."

Len takes his gloves off, stuffs them in his pocket. His big hands creased with black lines.

Dirty hands.

"Where's my son?"

"That's a secret."

"You're going to hurt him, aren't you? You already have."

"Now, now. You'll only upset yourself."

"He's just a child. Doesn't that make a difference to you?"

"We were *all* children once."

I cough back a surge of sick. My throat burning from the inside out.

"It was you," I say. "You took those girls in Whitley."

"Before my time."

"Then who?"

"That was *him*."

"Mull? You sure it wasn't you shadowing your little sister? It wasn't you who wanted her?"

"I *protected* her."

"How?"

"By making Daddy go away."

"You killed him?"

"We needed to make a new world," he says, showing the ground stumps of his teeth. "And he couldn't be in it."   •

Len watches the eyes roll back in my head.

"I don't feel so great," I say.

"It's the dehydration."

"Can I have some water?"

"That's good. That's *funny*."

He steps over to the fire. Picks up a branch and considers adding it to the flames. After a moment, he puts the branch back on the pile he got it from.

Upstairs, Angela is opening doors, closing them, putting things into a bag. If I'm counting the bedrooms right, she's almost done.

"Who was it?" I ask. There's the idea I'm about to throw up but there is little time left now. "The body I thought was you."

Len comes to stand directly in front of me. He unclasps his hands so that they swing against his hips.

"The *National Star* should have a job opening pretty soon," he says.

And then I do throw up. A painful choking that summons a half-cup of bile on to the floor.

Angela appears in the hallway holding a duffel bag. Black stains seeping through the canvas. She shares a look with Len.

"I think it's time," she says.

She starts away, then stops. Comes to me and slips her hand into my pocket. Pulls out the dictaphone.

"I made other tapes," I say.

"We have them all now."

"There's copies."

"No, there aren't. And we have your journals too. Right up to you arriving here. You left that one in your car's glove box."

Angela asks Len if he's checked the kitchen, and he lowers his head slightly when he admits he hasn't. She looks at her watch. Gives him two minutes.

He does as he's told. Leaving Angela leaning against the archway, looking past me out the window. Like I'm not even here. Already dead.

"You got me wrong," I say, and the unexpected laugh that comes after spills warm spit down my chin.

"Oh?"

"You don't have my whole story."

"The voice of desperation."

"It's the truth."

"I know everything I need to know about you."

"No, you don't. There's a secret I've kept so long that even I don't remember it half the time. Something that changes everything."

"This is *sad*," she says. But she's watching me now.

"I'm the last character in the circle. And without this, something will be missing. Your book will have a hole in it. Because Mr. Boring is not who you think he is. He has a twist."

In the kitchen, Len pulls a cutlery drawer out too far

and it falls to the floor. The clatter of knives and forks. A barked profanity as he bends to pick them up.

Angela comes closer.

"Go on then," she says.

"Promise me. I'll tell you if you promise Sam will be safe."

"I told you. I wouldn't –"

"I *know* it's not you. Killing isn't your department. It's *his*."

"Maybe it's already been done."

"Maybe it has. And if it hasn't, he's going to. To keep Sam quiet, or to punish me, or just because it's what he does."

"You think your little secret might stop him?"

"No. I think you might."

"Why should I do anything for a dead man's lie?"

"Because it isn't a lie."

"How would I know?"

"You'll know as soon as you hear it."

Down the hall, Len slides the drawer back into its slot. Claps his hands together for warmth.

"Fine," she says, unable to entirely hide her interest. "I'm listening."

So I tell her. In a rushed whisper of run-on sentences and bullet points, clipped and unadorned. It's not what I say that proves it's true. It's the voice. Breaking as soon as I begin, a thin note that thins even more over the telling.

What I tell Angela is how I killed Tamara. My wife. How what I did makes both of us murderers.

It wasn't an assisted suicide either, not the carrying out of a consensual plan. It was my idea alone. I must be clear on this. Yet even though she was asleep when I pressed the needle into her arm, I believe that when Tamara wakened and saw what I was doing she was thankful, that she understood it was for love. Because it *was*. It may have been wrong according to certain laws or gods, it may have stolen restful sleep and guiltless dreams from me for the rest of my life, it may be where the out-of-nowhere tears have been coming from these past years—it may have been done *too early*—but I wanted only to take her pain away, to prevent the worse pain to come. To show as much courage as she showed, working up a white-lipped smile whenever Sam was around. Cancer did most of the killing on its own. It was the villain who stole into her room without turning on the light, not me.

These are the kind of thoughts that made what I did no easier. What I now share with another for the first time. With Angela, who watches the words drift out of me in grey puffs of steam.

Len returns to the doorway. Takes a breath as though savouring a scent in the air.

"Ready," he says.

Angela turns to him. There is nothing in her expression—nothing at all—that would suggest she has just heard something surprising. She is good at hiding things. Or maybe it is only that there is nothing for her to hide, as she's decided that what she has heard is little more than an overplayed bluff. The hollow glance she gives me as she follows Len to the door makes it impossible to tell.

I hear her step outside. A pause as Len takes a last look down the hall. When he leaves, he pulls the door only partway closed. The wind moaning through the house, grieving. Sorry to see them go.

35

It's been some hours since there's been any feeling in my legs. I was hoping this was one of the benefits of dying from exposure—at least it kept the pain to a minimum. Now it seems I was wrong about that. The body doesn't let go of feeling easily, even if the only sensation left to it is setting itself on fire. Frostbite? Sounds *chilly*, doesn't it? Try gripping an ice cube tight in your palm. It's only cold at first. Then it burns.

The screaming helps. My voice pushing back against the darkness that draws closer as the flames diminish in the hearth. And even now there is an idea that someone might hear me. Perhaps Angela has arranged for a *deus ex machina*—a kindly neighbour? a local cop?—to walk in the door and give me a lift to the Sportsman for a hot shower and a stiff drink. And I will be reformed by my experiences, the one she'd chosen as the recipient of her tough love. Wasn't *The Magus* her favourite book, after all?

But this isn't a book.

I'm taking in a breath to let out another howl when I hear the radio.

It must have been on for the whole time of this most

recent wakening, but it doesn't have a firm grasp on the frequency, so that the signal drops out from time to time. Now, abruptly, it has found itself again. The last fading bars of "Raindrops Keep Falling on My Head," crackling out of the dark.

An old transistor unit on the floor by my feet. The antenna fully extended, wavering in the drafty cross-currents. A dim blue light from the tuning dial that turns the floor around it into a shallow pool.

The announcer comes on to inform me that it's Whitley's easy listening station ("The smoothest sounds north of Superior"). Coming up: Perry Como, Streisand, The Carpenters. "And pull your sweetheart a little closer," the DJ says with an audible wink, "because next we've got a real blast from the past—with Paul Anka!"

It makes me wonder: did Angela leave the radio with me for comfort, or further punishment? *Easy listening?* Maybe that was the only station she could get. Or maybe there's a message in its selection. Milquetoast music to send off the man with no imagination.

And they call it puppy love. But I guess they'll never know . . .

The fire nothing more than a stack of hissing embers. Red stars twinkling against the black bricks. Soon it will be cold and dead. Ditto the slumped man turning into a shadow.

I told her.

This comes with a stab to the chest. Followed by a shuddering fight to pull a whole breath in. A blown nose leaves a spray of blood over my pant legs.

I told her the story. It wasn't a dream. I told her.

Two bits of discouraging news from the radio between the Jefferson Airship retrospective and "Careless Whisper": it's 3.42 a.m. and minus nineteen outside. I'd been nurturing some hope that I might make it to the morning, if only to see the patterns of frost over the glass, the stark line of trees beyond. But it seems these small consolations are to be denied me.

Engelbert Humperdinck next. Always loved that name. *Please release me. Let me go . . .*

The news comes on. The second item (after the day's Middle Eastern death count) is a breaking story. One I only focus on halfway through the reception's broken account.

"The son of author . . . street corner in Dryden, Ontario . . . taken to the local hospital to be checked over for any possible . . . unknown at this time . . . appeared unharmed, though a statement has not yet been released regarding information on his kidnappers' identity . . . also apparently missing, and therefore not available for . . . unconfirmed initial reports that the boy has offered information which may lead to his father's whereabouts . . . repeated their policy of not answering questions until they have followed . . . In sports, Leafs lose another close one . . . ."

There's to be a follow-up report a half-hour later. It gives me something to keep breathing for. Fighting sleep that isn't sleep. Humming along to crackly patches of "Everybody Plays the Fool" and "Someday We'll Be Together."

Then the news again. This time around, the reception is good enough to get the facts down.

Sam Rush, son of the bestselling author, was discovered wandering alone on a residential street in Dryden, the next town along the Trans-Canada from Whitley. Early reports indicate that he appeared in good health, and has made a statement to authorities that may assist them in locating the boy's father, who has also been recently designated a Missing Person. Police are now working to locate a farmhouse where the boy was kept, and are using geographic parameters he has provided regarding its location in relation to the stars. There are currently no leads as to the identity of the boy's abductors as he was unable or unwilling to provide detailed physical descriptions. Parents are urged to monitor their children more closely than usual over the coming days, though they can be assured that the Rush investigation is now a top priority. The police spokesperson went out of his way to emphasize that, despite the boy's statements, there is no evidence to support the contention that Sam Rush's abduction and his father's missing status are related.

There's no mention of Ramsay. Nothing about Tim Earheart either, though the police have surely made a positive identification by this point. Soon, they'll start pulling some of the connections together. But they'll never find Angela and Len. I'm sure of this. They're gone and won't come back. With different names and faces they will slip across borders, shedding themselves as they go. Somewhere else, eventually, they will join another circle. And someone will start believing in the Sandman again.

The radio's reception starts to fade. The batteries mostly used up to start with. She wanted me to hear the news, to let me know. But once I had, she wanted the silence to return.

And now, with a last rustle of static, it has.

Outside, the wind stills to nothing. The snow drifted up against the walls like breaking waves. Even the house holds its breath.

Sam is alive.

It's this fact, this painkilling knowledge, that allows me to let go.

I've been fighting harder than I knew. To be here for him. Just in case he found his way out of the storm. Instead, he is far away, in the care of others. I wish it were my arms that held him, my comfort that will send him off to sleep. No matter. We've had our bedtime stories. There will be my voice for him to hold on to.

Goodnight, son. Sweet dreams.

They may find me, of course. And maybe even before my breath has turned to crystal in my chest. The radio said they were looking for me, following the directions Sam gave them, the Norths and Wests and Easts he read from the stars. Odds are it will be too late to make any difference. And yet, even as I resign myself to the inevitable, there is a renewed struggle to stay here, in this moment, a thinking, remembering thing. Fighting for another minute, for the possibility of dawn. Of seeing Sam again.

There is even the time to dream of revenge. A plan to sell the house on Euclid, leave the city altogether and disappear with Sam, make ourselves safe. Then, a thousand miles away, I will set myself to work. To take something from Angela, the only thing that might matter to her. *The Killing Circle*. If I make it out of here, maybe I'll write it myself. Stick a knife in her heart. Steal back the book she's been assembling from the stories of the dead.

But these are only lullabye thoughts. The drifting weightlessness before the crash. For the first time in what feels like forever, I'm not striving for anything, not searching. No envy, unrequited admirations, the hollow yearning to be noticed. Not afraid.

Last thoughts?

There's the notion I might have some kicking around, perhaps a lesson or two of the kind you find at the end of novels. Something affirming and buoyant. I'm sure I could come up with something if I had the time, but I don't. Because here it comes: a wool blanket being pulled up over my shoulders, my head. Darkness. Blocking the light from the inside out. But before it takes me I surprise myself by laughing. A terrible, shaking, coughing mirth that echoes through the empty rooms of the farmhouse. A ghost sound. The laughter of a man without a story who sees that what has brought him here might have made a good one, if there was only someone else, one Dear Reader to tell it to.

Acknowledgments

My thanks to those who have helped this book—and helped me to write it—whether as listeners, questioners, editors or friends: Maya Mavjee, Julia Wisdom, John Parsley, Peter Joseph, Anne O'Brien, Anne McDermid, Martha Magor, Vanessa Matthews, Sally Riley, Lesley Thorne, Brent Sherman and Sean Kane.